Love Stories
from days gone by

Love
Stories
from days gone by

Illustrated by Tony Masero

This edition produced for **BHS** LONDON
By Hamlyn Publishing,
a division of The Hamlyn Publishing Group Ltd.
This edition 1985
© Copyright 1985, Hamlyn Publishing, a division of
The Hamlyn Publishing Group Ltd.

Printed in Yugoslavia

ISBN 0 600 31087 6

CONTENTS

THE PRISONER IN THE DUNGEON

Richard Grimsden

LADY MARGOT MCLEOD gave a gasp of horror, covering her mouth with her gloved hand, as she read the note brought in by Jeannie, her maid.

'Sir Rory Stuart has been arrested!' she cried. 'The Butcher has sent him to the dungeons at Fort Augustus.'

'Oh, ma'am!' Anxiety filled Jeannie on her mistress's behalf as the impact of the words sank in. *The Butcher . . . the dungeons at Fort Augustus*. And Sir Rory Stuart! The beautiful Lady Margot's handsome Highlander, who was the inspiration of clansmen from Thurso to the Border.

Lady Margot brushed the tears from her cheeks and stiffened her back. She would not give way. Everyone had expected Sir Rory's arrest, after all, and her *beau* was not the sort of man who would hide himself from the marauding English redcoats. Sir Rory would have gone defiantly to the dungeon, his head held high.

'Tell James to prepare the coach, Jeannie,' Lady Margot said. 'We shall go to Inverness. I shall ask an audience of the Butcher and plead my fiancé's innocence.'

'Go to see the Butcher himself? But, ma'am!' The maid's hand rose involuntarily.

'Do as I say. And remember not to cross yourself thus in front of the redcoats. If you show your Catholicism they will take you for a Jacobite and hang you for it.'

When the maid was gone Margot sat down in despair, still clutching the note headed, 'From the Headquarters of His

Royal Highness the Duke of Cumberland'. This was truly the hour of her beloved Scotland's agony. Her thoughts turned back mechanically over the past months, during which peace and plenty had been savagely sundered and the Highlands had fallen into the fearsome grip of the Duke of Cumberland, the Butcher, as everyone called him.

It had all begun many years ago when Queen Anne died and the government in London, fearful of the return of another Catholic king from the House of Stuart, sent to Germany to invite the Hanoverian King George to come and reign over them.

Margot had never been to London, but she was convinced that the English Protestants were terrified of Catholics and looked under every chair before they sat down, for fear there was a Catholic hiding there. The new King George was a good Protestant and would do what any Englishman said, mostly because he spoke no English anyway. But the land George the First was to rule included both England and Scotland, for the two nations were united as one.

Many of Margot's Scottish countrymen did not want a German king, neither the first George nor the second, who now reigned over them from London. And as most of them were Catholics, they didn't even want a Protestant king. They wanted their own Charles Stuart, whom they claimed as true heir to the English throne – and who was a Catholic.

The Highlanders rose in rebellion against King George. Rory – her brave, impetuous Rory – rallied to the clansmen's standard. Margot recalled with a swell of pride their last meeting before he joined his regiment. How magnificent he looked in the Stuart tartan, with his gleaming sword at his side!

Dreams – all dreams! The government in London had sent a huge army of English and German redcoats into Scotland, led by the notorious Duke of Cumberland, the German

King George's own son. On Culloden Field, a couple of miles from Inverness, the proud army of Scotland had been cut to shreds.

Dishevelled and shattered, Rory and thousands of his comrades had fled to seek refuge wherever heather moor or high mountains would hide them – only to find that Butcher Cumberland was not content with victory. He wanted every fugitive, every Scotsman who had fought with such gallantry, hunted down like an animal and killed.

Margot shuddered as she recalled the stories that were circulating in Nairnshire ... of exhausted men trapped in woods and coverts, encircled by English redcoats, then hacked to pieces ... of summary hangings going on even now in the countryside all around.

She had not seen Rory since he had marched off to war, and it was three weeks since the disaster of Culloden. Friends had told her that he had escaped and was hiding, and clearly, while the hunt was on, he was prudently keeping away from her, for fear that his presence would draw attention to her. And now he had been caught, a prisoner of the dreaded Butcher – a man who had sworn to kill all the Scots who had fought at Culloden.

Maybe just once, just this time, the Butcher would relent. A scented gloved hand, a radiant smile, a charming curtsey ... Margot was still rehearsing in her mind a whole repertoire of feminine charms as her coach rattled through the gates of the Duke of Cumberland's temporary headquarters in Inverness, past saluting sentries in scarlet tunics with primrose and green and blue facings, and militiamen marching up and down.

Margot gave her letter asking for an audience to an officer, who bowed stiffly. A form to sign, then keys rattled and she was ushered from officer to officer until she was told to wait in a big, tall-ceilinged anteroom. Ten minutes alone – then a soft-footed orderly bade her follow him. The orderly silently opened double oak doors, ushered her in, and closed them behind her soundlessly.

It was a big room with tapestry hangings, pictures, a chandelier and, in the far corner, seated at an oak desk, the man whose name was dreaded across the length and breadth of Scotland. The Butcher, square-jawed, Germanic, surprisingly young but already plump, rose at once, pushing aside Margot's letter, which he had been reading. She curtseyed, remembering each well-rehearsed detail.

'You have come to see me about the prisoner Rory Stuart, I understand.' The voice was like a steel file, each heavily accented word pronounced with care.

'Your Grace, I have come to ask your pardon for him. He is a good man and most assuredly innocent of any crime.'

'Innocent? *Innocent*?' The words were barked out gutturally and with false astonishment. 'Madam, your capacity for self-delusion is overwhelming. Your fiancé is a traitor to my father, the anointed King of this country. Any man who takes up arms against his sovereign takes up arms against his nation, and the nation must not falter in the face of treachery.'

'But, Your Grace, this is war, and Rory Stuart is a prisoner of war ...'

'Stuart is a rebel, madam, a follower of his namesake – possibly his kinsman – Charles Stuart the upstart Pretender. He has sought to overthrow the King. He is a citizen of the new Great Britain and he has defied its laws by murdering other citizens of this realm on the field of rebellion, in pursuit of his traitorous aim.'

Margot was aghast. In the face of this man's cold ruthlessness her charm was of no avail. All resolution was ebbing from her.

'What – what are you going to do with ...' The words trailed away in a muted sob.

The Butcher adjusted his wig and clicked his heels

impatiently as he walked up and down in front of his desk.

'He has access to secret information about rebels and their future plans. We shall extract this information from him, and then we shall hang him, after a fair trial, as we hang all traitors.'

Margot recognised the veiled threat and tears welled up in her eyes. Although torture was against the law, she knew very well that this English army, led by a man as merciless as the Butcher, had their own ways of persuading prisoners to talk, even men as brave as her own Sir Rory.

'Can't you have pity ... he's a good man ...' she sobbed.

Butcher Cumberland came round his desk in a full circle. His boyish air of indifference was etched now with a touch of impatience.

'Madam,' he said brusquely, 'I have permitted you this audience only on account of your name. But I must warn you of the peril you face by associating with my father's declared enemies. Had you not been of noble birth, you would have been arrested by now and no doubt would most likely be hanged, too.'

Desperately, Margot fought for some lifeline, some feeble bridge to build between the Butcher's intractable determination and her own all-consuming love.

'Will you let me see him – just once?' she pleaded. 'Let me take him some food, some comforts before ...' the words trailed away in another heart-rending sob as the tears, no longer controllable, flooded down her cheeks.

Butcher Cumberland, stopped short by the total demolition of the proud young noblewoman, smiled grimly. There was nothing he liked more than grovelling submission – in men as well as women.

'Very well,' he said. 'You may visit the traitor, once only.

Take him victuals if it pleases you.' He laughed contemptuously. 'A man should certainly have a full belly before he is hung.'

Outside, Margot's mind was racing. Her thoughts were all on Rory – there wasn't even time to explain her unfolding plan to her maid. She climbed quickly into the coach, commanding, 'Home to Kintessack, home to Kintessack!' to the dozing James, slumped on the coachman's seat. She needed to compose her mind, to complete her half-formed ideas, to sharpen each detail, to rehearse the scene ...

In the next twenty-four hours Margot scarcely slept. When exhaustion forced her to take a nap, the sleep that came was fitful and troubled. In a shallow dream she saw a man dressed in the full Highland dress of a warrior clansman chained to a wall. Shadowy figures surrounded him and the man's screams penetrated her mind like jabbing needles. Suddenly the man turned in anguish towards her and his face was Rory's.

When morning came she prepared a basket of food with infinite care, bought a new tartan shawl for Jeannie and sent messages to Rory's friend, the Abbot at Kinloss Abbey, at Burghead Bay, and to Andrew McKay, a boatman who had once served her father, at Lossiemouth, a half dozen miles from the Abbey.

At midday the day after her interview with the Duke of Cumberland, Margot commanded James the coachman to prepare the horses. She and Jeannie climbed into the coach, the maid clutching the basket of provisions. As they rattled over the cobbled road along the Moray Firth, the westering sun dappled the broad river's waters, playing on the fishing boats at Campbelltown and on the wet sand at Whiteness Head.

At Fort George half a dozen English redcoats sallied forth to halt the coach. Margot handed her pass to the young corporal, and at sight of the signature of Butcher

Cumberland's Chief of Staff, the soldier stiffened with awed respect and hastily waved the coach on. As they turned towards the Loch Ness road Margot watched the thin sun, pinned like a medal on the sky, high over the Monadhliath mountains, and prayed silently for a mist that evening – a mist that would shroud the rest of the day from the searching gaze of all English redcoats.

She was glad to see that Fort Augustus scarcely looked like a prison. The sergeant at the gate stiffened with the same awed respect as the corporal had shown at Fort George at the sight of Margot's pass. With quick steps and sword held upright within an inch of his nose, the sergeant led Margot and the hunched, worried-looking Jeannie into the orderly room. There, seated at a scrubbed table, was the Officer of the Guard.

When he saw Margot the moustached officer rose smartly and saluted. Margot recognised instinctively the type of man he was. She felt chivalry exuding even from the bright brass buttons of his tunic, and knew at once that she had to play the haughty, high-born woman to impress this man.

'I am given leave by His Royal Highness the Duke of Cumberland to pay my last respects to a friend, Sir Rory Stuart, who is in your charge . . '. Not so much as a tremor of her lips betrayed the authority of her tone.

Now it was the officer's turn to be overcome with awe. He glanced at the pass just long enough to read the Duke's name at its head, then obsequiously commanded the sergeant, stiff like a toy soldier, 'to conduct Her Ladyship below with all due diligence.'

'You'll find it a bit draughty, like, down 'ere, ma'am,' the sergeant said, half apologetically, as he led the two women down a flight of spiral stone steps. Margot suppressed a shiver, a mingling of fear and bone-chilling cold. She wanted to watch every step, note every footfall, each unusual mark, along the way.

At the foot of the spiral steps the route led along a narrow gloomy corridor, faced with granite blocks blackened by smoky lanterns. The sergeant led the two women through three sets of doors, at each of which was a redcoat sentry who seemed to come awake, Margot noted, only as he heard their footsteps approach. Beyond the third door the sergeant stopped at a brass-bound oak door and selected a key from a bunch hanging at his belt.

'I'm afraid my orders is you can have only ten minutes with the prisoner, ma'am,' he said in the same half-apologetic tone. He turned the key, swung the door inwards and stepped back. 'I'll be waiting for you at t'other end of the corridor, remember, at the foot of the steps. Just call the sentry when you're ready to leave.'

Margot stepped through the door, pulling Jeannie with her, and heard the heavy lock turned behind them. For a few seconds she blinked at the unaccustomed gloom, trying to define shapes. Then she saw Rory – and she ran to his arms.

She clung to him for what seemed an age, lost in the warmth of his body, the soft murmurings of surprise and protest in her ear. Suddenly, with an effort she would not have thought possible, she broke free of him, remembering the swiftly passing time, the need for explanation, urgency, calm.

'Undress yourself, Jeannie!' she whispered fiercely.

'Ma'am?'

'Undress yourself. In the corner, where it's dark. Be quick, I say.'

Margot ripped off Rory's threadbare tweed jacket and his tam o'shanter and unbuckled his sporran.

'You are coming out with me dressed in Jeannie's clothes,' she hissed. 'It's the only hope we have to save you. Jeannie will stay here. No harm will come to her – a simple serving girl obeying orders. It is me they will blame when they discover you're gone. Be quick, Rory, put this skirt on in place of your trews. It's lucky that she is almost your height.'

'But Margot, I *can't* dress ...'

'Do as I say, if you love me!'

Stifling the horror that his kinsmen would undoubtedly have expressed had they seen their leading clansman, the gallant Sir Rory Stuart, thus attired in a serving maid's clothes, Rory did as he was told, silently thanking Providence for the masking gloom of the Fort Augustus dungeons. And when, from within the distant corner of that gloom, he heard the servant girl's frightened snivelling, he even felt a touch of remorse.

'Put this on ...' Without waiting, Margot knotted Jeannie's new shawl around her fiancé's head and, as a final touch, drew the neck of the girl's cape up around his neck.

'Now, remember,' she whispered fiercely, trying to calm the thumping of her heart, 'we must *lament* as we go down the corridor. We must sob and choke and grieve enough to embarrass the sentries.' She turned towards the dark corner where Jeannie, dimly resembling the shape of Sir Rory in his trews and tam o'shanter, was weeping into her kerchief. 'Now stop that, Jeannie, or they'll catch your master and hang us all. Lie quiet and still on the bed until the soldiers come with the laird's dinner.'

Margot called to the sentry to open the heavy wooden door and, affecting to be comforting her 'maid', she began the endless journey down the granite corridor.

'Sob!' she hissed at Rory. 'Bury your head on my shoulder and *weep*!'

The proud, high-born laird of the Stuarts dutifully lowered his head and emitted a strangled, weeping sound. By the time they reached the first door Rory was making guttural sounds which, in the gloomy echoing chamber of that sinister underground cavern, were passable as a serving maid's grievings. The sentry looked away uncomfortably as he let

Margot gave her letter asking for an audience to an officer, who bowed stiffly.

them through and the two weeping women glided past him.

At the second door the redcoat sentry charitably held open the wooden rectangle for the 'mourners', while at the third the young redcoat averted his gaze sheepishly.

'Ah, here ye are, then!' It was the voice of the sergeant coming from the shadows at the foot of the spiral steps. The sergeant cleared his throat as the two women sobbed anew. 'Now come along, ladies. Time enough for that sort of thing later!'

Gallantly he propelled Margot the last few paces towards the foot of the steps, placing his hand on the small of her back in a style that indicated that she should precede him. Quick as a flash, Margot pushed the sobbing maid in front of her, hoping desperately that in the dark shadows 'Jeannie's' huge feet and ankles would not be revealed to the sergeant as he came up the steps behind them.

Not to go too fast, or stumble, that was it! Margot faltered, easing herself back on to the outstretched palm of the bemused sergeant.

'Now, come along, ma'am, all this weeping and wailing will not do at all!' The sergeant, however sympathetic, had clearly never before found himself alone in a dark dungeon with two weeping women.

At last they were at the top of the steps. Margot nudged 'Jeannie', forcing her to cling to her shoulder. In front of them now was the orderly room. The Officer of the Guard looked up sympathetically, then coughed behind his hand and looked away, embarrassed. As, with heads bent and sobbing, they went out through the fort's main gate, the officer called good-naturedly after them, 'Good night, sweet ladies. All will seem much better on the morrow!'

'Indeed it will' cried Lady Margot McLeod, laughing, as she pushed her 'Jeannie' into the waiting coach and closed the curtained door behind them. Peeling back Rory's tartan shawl she hugged him with relief and love and laughter.

'My beloved Margot,' he said, taking her in his arms. 'You risked everything for me.'

'There's time only for a quick kiss, my·love!' She smiled radiantly. 'You must keep your shawl on and look like a maid for many miles yet. The redcoats are everywhere, and it would be terrible to be discovered now.'

'Where are we going? You have a plan?' Rory's voice was hoarse with fraudulent crying.

'First to the Abbey at Kinloss, where my Lord Abbot will keep us until the hue and cry has died down. Then to Master Andrew McKay's boatyard at Lossiemouth. He is expecting us, and he'll be well paid to ensure we are shipped to France.'

Sir Rory chuckled appreciatively. 'I'd give a purse to see Cumberland's face. Tricked by a woman, egad!'

Outside, the hoped-for evening mist was rolling across the glens, blanketing the road that led through Glendoe Forest.

'At last we must be almost safe, my love,' whispered Margot as she nestled into the tartan shawl.

Butcher Cumberland was consuming his usual large breakfast when they brought him the news. He stared at his Chief of Staff in a mixture of anger and disbelief. When he spoke his voice was precise and without emotion.

'Place the entire guard at Fort Augustus under close arrest,' he said. 'Publish an order commanding that all the lands belonging to Lady Margot McLeod are sequestered for His Majesty the King. Put all search parties on constant alert.' He paused, went to the window and studied the grooms in the courtyard below for a moment. Then he laughed, a short, sardonic laugh.

'We'll never find them, you know, Hans,' he said. 'The pen may be mightier than the sword, but I'll wager that in this case love is mightier than both of them.'

ROSEMARY AND RIBBONS

Beverley Watts

ALONG THE RIVER BANK not far from Richmond-upon-Thames in Surrey, work had finally been completed on Hampton Court Palace. Cardinal Wolsey's plans had been fulfilled and in the year 1526 the beautiful buildings had been presented to Henry VIII.

The hundreds of craftsmen had done a fine job and their mastery showed in every corner and crevice. Inside the palace, the furnishings were rich and luxurious, too. Members of the royal household lived in splendour and dressed in the latest elegant French fashions.

Outside, the garden of the palace was also a truly wonderful sight to behold. Whilst the builders had been busy with constructing the magnificent rooms of the palace, a whole team of gardeners had been just as busy planning and laying out the grounds. One of those gardeners, Wilf Ruddock, now stood with his daughter Elizabeth on the edge of the flowerbeds, as did many of the local farmers and tradesmen, watching an archery competition in the outer grounds of the palace. Scores of young men from far and wide had come to enter the contest, travelling down the Thames in boats which now bobbed up and down with the swans and moorhens on the river.

Elizabeth was enraptured by the occasion. This was her first visit to the palace. Her father was not a full-time employee of the royal Court; he had simply been recruited to help with the planning and construction of the garden. Soon he would return to work on their own smallholding which provided just enough food for them to live.

The palace gardens seemed magical to Elizabeth. She was impressed by absolutely everything she saw. Colourful flower-beds stretched out around her in decorative patterns, edged with rosemary, lavender and thyme. Fountains gushed up into the warm air and she could feel their spray touch her cheek as it was carried by the gusty wind. Over the way were orchards laden down with ripening fruit – apples, pears and plums – and she could see the green leafy tops of rhubarb next to glistening bunches of redcurrants. The yew hedges were skilfully clipped into wonderful shapes of animals and birds and there was a huge maze. It was all so exciting!

Although she didn't recognise some of the big blooms that swayed in the sunlight, Elizabeth could appreciate their beauty. Her father had told her that many had been specially brought from overseas at great expense. He'd sneaked her a tiny sample one night – a lovely pink flower called a geranium which was the prettiest thing she'd ever seen. There were never any flowers on their own land – only pumpkins, radishes, turnips and parsnips, things they could eat.

Elizabeth stood on tiptoe to watch the next archer shoot. She could only just see over the heads of the other spectators as she was a small girl, with tiny hands and feet. Her long, straight hair, the colour of ripened barley, was shiny and clean and her eyes glistened with their natural sparkle.

An old man, noticing her predicament, kindly edged aside and allowed Elizabeth to stand in front of him where she had a clear view. The young man about to take his turn saw Elizabeth move to her new place and smiled across at her. He had a pale but handsome face and Elizabeth lowered her eyes, afraid to meet his. The boy continued to stare for a few seconds, then went about his task.

Taking up his yew longbow with its flax string, he loaded it with a wand of birch pierced with grey goose feathers. His movements were confident and quick, and his aim was true. Once, twice, three times he shot – all perfect bullseyes. The crowd applauded heartily. His was the best score so far and there were only two more contestants to go.

Elizabeth could no longer concentrate on the other marksmen, however. She stole a sideways glance at the young man who'd caught her eye. He was dressed very simply in comparison to some of the other boys. His breeches were short, his shirt delicately embroidered and he wore a plume in his flat velvet cap, but he did not sport enormous slashed sleeves or breeches or a thick coat lined with wool as did many of his competitors.

The fascinated girl wondered who he might be. A tradesman, perhaps, she thought – or a merchant's son. Whatever his background, he was too fine a person for her, simple Elizabeth Ruddock, to set her sights on. She knew that it would be time for her to marry soon and she'd half promised herself to Willy Lavender whose father's field bordered their own. He was a kind boy, but a dull one. Elizabeth longed to meet other young men, men who were exciting and fun and with a sense of adventure, but she waited still ...

'Go and pick yourself some peaches and plums,' a voice whispered in Elizabeth's ear. It was her father, who had sidled up behind her. 'There are grapes too, on the south-facing walls. Try the quinces and medlars.'

Elizabeth knew she shouldn't really help herself to the fruit in the garden, but a few peaches wouldn't be missed, and she had never tasted some of the other delicious offerings. Her father gave Elizabeth a conspiratorial wink and she slipped away behind the cheering crowds and made her way to the orchard where oranges were growing under glass and apricots hung ripe and ready for picking.

Gathering the ripe fruit in her apron, Elizabeth sat with her

Elizabeth sat with her back against a large apple tree and sank her teeth into a huge furry peach.

back against a large apple tree and sank her teeth into a huge furry peach. The juice ran down her chin and she wiped it off with the back of her hand, then licked the skin, so as not to miss a drop. The sun beat down on her freckled forehead and she only lifted up her head when she realised a shadow had fallen across her face. There, standing laughing in front of Elizabeth was the handsome marksman.

'Are those peaches as good as they look?' he asked. Not knowing what to say in reply, Elizabeth handed him one and grinned nervously.

The boy sat down beside her, nibbling the soft fruit, and watching Elizabeth's every move.

'We shouldn't really be here,' she told him after a few minutes. 'This is part of the palace gardens and it's out of bounds to us commoners.'

'Oh, I'm not afraid,' the young man replied. 'Here, let me try one of those plums.' Elizabeth passed him the burgundy-coloured fruit and began to relax again. The lad had a happy way about him and laughed and joked with her easily. He'd come to Hampton Court specially to enter the archery contest, he said, but didn't live far away from the palace. His name was Francis and he was nineteen years of age.

The way Francis talked was bewitching for Elizabeth – he knew such a lot about so many things. He could read books and had read all of Chaucer's works which he told her were very funny indeed. Elizabeth could not read, but she'd heard about Aesop's Fables and remembered a few of the stories which Francis told her had now been printed in a book.

The young couple chatted easily, about dogs and music and their families. At least, Elizabeth told him about her family, and the smallholding with the crops and chickens that she helped her father run. Francis seemed rather reticent about his home. But she found it so much easier talking to Francis than to Willy Lavender who only had one subject that interested him – sheep. Willy wanted a good wife who would bear his children and he'd settled for Elizabeth. He didn't love her, though; Elizabeth knew that. Any one of several girls would have suited Willy – Nell Bradwell, Mary Salter – they were all the same in Willy's eyes. Elizabeth just happened to live near to him.

As she looked at Francis, a warm feeling began to grow in Elizabeth's breast. She'd never felt the sensation before but guessed that this must be the beginning of love. Could he be feeling it, too? No, it was too much to expect, too much to hope for. He was the kind of boy who would marry a rich merchant's daughter, not a simple farmer's girl. And yet . . .

When Elizabeth and Francis parted that afternoon, it was with a gentle kiss. Francis had promised to meet her every afternoon in the same place, at the bottom of the orchard, and the young girl was thrilled. She ran home with bluebirds singing in her heart and could hardly wait to tell everything to her dear mother who was waiting for her at home. But as the words tumbled out, her mother looked grim and would not share in Elizabeth's joy.

'He's toying with your affections, lass,' she warned. 'Why would a smart young man like that be wasting his time with simple folk like us?'

Elizabeth's father, returning home later, echoed his wife's words. Francis had won the archery competition and it was obvious that he was from a fine family. He doubted the lad's honourable intentions towards his daughter and forbade her to meet him again. That was that. His word was final.

Elizabeth knew it would be no use arguing. Once her father had made up his mind about something, there was nothing that could change it. Words would be useless. But she could not, would not, obey him.

For the first few days, Elizabeth's parents kept a sharp watch on their daughter, so she could not slip away, but on the fourth day they were less attentive and she managed to make her way down the narrow, winding lane to the palace. She doubted whether Francis would be waiting, but as she turned into the orchard, Elizabeth saw his slim figure propped against a wall.

She called out to him and Francis ran to greet her, swinging her round in his arms and laughing merrily.

'My father forbade me to meet you,' she explained sadly. 'I had to disobey him to be here.' She did not elaborate on why her father disapproved of her association with Francis for she wondered herself if there might be some truth in his fears. Within a few minutes of being in Francis's company, however, her doubts disappeared.

They had a wonderful afternoon together. Francis took Elizabeth to some open ground nearby and they flew kites in the strong winds. They bought a halfpenny worth of peppermint drops and sucked them as their kites soared above the trees. Elizabeth felt complete somehow, as if she'd found the other half of her that was always missing, the boy who was in her destiny, waiting for her – her one true love.

Over the next few weeks, Elizabeth and Francis met many times for an hour or so, just sitting, cuddled in each other's arms, or for the whole afternoon when they sometimes went along the Thames in Francis's boat or for a walk in the local countryside. Just being alone together was enough for them.

Elizabeth began to feel more and more confident about her love's intentions. It worried her that he spoke very little about his home life, but he was an honest and true boy, of that she felt sure, and he told her that he loved her.

One day, in the garden of the palace, with the bees buzzing around and the butterflies fluttering from bloom to bloom, Francis knelt down on one knee and asked Elizabeth to marry him. It was the moment she had longed for, wished for ever since their first meeting, and she accepted happily. But something told her that Francis wasn't as happy as he should be; he seemed rather quiet and withdrawn. When she asked what was troubling him, he insisted it was nothing important, a mere trifle, and promised to explain to her at their next meeting. First, he said, she must tell her parents of their planned marriage and ask if Francis could visit their house in order to ask her father formally for Elizabeth's hand.

Elizabeth knew her father would be very angry about her disobedience but hoped that this proof of Francis's honourable intentions would smooth the matter over. She was right. Although Mr Ruddock exploded when Elizabeth admitted she had gone behind his back, he was deeply devoted to his daughter, and realised that she was genuinely in love and that she had found a husband who had promised to make her truly happy. He agreed that Francis could visit their cottage the following week.

Next day, Elizabeth and Francis met by the plum tree as usual and Elizabeth was bubbling over with her good news. Francis smiled when he heard that Elizabeth's father was prepared to give his approval, but his eyes were troubled and his manner hesitant.

'I have a confession to make,' he told her finally, and there was guilt written all over his face.

Elizabeth did not know what to expect next. Was he already married? Did he not truly love her? Her mind flitted from guess to guess like a butterfly dancing from flower to flower. What could this confession possibly be? She braced herself for the truth, however terrible.

'I misled you about my family and my home,' Francis confessed. 'My father is no merchant, he is a member of the nobility and connected to the royal family. This means that I too am distantly related to the King. We have been staying here in Hampton for a while, but we must return to our home in Cornwall soon.'

The pretty peasant girl was overwhelmed. It was all too much to take in. This man could not possibly want her for his wife – he was of noble blood and she was little better than a servant. If she had doubted his sincerity as a merchant's son, this was even more beyond belief. How could he be so cruel as to use her in this way? Their courtship must have been one big joke for him – something to pass the hours.

She felt that a chasm had suddenly opened between them and could see no way of bridging it.

Francis took Elizabeth's hand and looked down at her confused face. His eyes were troubled and full of concern. As if reading her thoughts, he said, 'I know you doubt me, but my love is firm and true. I want you for my wife. My parents know of my wish, and I have my father's consent. They say it is my happiness that they desire and I am free to take a bride of my own choice.'

'I cannot believe . . .' she began.

A slight smile passed over his lips. 'I won't pretend that at first they were overjoyed,' he admitted. 'But when he saw I was truly determined, my father relented. He is much sickened by the follies of the Court and wishes to see me settled on the family estate with a wife who will be content with a simple country life.'

Elizabeth was torn in two by fear and longing and wanted to believe that Francis was speaking from the depths of his being. They held each other fiercely and he kissed away her tears as they trickled down her cheeks.

'Please trust me, Elizabeth,' he begged. 'I cannot lose you now, I must not . . .'

The following week dragged for Elizabeth. She and Francis had agreed not to meet again until he came to see her father and she waited for the visit impatiently.

Her own parents were sceptical and had little faith in promises.

'He is playing with you, child,' warned her father. 'Think no more of him – he will not come. Fine nobles such as he may choose their bride from the pick of the kingdom.'

Eventually the morning arrived and as the minutes crawled by to the appointed hour, all her old doubts and worries kept surging into her head. Was her father right? Would he not come? Had he left for Cornwall without her? Had he just spun her a web of ridiculous lies?

Then, just as she was beginning to despair, a tall, handsome figure appeared in the distance, riding a mettlesome chestnut. Francis – he had come! Now at last Elizabeth knew all was well. It had been against all odds, but she had found a true, unyielding love. A love that would last a lifetime.

Their wedding day was an occasion for great celebration in Hampton. Everyone wanted to see that peasant girl who was to marry the lord. Was she as pretty as was said?

The crowds were not disappointed. The wedding procession was a sight to see with the bridegroom coming first, along with the young bachelors, each with bride lace upon branches of green broom tied to his left arm. Elizabeth, in her bridal gown, with her hair plaited, was led to church between two young boys with bride laces and rosemary tied about their silk sleeves. The bride cup of silver was carried with a gilded branch of rosemary inside, hung with ribbons of all colours.

Musicians followed, then a group of maidens, some bearing bride cakes and others garlands of gilded wheat. Everyone cheered as the procession passed by.

Elizabeth trembled as she spoke her vows but her young husband didn't have a quaver in his voice. When the priest asked, 'Do you take this woman to be thy lawful wedded wife?' he smiled at her and firmly said, 'I do.'

THE WHITE ROSE OF YORK

Mary Hooper

'Is it much further, mistress?' Isabel asked wearily. 'I've been on this horse so long I fear I shall never be able to walk again.'

'By nightfall we'll be there,' Mistress Martin replied. 'Shortly we'll be across the moors and able to see the castle in the distance.'

'By *nightfall!*' Isabel said, and sighed heavily. 'Who would have thought that any place could be this far from London?'

Mistress Martin looked at her kindly. 'It must seem so to you,' she said, 'but I've been to our master's northern castle before and knew it was many a weary day away.'

Isabel sighed again. She wasn't yet sixteen years old, no more than a child really, but girls had to grow up fast, especially in troubled years like 1486.

The sun came out from behind a cloud and briefly warmed the four travellers bound for the castle at Sherriff Hutton: Isabel, Mistress Martin, who was cook and housekeeper to her master and, some distance in front and scouting for possible trouble, Master Martin, skilled blacksmith and Mistress Martin's husband. In front of *him* and out of sight of the other travellers was young Jack Kirkby, groom and jack-of-all-trades.

Isabel was just a maid servant, used to waiting at table and being at everyone's beck and call. She was a quiet, hard-working girl, though, and it was this which had caused her to be sent to Sherriff Hutton in the first place.

'We'll need a maid in the castle, as well as you and your good husband,' Mistress Martin's lord and master had said to her some days ago. 'But we'll need one who'll keep her mouth shut, not blather to tradesmen about the masters she'll be serving.'

'Then that's Isabel, to be sure,' Mistress Martin said. 'She's a quiet girl, a good worker – and loyal, too. She'll not tell secrets.'

'Isabel it is, then.' He hesitated. 'It'll be lonely and drear for you at Sherriff Hutton – none of your London entertainments nor any visitors to lighten your day.' His voice fell. 'And just the two young lords to be cared for.'

''Tis not entertainment I'd be seeking at my time of life,' Mistress Martin said tartly. 'I'll be well content to serve in any of your castles, sire, and wait on whomever you choose.'

'You're a good woman! And when your duty's done in Sheriff Hutton there'll be a gold reward for you.'

Mistress Martin blew out her cheeks indignantly. '*My* reward will be to see that usurper Henry Tudor put off the throne!' she said, causing her lord and master to look round hastily and make sure she'd not been overheard.

'Hush!' he said. 'I know feelings run high but these are times of great unrest. One cannot speak one's mind freely. One *dare* not.'

'But he fought and killed our own King Richard! He – Henry Tudor, a Welshman who'd hardly set foot in England before – and who had no more right to the throne than two dozen others!'

'I know, I know,' the answer came back soothingly, 'and now we must work to put things right.' He walked to the window and looked out for a moment reflectively, as if remembering how he and Richard had played together as boys. 'Yet I fear that even now people are poisoning his memory. Now there is a Tudor on the throne it is not safe to talk of our late King as the fine leader he was, but instead they tell lies about him.'

'Indeed they do,' Mistress Martin put in. 'Already I have heard that he was a hunchback with a club foot and a withered arm – yet he stood as straight and fine as you or me!'

Her lord gave an exclamation of anger. 'Mark my words, if this Tudor keeps the throne then the day will come when our King Richard is only rememberd as a crooked, wicked hunchback. Henry Tudor will have history rewritten to suit him!'

'Never, sire!' Mistress Martin cried indignantly. 'We must all work together to restore the throne to the Yorkist line.'

At last the weary day was ended, and the castle was reached. Isabel saw it ahead of them on a small hill and shivered, for it looked bleak and unwelcoming.

'Why did we have to come here?' she said to her mistress as they rode through the vast doors. 'Why could not these mysterious persons whom we must serve have come to London?'

'The whys and wherefores do not concern *you*,' was the sharp reply, and Isabel looked at her in surprise. Mistress Martin was not usually so blunt – but perhaps she, too, was tired, her bones aching like Isabel's from the sheer effort of staying upright in the saddle day after day.

The steward came into the courtyard to greet them and bid them welcome.

'The young lords arrived yesterday,' Isabel heard him say to Mistress Martin in a hushed voice, 'and very weary of being pushed around the country they are, too. Methinks they'll be well pleased to rest here awhile.'

'Then 'tis nurture and fond care they'll get from me,' she replied with satisfaction, for she liked nothing better than having someone less than strong to build up with her pies and

31

pastries and the sweetmeats for which she was renowned.

She went to look round the kitchen which was to be her domain, and Isabel looked round, too. It was a vast room with foul-smelling rushes on the floor and two large spits above the fireplace. Underneath the long, long table were an assortment of dogs – and an even bigger assortment of half-gnawed bones.

'This lot will have to be cleared up for a start!' Mistress Martin said, wrinkling her nose at the smell. 'You can send out for some fresh rushes straight away.'

She glanced over at Isabel. 'You're asleep on your feet, child. Take your bundle of clothes and find yourself a space to lie in the big hall. Tomorrow will be time enough to sort out a more fitting place for you to sleep.'

Isabel did as she was told, and though her face was pale from tiredness and her eyes heavy the steward looked at her appreciatively, for with her glossy chestnut hair and small, heart-shaped face he thought she was one of the prettiest girls he'd ever seen – and just what the castle needed to make it a more cheery place.

Isabel knew nothing of how she looked just then, however, and cared even less. Grateful to be off her horse she found her way to the great hall, laid her clothes on one of the benches and went straight to sleep.

She awoke when the sun was high in the sky, and ran out to the yard to splash her face with water from the pump and look around her. It was not like her lord's busy and bustling London home, that much was certain. A lone cow stood tethered near the gateway, but apart from that there were little signs of any life. It was as if the castle had stood empty for some time.

'There you are, lazy stay-a-bed!' Mistress Martin said, coming out into the yard and filling a pan with water from the pump. 'What time is *this* to rise?'

'I didn't know what hour it was,' Isabel explained quickly. 'There were no roosters to waken me, nor tradesmen calling, and no mistress shouting for me to lay her clothes out ...'

'Aye, it's quiet enough,' Mistreess Martin said, 'but we won't be welcoming callers here. There are secrets which must stay within these walls.'

'Secrets?' Isabel said, and she reached to her belt and pulled out a comb which she began tugging through her hair.

'Aye, secrets. You'll know them soon enough. And you'll keep your pretty mouth closed about them, too.'

Isabel shook her head and her hair shimmered down her back. 'You can trust me, mistress, you know that. But what are my duties to be while I'm here?'

Mistress Martin's voice fell, even though there was no one else around. 'You are to attend to the young lords,' she said, 'you will bring them food, be a companion to them, and see to their wants.'

'But what young lords – and have they not menservants to do this for them?' Isabel asked in astonishment, for the only young lords she'd ever seen had had a positive army of servants dancing attendance on them.

'Not *these* young lords. The less people who know about them, the better.'

Isabel shrugged. 'Are they prisoners, then?'

'Not prisoners, no. Kept privy for their own good, Isabel. There are people who would have them killed.'

'But ...'

'Enough!' Mistress Martin picked up the pan of water. 'You know all you need to know for now. Go now and begin your duties — greet your lords and take them ale and bread to break their fasts.'

Isabel tied back her hair, adjusted her dress and did as she was bidden. She was directed to a spiral staircase which led to the nursery wing of the castle – which made her wonder, fleetingly, if the young lords she had to care for were babies.

She reached the doorway at the top of the tower and knocked, anxious to see her charges.

'Come in!' a boy's voice called, and she opened the door, stared in shock and surprise at the two youths and then went down in a deep curtsey. If only Mistress Martin had prepared her for this!

'Rise! We are not used to Court manners up here,' a voice said, and the other boy added, 'Do you know who we are, then?'

'Sires . . .' Isabel stammered. 'I have seen you both in royal processions in London. You are – you are my Lord Edward, who was King but never crowned . . .' she turned to the other, smaller figure, '. . . and you are young Prince Richard, Duke of York!'

'That we are! Or were, at least,' Prince Edward said.

'The – the princes in the tower!' Isabel said. 'But I thought you had perished – been put to death by order of King Richard, your uncle!'

Edward, a slight lad of sixteen, smiled wearily. 'So you believed the rumours, too.'

'The people did not know what to believe when you disappeared, sire.'

'My uncle had us removed from London to keep us safe. He knew that if he was defeated in the uprising led by Henry Tudor then we would be put to death by him.'

'By Tudor's men?' Isabel said fearfully.

Edward nodded. 'My claim to the throne is better than his – even though he has now married my sister Elizabeth to strengthen his hold on it.'

'But – so what can be done?'

'Though King Richard, my uncle, was killed at Bosworth his friends live on. They will fight for me – even now forces are gathering and soon Henry Tudor will be no more.'

Isabel put her hand to her mouth, alarmed, for she had never heard such treason spoken against the King's person. Yet she knew the two young princes standing before her – knew, too, that what Edward said was true. His claim to the throne was greater than anyone else's, for he was the eldest son of Edward IV.

'Sire . . .' she said shakily, making another, deeper curtsey.

The younger of the two boys laughed and Edward went to Isabel and, taking her hand, gently lifted her upright again.

'Come,' he said, 'for our stay here we are not sires to be curtseyed to and kneeled to, we are just ordinary folk. No one must know we are princes of the royal blood.'

His voice was gentle, his hand warm and reassuring and Isabel relaxed and smiled back at him.

'I do not think I can regard you as ordinary folk, though,' she said, shaking her head so that a few coppery curls escaped from their ribbon. 'I cannot forget that you are King Edward's sons!'

'You must try,' Edward said, his eyes lingering on Isabel's hair. He, too, would be passing glad to have a young maiden around the place again, for he missed the company of his younger sisters and the busy life they'd led in London.

Two weeks later Edward realised that he was not looking upon Isabel as a sister at all. While young Richard spent most of his time with Mistress Martin in the kitchen, chattering and laughing for the first time since he'd been parted from his mother, Edward and Isabel were inseparable. They rode horses across the moors together, went hawking and hunting and once, with Edward disguised as a footman accompanying a kitchen maid, went to the local fair. On occasions like this, with Isabel at his side, Edward could forget that he was someone with a price on his head and be like any other young man smitten by a pretty girl. Isabel, for her part, was equally taken by the fair good looks of her new companion.

'Do you have to go back?' she asked wistfully one day. 'Can't you live here at Sherriff Hutton for ever and ever?'

Edward shook his head. 'Would that I could, but I have a duty to the Yorkist line. I must try to put the white rose of York back on the throne.'

'But there is such danger!' Isabel said, shuddering with sudden chill. 'I have heard that Henry Tudor is a ruthless man. When he finds out you are still alive . . .'

'Hush!' Edward said, 'I have many friends. They'll help me.'

'The people, though,' she faltered, 'they've seen much bloodshed in the past years. Mayhap they don't want another change – another king on the throne and another war.'

'The people would have fair play,' Edward said resolutely, for Plantaganet blood ran in his veins and he was a young man of courage. 'They loved Edward my father and they would want me to inherit the throne.'

'Perhaps,' Isabel replied worriedly, and as she looked at Edward she knew all at once that the reason why she feared for him so much was that she loved him; loved him with a wholehearted intensity which took no notice of her years.

His eyes caught hers and read the message in them and he put his arms around her and buried his face in her hair. 'We must try and forget tomorrow,' he said huskily, 'while we're here we have each other and that is enough.'

They kissed several times, happy in their discovery, and then Isabel drew away and looked at him wonderingly, realising that she might possibly be holding the future King of England in her arms. 'What if you should be King again?'

'If I am, then you shall come back with me to the royal palace of Westminster and be my queen!' Edward said. 'You shall have servants and maids of your own.'

Isabel gasped and laughed aloud, for she knew such a thing

'We must try and forget tomorrow,' he said huskily.

could never be.

'Tush!' she said. 'If you were King you would have to marry a royal princess – someone of foreign blood who would unite our country with another.'

'I would not!' Edward said soundly. 'I'd be like my father and marry whomever I chose. I would be King, after all – my word would be law.'

'But you couldn't marry a maidservant!' Isabel protested.

'Then you'd not stay a maidservant; I'd make you a countess!' Edward said, and they laughed and kissed again and made a solemn pledge to stay together for ever.

Three weeks after that a band of travelling entertainers came to the castle: three musicians playing pipes, harp and rebec and a team of jugglers and actors. Mistress Martin didn't want to let them in because she still feared spies, but the other servants and the two young lords begged that they should be allowed to enter, for it had been many a long week since there had been any gaiety and music at the castle and time passed slowly.

It was an evening that Isabel was to remember afterwards as the happiest of her life. They sang and danced together and then, while the actors performed a play, Isabel sat by Edward's chair, stealing glances at him and marvelling at how happy and relaxed he was. He looked many times at Isabel, too, and reached out and touched her hair, shimmering in the firelight, and it was quite obvious to all the company that they were in love.

'They say love can work miracles,' Mistress Martin said quietly to her husband, nodding towards the young pair, 'but it would take nothing less than that to ensure a happy life together for *those* two.'

'Indeed!' Master Martin said. 'A deposed king and a serving maid – 'tis like a fairy story and no mistake!'

Isabel retired to her bed that night happy and believing that fairy stories might sometimes come true.

A few days later riders came from London to the castle after dark and Mistress Martin was informed that her two charges were in grievous danger and must leave the country for France that night.

In a panic, she ran up to Isabel's room to warn her.

'Make ready the young lords!' she cried, banging on Isabel's door. 'They must leave the castle at once!'

Isabel flung a cloak over her shift and ran to the door. 'What is it? What's amiss?'

'Riders from London – friends of the House of York!' Mistress Martin panted. 'They have heard there is a plot to capture our lords – Henry Tudor has discovered they are hidden in this part of the country. We have to get them away!'

'Was it the musicians?' Isabel asked fearfully. 'Surely they could not have . . .'

'No one can be sure – but we must help the young lords get away without delay. Hurry, girl!'

Isabel ran towards the tower, fear and alarm making her feet fly along the passageways. One of the messengers had already woken Edward and Richard, though, and they were buttoning their surcoats by the light of a candle.

She ran towards Edward and, unmindful of protocol, flung her arms around him. 'I can't bear you to go!' she cried. 'I'm so afraid you'll never come back to me again!'

Edward kissed her on the forehead. 'Be brave and pray that we reach France safely,' he said, striving to remain calm.

'And what then?' Isabel asked, panic stricken.

'There I may raise support and fund an army to fight for my throne. Have courage, Isabel!' He gently removed her arms from his shoulders and began rolling up the papers and documents that were scattered round the room.

Isabel, remembering her duties, hastily piled some clothes into a bundle and wrapped warm fur rugs about it, her hands shaking and her heart heavy.

'My wife is preparing some food,' Master Martin said, appearing at the door, 'and the grooms are bringing your horses round. You should delay no longer in getting away, sires, for they say that the King's men that seek you are armed and determined.'

Edward ushered Richard towards the door and then he gathered Isabel in his arms and covered her face with quick, urgent kisses.

'Goodbye, sweet Isabel,' he murmured. 'Think of me often – and pray for my safe return.'

Isabel began to cry, but there was no time even for that.

'When I return to England I shall find you and we will be together for ever,' Edward promised, and then he was gone and Isabel was quite alone in the room.

She stood there motionless until she heard the sound of horses' hooves across the drawbridge and then she ran up to the castle battlements and, leaning over, saw six dark shapes riding off over the moors.

Heavy tears began to fall from her eyes then and the grief inside stabbed right through her, for in her heart of hearts she knew the truth – that Edward, her beloved prince, would never return.

'I love you, Edward! God keep you safe!' she cried into the darkness, but her words were carried away by the wind and there was no one to hear them.

KISSES ARE SWEETER THAN WINE

John Sanders

LUCINDA MARCHMONT SET HER BAY GELDING, Champion, into a canter down the empty village High Street. She was tired after a long afternoon's ride and Ferndale House was still two miles away.

She could see her breath rising in the cold air in front of her and she had a tempting vision of muffins toasted against the blazing log fire in the drawing-room, where Lady Cynthia Ferndale would be reclining on a sofa waiting for her to return and pour out the tea.

The handsome, black-caped rider whose mount was cantering down Cherry Blossom Lane at right angles to the High Street was tired and in a hurry, too. His hostelry was another mile beyond the village, and tonight mine host was serving an *escalope de veau* with mushroom sauce which promised to be almost as succulent as any he could buy in his native France.

Neither saw the other until it was too late. As the two horses met at the corner, they swerved sharply, and the riders were thrown against each other. The impact hurled Lucinda like a lance from the saddle and she struck the ground with a force that jarred from her toes to her ribs. Next moment it seemed as if the black cape was spread all around her.

'Mam'selle, a thousand pardons! I had no idea . . . I did not keep a look out, as you say. Are you hurt? Shall I call some assistance?'

Lucinda felt first her arms, then her legs, gingerly, as if in disbelief that they were still there. Satisfied that they were, she turned her attention to the rider in the black cape.

'I – I don't think I was looking, either,' she faltered.

The man got to his feet slowly, helping her up with an outstretched arm. Lucinda was surprised at his height and found herself craning her neck backwards to look into bright, nut-brown eyes which were now looking at her with genuine concern.

'Forgive me,' he was saying. 'A thousand pardons. I am a stranger here and I do not know the road well.'

'You — you're French, aren't you?' she asked.

'I am indeed. Just a merchant visiting your lovely land. Now tell me, are you hurt at all?'

'I'm quite all right.' Lucinda smiled back. She was suddenly conscious that she was pleased at his concern. Try as she might, she could find no real injury, beyond a few bruises. 'It's kind of you to be so troubled on my behalf.'

'Not at all. Here, let me help you on to your horse. Your dress is dusty, I fear, and you must be a little shaken – *un petit peu*, perhaps.'

Boldly he picked her up and set her down on her saddle as if she were as light and fragile as a Grecian vase. Then, for a magic moment that made her thrill with mingled pleasure and embarrassment, his hand continued to clasp hers.

'Have you far to go?' he asked anxiously. 'Are you sure you'll be all right?'

'I'm only going to Ferndale House. I live there,' Lucinda explained, aware of a false pitch in her voice. 'I am companion to Lady Cynthia Ferndale.' She raised her riding crop and touched her horse's flanks. 'Come, Champion.'

She rode on, though she couldn't resist one backward glance. The handsome Frenchman was still standing beside his horse, watching her. He raised his hand in a farewell gesture.

She rode back across the park faster than she'd ever ridden before, as if her life depended on it. Gone was the peaceful vision of toasted muffins by the fire. Instead she could only conjure up the disturbing image of a handsome face with nut-brown eyes that contained in their depths the suspicion of a humorous twinkle. Remembering the proximity of that face and the enveloping folds of a black cloak, Lucinda felt her cheeks burning despite the whip of the cool wind.

A Frenchman! And so handsome! Who was he? And what was he doing in Ferndale village, two hundred miles away from his native land? She had heard Lord Ferndale talk of the rumblings of discontent between London and Paris, of the threat of war with the newly crowned Emperor Napoleon Bonaparte. As a result Frenchmen had become rare in England – rarer still in the heart of the rural Midlands.

Back at Ferndale House Lucinda was obliged to put the memory of that violent encounter behind her as she attended Lady Cynthia and sympathised with her murmured complaints. She poured out the tea and placed cushions behind Her Ladyship's back when she complained of a pain, trying to forget the ache of her own muscles from the bruising she'd received in her fall.

Lucinda rarely saw her employer. She knew that his wealth came from farming his thousands of acres; that he went regularly up to London where he had banking interests; that he was one of the new breed of English aristocracy who believed there was real merit in trade and that no longer should anyone scorn the profits and rewards of industry just because he was a member of the nobility. Such a man in this new and exciting nineteenth century had plenty of work to do. So Lucinda was surprised, not to say disquieted, when a week later Dickson, the butler, opened the door and announced gravely, 'His Lordship would like to see you in the study, Miss Marchmont.'

Lucinda knocked timorously on the study door, still not quite believing that Dickson had delivered the message to the right person. Lord Ferndale was sitting at his desk, and standing beside him in deep discussion, which Lucinda was aware had been abruptly broken off as soon as she'd appeared, was his eldest son and heir, George.

Lucinda stiffened involuntarily. She knew she had no right to dislike her employer's kinfolk, but she was willing to admit that George was perhaps the Ferndale she liked rather less than the other members of the family. He seemed a cold, aloof young man; you knew your place with George and, furthermore, he expected you to know it.

'Ah, Miss Marchmont.' The kindly Lord Ferndale rose from his desk and came towards her. 'Sit down, sit down. We have a small problem, George and I, and we think that you may be willing to help us.'

'If I can . . .' Lucinda murmured.

Lord Ferndale went on, 'I have recently finalised a potentially profitable agreement with a company in France called Duhamel Frères – you may have heard of them. They are distributors of very good claret wines produced in the vineyards of their own château, and they have agreed to take wool from our farms and market it in France, while we shall take their wines and sell them through our numerous outlets in London.

'As you may know, the head of Duhamel Frères is a business friend of mine, Marcel Duhamel. My son George here has been acting as intermediary between the two companies, travelling regularly to France, and –' he glanced across at his son, with a faint smile – 'in the course of his frequent visits to the home of Monsieur Duhamel he has become attached to the eldest daughter, Yvette. The connection has met with the entire approval of both families and I am happy to say the couple are now formally betrothed.'

Lucinda smiled warmly at George. 'My congratulations, sir. I had no idea …'

Lord Ferndale held up his hand for attention. 'The problem is this … my wife would dearly love to be present at the wedding. However, it is a difficult time for an English family to be visiting France. With the unstable political situation there is an element of uncertainty – the journey will be very fatiguing and English travellers may not always be welcome.' He cleared his throat. 'Fact is, Miss Marchmont, we should be glad if you would accompany my wife on this occasion. I may not be able to be with her at all times and she will need a companion.'

'Why, yes, of course,' Lucinda agreed wonderingly. 'I should be happy to attend Lady Cynthia.'

France! The home of the young man she had so recently encountered! The dangers of such a journey scarcely entered Lucinda's head, as she made her preparations with mounting excitement. Just to travel, to have the chance of seeing a foreign land, even though she knew she would hardly be allowed a free moment. In her uneasy position as companion, in which she counted neither as family nor as servant, she could scarcely expect to attend the wedding itself. But she would be abroad – it would be an adventure!

She did not pause to wonder at the readiness with which Lord Ferndale had accepted the match. There had been a whisper, she had heard, that before the Revolution the Duhamels had been a family not only of substance but also of noble connections, and that they had survived the Revolution due largely to their willingness to suppress the noble connections.

Lucinda was astonished when Lady Cynthia remarked casually a few days later, 'I have ordered my dressmaker to make a new gown for you, my dear. If you are to accompany us to France it is important that you are dressed in a fitting manner for all occasions. Lord Ferndale insists upon it.'

It was an unexpected piece of generosity, and Lucinda could only wonder what opportunity she would have for wearing such finery, when her time would doubtless be occupied in reading to Lady Cynthia, or in fetching her smelling salts, her book or her needlework. Lucinda had no illusions on that score: when she had joined the family as Lady Cynthia's companion it had been made perfectly clear to her that it was a great privilege she was being offered – she, the daughter of an impoverished clergyman – and it was entirely on account of her mother having been a distant cousin of Lady Cynthia's. She had been repaying that debt of gratitude ever since.

She had to admit, however, that whenever Lady Cynthia could spare a thought for anyone besides herself, she had been treated with kindness. Nor had the position proved too demanding, though there were times when Lucinda couldn't help feeling like the proverbial bird in a gilded cage.

The brougham came jarring and jolting down the hill and suddenly spread out in front of them was the broad sweep of the Channel and, in the foreground, the Calais packet, with her sails furled and the wind set fair for France. Lucinda couldn't suppress a strangled cry of delight, which caused Tilly, Lady Cynthia's maid who was sitting beside her, to giggle. In the seat opposite, the Honourable George Ferndale merely stiffened and twitched his forefinger on his silver-knobbed cane, to show that he was well accustomed to such ordinary sights – as indeed he was, being a seasoned traveller.

In front of them Lord and Lady Ferndale were travelling in the first carriage. Lord Ferndale's valet sat on the box beside the coachman. It seemed to Lucinda an extravagant luxury that Lady Cynthia should have required her presence as well as that of her maid, but she was thankful for it as she sniffed the

'. . . suddenly spread out in front of them was the broad sweep of the Channel and, in the foreground, the Calais packet.

sharp sea air and savoured the scent of salt water and tarred ropes.

It was a different story a few hours later when they were halfway across the Channel and the little ship was riding a deepening swell. On coming aboard Lady Cynthia had instantly taken to her bunk, and Lucinda and Tilly had been in constant attendance ever since, bathing her aching forehead, soothing her terror when the ship heaved and rolled with every timber shrieking, and finally nursing her through bouts of seasickness that became ever more severe as each hour passed.

Lucinda herself felt increasingly queasy and longed for the fresh, clean air on deck, but she was unable to leave her patient and had to bear the ordeal as best she could.

The tortures of the voyage were soon forgotten, however, when they disembarked at Calais. There they transferred to two carriages which had been sent by the Duhamel family to meet them, and were driven to an inn just outside the town. Exhausted by sickness, Lady Cynthia wanted nothing but sleep, and Lucinda found herself free to sit at the window and gaze over the moonlit French countryside. Where was he now, her handsome Frenchman? Was he back in his own country? she wondered. How strange it seemed that she should now be here, in *his* land, hearing *his* tongue spoken all around her ...

At dawn next day, with Lady Cynthia fully recovered they were away again and heading south towards Paris.

Paris! Lucinda's heart leapt as they approached the broad Seine river, and the horses seemed to pull faster, more triumphantly. Suddenly, in front of them was the Tuileries Palace, where, only a few years ago, the King was ruling before they took him out and cut off his head. Lucinda shuddered. The people in the streets looked cheerful enough as they went about their work.

'They don't look like regicides,' she said aloud.

'Peasants!' George snorted. 'May they all answer before God for their murderous crimes.'

George had been like that for the past two days, Lucinda reflected. Hardly friendly, and scarcely like a man on his way to his own wedding. I'm glad I'm not getting married to him, Lucinda thought. It didn't occur to her that he might be worried, well aware that he was the only one of the party who spoke fluent French and that he felt responsible for his family in this hostile land.

However, nothing untoward happened, protected as they were by the Duhamel livery worn by the coachmen and adorning the carriages, though there had been a brief moment of tension at an inn where they had stopped for a meal. The English voices had affronted the landlord whose patriotism seemed to have exceeded his hospitality, but using his haughtiest air of authority George had spoken to him in rapid French and Lucinda had seen gold pass between them.

They dined that night at the Porte St Denis with the Duhamel company agents and for the first time George began to relax. He had clearly known the senior agent for some time, Lucinda noticed, and he seemed totally at ease in their company.

Next day they were on the road again, and all that day and the next they rattled southwestwards to the Duhamel château. As the miles swept by George laughed and joked with the agents who rode beside them. Lucinda had never seen him in such a merry mood, so cheerful and eloquent.

On the last morning one of their horses cast a shoe, and Lord Ferndale's carriage went on ahead. Lucinda was used to the English elegance of the Ferndale estate, but the long drive across the Duhamel vineyard and then through the private park that surrounded the château in the centre of the Burgundy country made her catch her breath in wonder.

49

At the magnificent main entrance liveried servants whisked away her trunk and a soldier-straight butler led them into the great hall. There Lucinda received her first surprise.

From the top of the broad staircase a shrill voice screamed '*Georges!*' and a girl came flying down the stairs, ran across the hall so fast that her feet seemed hardly to touch the floor, and without pausing, leapt into George Ferndale's arms.

'*Mon chérie, tu es revenu! Chaque jour, je t'attendais!*' Before Lucinda's astonished gaze, she covered George with kisses – stiff, pompous George Ferndale – punctuating each word with a passionate embrace. And George, Lucinda couldn't help noticing, seemed to be enjoying every moment of it, returning kiss for kiss with equal passion, oblivious now of her and of the servants scurrying all around them and the impassive attitude of the ramrod-stiff butler, standing discreetly several paces away.

Suddenly his fiancée noticed Lucinda. As the French girl looked round, still locked in the embrace of the Honourable George Ferndale, Lucinda was surprised by the loveliness of the laughing, flushed face. It was a classical face of soft tenderness with smiling, darting eyes and firm, expressive mouth, all framed in a mass of dark, quivering ringlets. In a single instant Lucinda was conscious of a young woman of rare beauty.

The girl struck her forehead with her hand in a theatrical gesture of apology.

'Pardon me, Mademoiselle. I did not mean to ignore you. I am Yvette Duhamel, and it is I who will marry this one!' She laughed, and hugged again her grinning fiancé.

Lucinda could not help feeling a twinge of envy as she looked at the glowing happiness of the couple before her. Although her opinion of George had mellowed in the last few days, it was certanly not for him that she envied Yvette. It was simply that it must be wonderful to be so much in love and to know that love was returned a thousandfold ... to be getting married in two days' time to the man of your dreams. She sighed, as quite involuntarily the image of a handsome face with nut-brown eyes and a humorous twinkle rose up before her. Other people's happiness was sometimes hard to live with ...

She turned away to follow the butler up to a great bedroom with tall windows opening on to a balcony that looked out over the splendid formal gardens in front of the château.

She was surprised when, a short time later, she called at Lady Cynthia's room, only to be dismissed by a wave of the hand.

'I shall not be needing you, Lucinda,' Her Ladyship said in her faintly querulous voice. 'I shall be driving out with Madame Duhamel this afternoon. You may amuse yourself.'

Lucinda returned to her room, wondering again why Lord Ferndale had considered her presence at this wedding really necessary. After all, the Duhamel family were more than adequate hosts and the house seemed to be fully supplied with servants. But she was here, and she was free, and this could only be looked on as a delightful holiday. With a lift of her spirits Lucinda ran out of the house on to the sweeping lawns to enjoy the spring sunshine.

'Mademoiselle Lucinda!'

She heard her name being called and turned round. Yvette was running across the grass toward her. The girl took her by the arm in a gesture of familiarity.

'I thought I should come and talk to you about the arrangements for tonight,' she said. 'George and I have to go to see my father's lawyers about the marriage contract this afternoon. I think you would prefer to stay here and rest because tonight is the night of the Burgundy vintner's ball and it will be held here in our own ballroom. It's the big occasion of the year in our district, so you must wear your best gown. All the world will be there – everyone important.'

'But Mademoiselle,' Lucinda protested, 'I don't think it is seemly – I mean, I am here as Lady Cynthia's companion. She may need me – she may not wish me to ...'

Yvette laughed prettily. '*Au contraire!* I have the permission from Lady Cynthia to tell you that she does not need you to attend her this evening. Tonight you will be our guest! I promise you we will make your visit worthwhile. The ball starts at nine o'clock. I shall be waiting for you then in the great hall.'

She turned away quickly and before Lucinda had time to ask another question she was running back to the house.

Lucinda followed slowly, her thoughts in a turmoil. A ball! And she was to be a guest! Once again, she blessed the surprising generosity of Lady Cynthia for giving her such a lovely gown – what a happy coincidence! Obediently she retired to her room to rest before the evening's revelry.

Promptly at nine o'clock Lucinda descended the great staircase that led to the hall. Yvette, already waiting there with George, raised her hand to wave, then covered her mouth in delight.

'You look ravishing, *chérie*, absolutely ravishing!' she gasped. 'Now, to the ballroom, to greet our guests and meet the rest of the family.'

The château seemed suddenly alive with a thronging crowd: women in exquisitely cut ball gowns; men in white silk breeches, and occasionally a uniformed hussar of the Emperor Napoleon's famous *Grande Armée*, carrying his hat under his arm and his sword in a sheath at his side. Lucinda followed George Ferndale and Yvette Duhamel in single file through the surging mass, smoothing the folds of her cream silk gown, and enjoying the occasional admiring glances which, she was aware, were being flashed in her direction.

Yvette led them through the crowd to a table under the minstrel's gallery, where a dozen people, Lord and Lady Ferndale among them, were already seated with her parents. Lucinda found herself shaking hands with strangers, trying to memorise their names – women in low-cut dresses, men standing bowing ...

And then – a shock.

From among the people sitting at the table a man, resplendent in the full dress uniform of the French navy, rose to his feet. He took her hand, kissed it, and before she had time to do more than gasp, said, 'Hello. We meet again, Mademoiselle. And how is Champion?'

Lucinda raised her head to gaze into a pair of familiar nut-brown eyes smiling down at her.

'The Frenchman!' she whispered.

A silence fell around them, and she was suddenly aware that everyone was watching. Beside her, she heard Yvette say, 'This is my brother, Raoul – Captain Raoul Duhamel. But –' Yvette gave a tinkling laugh – 'I believe you have already met.'

Lucinda felt herself blushing furiously. 'I – I did not know ... did not realise ...'

Raoul was still holding her hand. 'That I was Yvette's brother? Ah, it was a well-kept secret, was it not?'

'Like George,' Yvette explained, 'Raoul must travel sometimes to England on family business. Last time, after he met you in the village, he decided he must see you again – that it is imperative! And, *ma chérie*, I can see why!' She hugged Lucinda impulsively. 'But alas! It is no longer possible for him to go to England. In his position it is too dangerous, you understand – his duty is here, and if war comes between our two countries ...'

Raoul broke in, 'As you can see, Mademoiselle, I am not really a business man. I have another calling. Since I could not visit you in England, it seemed instead that you must come to France . . .' he glanced across at Lord and Lady Ferndale, who were chatting to his own parents '. . . so I asked Lord Ferndale if he would bring you to the wedding!'

Lucinda gasped. 'You mean Lady Cynthia knew of this arrangement?'

'But certainly!' He laughed gaily. 'I insisted that she would need a companion – I assured her that my mother would desert her completely!'

Lucinda's head was in a whirl. As she looked across the table, Lady Cynthia raised her fan and graciously inclined her head in her direction, as if sending her a blessing.

Raoul guided her to a chair, seated himself next to her and calling a waiter over, ordered some wine. Above the babble of voices, an unseen orchestra struck a chord to begin the dancing.

'And so now you are here, Mademoiselle, how do you like France?' Raoul asked, his eyes scanning her face admiringly. 'Well enough, I hope, to make your stay with us a long one.'

As she looked back into those warm brown eyes, Lucinda's heart was beating wildly. She felt as if she were melting into a dream, the outcome of which had been settled long ago. I have a feeling that from now on I'm *really* going to enjoy myself, she thought.

'Oh yes, Monsieur,' she said fervently. 'I like France very much indeed. In fact, I feel – already I feel I should like to stay here for ever . . .'

TABBIES ARE LUCKY, TOO

Angus Allan

BARRY TREMAYNE'S MASK was securely in place. He checked it, unnecessarily, for the tenth time, and glanced down at the pistol in his belt. Primed. Pan closed. Hammer on half-cock. He felt the usual surge of excitement quicken in his breast, and leaned forward to pat the neck of his patient horse. 'Any moment now, Firefly, and we'll be in business.'

There could have been no lonelier place that moonlit night than the broad expanse of Hounslow Heath. The Bath Road was a ribbon of silver, and the only sound, save the occasional jingle of Firefly's harness, was the screech of a hunting owl.

Barry Tremayne had been a highwayman for most of what he could remember of his eighteen years. He was not the sort of young man who would make excuses for himself, but anyone who had cared to study his childhood and his upbringing would have been little surprised. Orphaned, he had been thrown on the mercy of a cruel and unfeeling parish workhouse. He had stolen bread – not just for himself, but for the other miserable inmates of the institution, and he had been flogged for it. Flogged and confined in a stinking cell not even fit for a rat. But his terrible crimes had not ended there. Oh, no. At the age of ten, he had had the audacity, the outrageous impudence, to talk back to the workhouse master who had forced one of his sickly companions to toil for twenty-four hours without a break. That particular villainy had earned Barry a thrashing he'd never forgotten, and had been, so to speak, the last straw. He had cut and run – falling in, inevitably, with 'the wrong crowd', 'the bad 'uns'. He had held up and robbed his first coach, amazingly, before his thirteenth birthday.

Now there was a price on his head, and the only possible alternative to his career as 'a gentleman of the road' was to be caught and hanged.

A faint and welcome sound came to his ears. It was the distant approach of *The Flier* – the London and Bristol coach. Barry drew his pistol and snapped the hammer back to full cock.

Here it was. The horses, the lurching vehicle, the driver, the guard, the outside passengers on the box ...

'Stand and deliver!' roared Barry, urging Firefly out into the coach's path, and the toiling team came to a slithering, undignified halt as the cursing driver hauled on the traces. The stage's body lurched and pitched, its squealing springs protesting to the night.

'I'd be obliged,' said Barry, 'if you'd remove your finger from the trigger of that blunderbuss, and toss it down into the road.' He gestured with his pistol at the angry guard, and the man did as he was bidden.

Although the outside passengers, only too well aware of their danger, quaked silently in their skins, there came a furious bellow from within the vehicle. 'What manner of outrage is this?'

The window came down with a bang, to reveal a choleric, purple face, a bob-wig all lopsided on the middle-aged head of a man with a port-wine nose and a livid sabre scar down one cheek.

'Tush,' said Barry. 'I'm only a poor tobyman, trying to make a living. You look out of sorts, sir. Like a man who carries too heavy a burden. Allow me to lighten it for you – starting, perhaps, with your purse?' He wagged the gun, meaningfully.

Spluttering, the fat man tossed down a leather pouch that gave out a satisfying, golden clinking as it landed in Barry's outstretched tricorne hat. Barry said, 'And your fob, sir?'

'Devil take you, gallows-bait,' snarled the man. But he fumbled the watch from his waistcoat, nonetheless.

'You're having difficulty with it?' prompted Barry.

'I'm removing a locket from the chain,' growled the man. 'It is of great personal and sentimental value to me, and I'll be hanged if I'll willingly part with it to the likes of you.'

'Let me see.' Barry snapped his fingers imperiously, and very reluctantly, the passenger handed it over.

The locket was a modest enough affair, for such an obviously wealthy owner. It was of engraved gold, but not of the purest quality. Barry thumbed it open, and found himself unable to suppress a gasp of admiration. For it contained a perfectly exquisite miniature portrait, surely executed by a master artist, of a beautiful girl. If there was such a thing as a speaking likeness, this was it. The sweetness of the face, and the half smile on her lips, would have melted the hardest heart, and Barry's was by no means that.

'Your daughter, sir?'

'Yes, plague take you!'

Barry smiled, and deftly took the locket from the watch-chain, tossing it back to the astonished passenger. 'No man with any sense of honour,' he said, 'would take such a thing from a devoted father.'

'Honour? Your kind talks of *honour*?' Now it was one of the uppermost passengers, beer-valour from the last posting halt overcoming his fright. Barry glanced up at him dangerously.

'Save your insults,' he rapped. 'Just make haste and empty your pockets. You and all your companions!'

Barry disdained to rob the driver or the guard. They, to his mind, were working men, entitled to keep whatever hard-earned pittance they got. Secretly, he envied them. If circumstances had been different, perhaps he too would have been able to pursue some equally respectable occupation.

However, no time for useless philosophy. 'Drive on,' said Barry, tossing back the blunderbuss, having rendered it harmless. The whip cracked, and the young highwayman chuckled as the lurch of the coach dropped the scar-faced man out of sight and into his seat, and the outsiders had to clutch desperately to save themselves from falling off.

'My thanks, gentlemen, and a very good night to you,' he called, mockingly. 'May you meet no more highwaymen on your journey. Some of my brethren get *very* angry when they find you've nothing left to donate!'

Barry made his way over the little-known tracks of the heath towards the Red Lion – a remote public house where the landlord was enough of a crook himself to be a friend to others outside the law. It had been a good haul. He had done well. But uppermost in his mind was the memory of the face of the girl in the locket. Barry sighed deeply. If only life could have given him a better deal. Fine clothes and a decent position. He lost himself in a daydream where he called at the scar-faced man's grand mansion – he was sure it would be a grand mansion – and payed court to his daughter. The devil! He should have asked the man her name! Was it Sarah, possibly? She looked like a Sarah. No – something grander. Amelie. Caroline.

Barry laughed, and cursed himself for a fool as he came back to reality. What was a hunted highwayman doing, thinking of romance? A creature of the shadows, always on the run. Flitting from one corner of England to the other. But try as he might, thoughts of that lovely girl returned to plague him, again and again . . .

It was well past midnight when he reached the Red Lion. He could see a light burning behind the warped shutters of the parlour window. Nothing was amiss. He swung from his horse, put her into the stables and saw that she was fed and watered from the supplies the landlord customarily left there for his shady clients. Whistling a soft tune, he strode to the door and gave the secret knock, hearing the bolts drawn back in immediate response.

And that's when Barry Tremayne received the worst shock he'd ever had in his life!

Did the familiar, ugly face of mine host look slyly out at him? It did not. Instead, the highwayman found himself eye-to-eye with the round 'O' of a musket-muzzle, and behind the horny hands that held it, the red coat and white cross-belts of a sergeant of the Middlesex Yeomanry.

'We've been expecting you, cully,' said the soldier.

Barry stood frozen. Beyond, there were perhaps half a dozen more of them. A preventive troop from the Isleworth Garrison. His throat suddenly felt as constricted as if the noose were already in place!

The purse of guineas that Barry had taken from the man inside the coach was in his right hand. Deliberately, he turned his wrist, and let the dazzling money spill on the ground, and absolutely nothing could have stopped the sergeant automatically looking down as the coins rattled at his feet.

Barry's right foot came up like a rocket. The musket, kicked off-aim, blasted its leaden bullet into the lintel of the door, and all Barry's force went into a flat-handed smash that sent the soldier hurtling back among his men!

Then the highwayman was running for the stable, his one hope to get to Firefly, unsaddled though she was, and vanish into the night.

He got no more than half a dozen paces. There were two of them, materialising from the rear of the outbuildings, on horseback. And they rode him mercilessly down, the flat of their sabres knocking the senses clean out of him. He knew

'We've been expecting you, cully,' said the soldier.

nothing of their crude laughter and bullying jest as they hauled his unconscious body to its feet and lashed his wrists behind his back ...

'What jail is this?' said Barry Tremayne, wincing with the pain in his skull. Blearily, he looked around him at the dark, plain walls of rough stone, the straw on the floor, the solitary man in coarse clothes who sat scowling at him from a table by the heavy oaken door.

'It's no jail, you poltroon,' said the man. 'You're in the cellars of Squire Maidment's house. Not,' he added, 'that they serve badly as a dungeon.'

'Squire Maidment?' Barry was having difficulty getting his wits back together.

'County magistrate,' said the other. 'The soldiers brought you here. The squire's the man with power of the warrant. He's out raising a jury right now. Come an hour or two, and you'll be all neatly tried, sentenced and dangling.'

Something brushed Barry's arm and made him jump. It was a cat. A tabby cat. And it began to purr loudly as Barry automatically reached to fondle its ears.

'Like animals, do you?' the jailer was sneering at him.

'They're better company than some humans I could name,' said Barry evenly. 'I could tell you a tale or two about those. Especially the rogues in the workhouse where I grew up. Made friends with the mice, we did. *And* the cats. Funny – they seemed to know they were all losers, like the rest of us.'

'*Very* touching,' said the man. 'Here. Bit of bread and water. That's all you're getting. I've got my orders to report you've come round.' He got up. 'Puss. Come on, puss.'

The cat stayed where it was, turning its back on the jailer, kinking its tail, and curling up deliberately on Barry's knee.

'Stupid varmint,' said the man. 'Can't think what makes Miss Ellen so soft on it.'

'Miss Ellen?'

'Squire's daughter. Rescued the thing from the mill-pond when it was just a two-day kitten. You'd think the creature was human flesh and blood, the daft way she treats it.'

The jailer left, and Barry shook his head as he tickled the tabby under the chin. 'Not much use your making a friend out of me, little 'un,' he said. 'I'll be crow-meat in an hour or two, so help me.' The tabby reached itself up and nuzzled strongly against his chin. 'Oh! *I* see! Telling me you think I'm not such a bad lad, and you'll miss me. That it? Daft little imp!'

Inevitably, the highwayman fell to thinking about his wasted life. Moments of self-reproach alternated with periods of defiance. Then there was regret. And there came, too, the closer memory, strangely powerful, of that locket, and the painting of the beautiful girl . . .

He spoke aloud, continuously, and all the time it was as though the cat were listening, head cocked slightly to one side, eyes narrowing and widening, the purring subdued but still there. Once or twice it yawned, and Barry laughed, despite the predicament he was in. 'You're a bonny one, and no mistake,' he said.

The fault was undoubtedly the jailer's. He had closed and locked the cellar door behind him, and had left a candle burning on a shelf in the corridor outside. Badly placed, that candle had overbalanced, and had flared on to the straw of the floor. The panelling out there had caught fire, and now there was a roaring blaze, the first inkling of which came to Barry as smoke began to seep beneath the crack of the door.

He was not tied, and desperately, he yelled at the top of his lungs and flung his weight against the heavy oak. Being hanged was one thing – being burned alive was another!

At the fourth assault, some part within the rusty lock mechanism gave way, and the door flew open. Barry recoiled with a gasp of dismay. The corridor was a mass of smoke and flames! Hurriedly, he drew his cloak over his head and plunged headlong through the blaze, racing up a flight of stone stairs with the blood pounding in his ears and the heat scorching his face. Somewhere he could hear a shrill voice yelling 'Fire!'

Abruptly, in a moment of crystal clarity, he realised that he was free! There would be panic – chaos, as whoever was around tried to raise help to fight the fire. With any luck he could get clean away! Better still – if the blaze really took hold, it might be thought that he'd perished in the inferno ...

Perished. In the inferno. Suddenly, he thought of the cat. It must still be there. Back in the cellar!

Barry took two more faltering paces forward. Stopped. He thought of the little animal, petrified with terror. Now a figure loomed up ahead: the jailer, carrying two slopping buckets. His eyes widened as he saw Barry, and he dropped them. His mouth opened to yell a new alarm, and Barry knew that it was now or never.

It had to be never. The young man turned, and gathering his cloak about him once more, hurled himself desperately back through the conflagration, blind instinct taking him to the cellar door.

The cat was there. Calling piteously, it crouched against the far wall, and though it fought and struggled, Barry pulled it close to him and thrust it beneath his shirt, ignoring the sharp claws. Indeed, the pain of them was minimal compared to the hot searing breath within his bursting lungs!

Now water drenched him as the jailer and other hastily equipped servants hurled bucket after bucket into the cellar area. One of them had rigged a crude canvas pump. Exhausted and helpless, Barry put up no resistance at all as someone grabbed him and dragged him out of danger up the stairs. There came the snap of manacles on his wrists, a door slammed, and his precious vision of freedom faded for ever.

The tabby cat struggled from his shirt and dropped to the ground. It ran a few paces, stopped, and deliberately began to wash its paws. Someone said, 'By all the saints! He went back to rescue Miss Ellen's *cat*!'

His wrists secured to the oaken rails of a heavy chair in Squire Maidment's study, Barry heard all the clatter attendant upon the magistrate's return. Now his footfalls were approaching, and the highwayman gave a gasp of amazement as the door opened to admit a man with a choleric, purple face, a port-wine nose and a livid scar, all beneath a lopsided bob-wig . . .

'Well, well, well! So it's *you* again!' The Squire threw his hat on to the table and walked round Barry, peering curiously at him from all angles. 'The young scoundrel who held up our coach! I'll see you hanged for that. Robbing honest citizens of everything we had!'

'Not everything, sir –'

At that moment a sweet, soft, melodious voice from the doorway said, 'Father. He had every opportunity to run free. Samuel said so. And yet he went back for Tabitha.'

Barry's voice stuck in his throat. He had eyes only for the girl – Miss Ellen. How was it possible that she was actually even more beautiful than the miniature portrait in the Squire's locket? At last, he found himself able to speak.

'Ma'am – I returned your picture. Ask your father if this were not so. I would not take it from him. But now –' The courage of desperation entered his voice. 'Now I have but one favour to ask. Would you permit a condemned felon to kiss your hand? I should die happy, Miss Ellen.'

She had the cat in her arms. 'You'll not die, my brave friend,' she said softly. 'My father may look every inch the stern, unflinching upholder of the law, but he is a good, kind man and I know he will do as I ask. I have much influence with him,' she added, going over to her father and kissing him on the cheek.

Maidment snorted. 'What nonsense, Ellen! Be silent, lass!'

'I know enough about it to recite the alternative punishment for highway robbery where no blood has been spilled,' said Ellen. She turned to Barry. 'Have you ever killed anyone?'

He shook his head. 'Not even in self-defence,' he said, quietly.

It took almost half an hour of argument, pleading persuasion on her part, angry bluster on her father's, but at last Squire Maidment agreed reluctantly that, in passing sentence, he would exercise his powers to have Barry not executed, but transported to the Colonies. It would mean a harsh and hard existence, where only the fittest and best survived. But – and it had happened in the past – a significant number of transportees had prospered. Even achieving honest respectability, enough to earn the King's Pardon ...

Gratefully, Barry pressed the hand that Ellen slipped into his, and the look that passed between them spoke of a time, who knew how far distant, when they might meet again, in better circumstances. At least, the highwayman had something definite to live and work for, and – it surely knew it too – the tabby cat, luckier for him than the blackest of its brethren, was purring loudly ...

LOVE IN DISGUISE

Mary Hooper

I RAN DOWN THE big circular staircase into the hall, my heels clicking on the marble. Mother had told me that my father wanted to see me, had important news for me, and I was anxious to hear what it was and then go out for my usual morning ride on my horse, Polly.

I wasn't in the least bit concerned, for, knowing Father, the important news would turn out to be nothing more than that he'd bought a fine piece of furniture, or a new brood mare – or that he had to go to London on some business deal or other and would I promise to be a good and dutiful daughter while he was away.

I opened the door of the drawing room. Father had his back to me and was looking out of the window at the maze he'd just had constructed, so for a moment I was able to look at him unobserved. What I saw made me sigh in dismay. Father was middle-aged, positively ancient, yet he liked to follow fashion as if he were one of the young dandies at Court. This meant, even at this early hour, that he was wigged and powdered and was wearing blue satin knee-breeches topped by a long embroidered waistcoat; *most* unsuitable for a man of his age.

He turned round and I saw he had on a white shirt with a frilly lace jabot at the neck that I'd never seen before. Fashions came and went so fast, though, that you had to be a regular visitor to London and the Court if you wanted to keep up with them. For myself, I didn't want to, preferring simple, unrestricting clothes. No vast, padded skirts or heavy wigs with fruit and flowers and ships in full sail decorating them for me!

'Ah, Charlotte,' my father said, and I bobbed a little curtsey. 'I'm going to London this morning to finalise a business deal – one which will affect us all.'

'Indeed, Father,' I said politely, looking over his shoulder at the fields outside just inviting themselves to be ridden over.

'And one which directly concerns you, child.'

I gave him my full attention. He took out his snuff box and took a pinch, and I knew he was trying to find words for what he had to say next.

'You are of an age, Charlotte,' he began at last, 'when we feel you should be married.' I drew in my breath sharply but he held up a hand for me to be quiet. 'I – I have effected an understanding with a certain Lord Winstanley – his son is of a similar age and – er – due to singular irregularities in his grandfather's will, cannot inherit until he is wed. As there are no suitable young ladies living nearby he is naturally considering . . .'

'Father!'

'Quiet, child. He is a most respectable boy – apart from being heir to a vast fortune. You could not ask for a better match. And what else is a girl of your age to do but marry? You've finished your education; you cannot idle away your life in vain amusements.'

Words could not express the horror I felt. I knew such matches were occasionally made, but I never dreamt that my own father would consider treating me as a mere chattel to be passed on to whomever he chose!

'You — you can't mean it!' I said, my voice shaking. 'It's unbelievable! I shall refuse!'

'You will not be given the opportunity to refuse. I have already accepted for you.'

I felt the blood drain from my face. 'Father!' I said

in anguish. 'You mean you have promised me to a stranger?'

'Come, come. Don't I always know what's good for you? Haven't I always put you first? You must trust me in this as you've trusted me before in your life. I won't let you down, Charlotte.'

'But – but that a marriage should just be a business deal,' I whispered. 'What of love, Father?'

'What would you know of such things anyway? Love will come later, child. When you are wed and have learned to live together.'

'No!' My stunned horror began to give way to anger.

'Come!' My father beckoned me over to his desk. 'The boy's father had his portrait painted so that you could admire him before you meet.'

'No, I . . .' I tried to back away but my father came towards me and took my arm.

'Just look at him, Charlotte. Get to know him and perhaps you may change your mind.'

I watched as he took away a piece of cloth which had been covering a small, rectangular picture. 'There. What do you think of your young knave?'

I stared at the portrait in fascinated horror. It was of a young dandy wearing a fine blue wig, curl upon curl piled high above his forehead. His face was pink with powder and rouge, and he had two black face patches on his cheeks and a simpering smile about his lips.

I let out a scream. 'Hideous! A dandy, a fop! I could not look upon such a man, let alone marry him!'

'Come, come, child . . .'

'I will not, Father!' I stamped my foot. 'You cannot make me! I'd rather die!'

'Charlotte!' my father called sternly, but I was running from the room, leaving doors wide open and racing across the fields to get away, my skirt and petticoats billowing around me. Never had I seen such a revolting and priggish dandy! I would truly die rather than marry such a man!

I sobbed as I ran, calling down unladylike curses on my father, shouting that I hated him, would never do as he bade me ...

At last I ran out of curses and out of breath – and reached the river's edge. I sank down, exhausted, and dried my eyes on the hem of my dress. My hair had escaped from its ribbon and hung about my face like that of a peasant girl, but I didn't care. A peasant girl was what I wanted to be: *they* never had to marry to suit their fathers. They would certainly never have to marry a dandy with a painted face and powdered wig.

I stared into the river, knowing myself truly miserable for perhaps the first time in my life – and knowing that if I did as my father wanted then the rest of my life could only be miserable, too.

I looked down at my simple flowered cotton dress, at my pink slippers. If I were married to a man such as the one in the portrait then I'd have to be a lady of fashion, and be obliged to wear stiff, embroidered linens and brocades, with hoops of iron underneath my petticoats so that I couldn't go in a doorway without turning sideways. I touched my hair: that would have to be tortured into waves, dressed high over cushions so that I couldn't travel in a sedan chair without having to have the top open. I shuddered. Never, *ever* could I be such a slave to fashion as was the custom nowadays. I couldn't bear to spend my life curtseying and paying meaningless visits, gossiping and playing at cards and making a pretty play with words all day! I wanted to be free to be myself – and free to choose the man I would marry.

I cried a little more and, finding no solution, at last got up and, leaving my slippers on the bank, began to walk along the river's shallows. I gathered wild flowers from the banks as I walked and the hem of my dress and my petticoats trailed behind me in the water but I didn't care. I'd stay here all day; I wouldn't go back – I'd run away!

I bent to push aside some weeds, sighing to myself. Running away was impossible. There was nowhere a girl like me could run to.

As I walked on, the river swerved and changed its course, then suddenly, before I realised it, shelved deeply so that all at once I found myself floundering in cold water up to my waist, with tangled weeds snatching at my ankles.

I let out a cry of shock and struggled to reach a branch on the bank, but my long skirts were clinging and cumbersome and the pull of the river was against me. I began to panic, let out a shout – and then there was a rustling sound and to my intense relief someone came through the briars at the top of the bank.

'Oh, please!' I called to the peasant boy of about my own age who had appeared, 'will you help me out?'

He grinned and jumped into the water. 'You'll not drown there,' he said, 'but don't panic or thresh around. I'll aid you.'

'Oh, you'll be rewarded!' I said, reaching out towards him.

He had me out of the water within seconds, his nut-brown arms clasping me firmly round the waist and pulling me to shore.

'A thousand thanks,' I said, blushing, because his eyes looked into mine in such a merry way and his hands surely clasped me closer than they needed to.

'It's nothing. As I said, you wouldn't have drowned in that depth of water.'

'Nevertheless,' I said, taking his hand to help me up the bank, 'it was not a pretty experience.' I was shaking all over with shock and he looked at me sympathetically.

'I'll fetch a rug from my horse,' he said, 'and perhaps some wine to warm you.'

'Oh please!' I called to the peasant boy of about my own age who had appeared, 'will you help me out!'

His horse was tethered to some bushes nearby and he was gone but a moment or two. When he came back he wrapped me in the rug and sat me on the grass with a reassuring arm about my shoulders, and soon I felt better. I wasn't used to young men being so close – the ones I'd been introduced to at balls and dances kept at a polite distance – but with him I felt strangely at ease.

He told me his name was William, and we began to talk — oh, of many things. I soon forgot that he was just one of the peasants from the village because he was honest and kind and forthright and there were many topics on which we agreed. After a while the sun came out strongly and I spread my dress across the grass to dry it out and, by and by, found myself telling him about my problem. When I'd finished William looked at me sympathetically and said that he'd always thought that marriages should be for love alone.

I looked at his honest face, at his simple leather jerkin and peasant's clothes, and smiled sadly. 'It's easy for you to say that,' I said. 'In your world that's the way things happen. In mine, though, people often marry for position or money or a title.'

'How tragic,' he said, and his eyes looked into mine searchingly, 'how tragic that one could live one's life through and yet never know true love ...'

My hair was still loose about my shoulders and suddenly he caught it up in his hands. 'Yet for today you are a peasant girl, free to love anyone you choose.'

I held my breath and his lips came close to mine and I felt the blood rush to my cheeks. I wanted him – oh, I desperately wanted him – to kiss me and I wanted to know, too, how it felt to be held in someone's arms, for until then I'd only heard the maids talking about such things.

'You are beautiful – my beautiful wanton peasant girl,' he said, and I knew that if ever I was beautiful then I became more so that day under his glance. His lips came down on mine and my whole body trembled in response. So *this* was what it was like to be kissed. And this was what it felt like to be in love ...

When we broke apart we were both shaking a little and I could not look him in the eye. I was little better than my own maid, sitting unchaperoned on a river bank and kissing one of the village lads! And yet – I looked at him out of the corner of my eye and yearned for him to kiss me again!

We spent the day thus: kissing and then breaking apart by turns, talking of many things and laughing together. At three o'clock he shared his lunch with me – a rough meal of cheese and apples and bread, but sitting under the hot sun with William I felt I had never eaten anything more delicious, and that no polished, silver-laden table could compare to the soft green grass which was our cloth that day.

'Shall we meet again?' I asked shyly when it began to grow late. I knew I'd have to go back soon or my father would be searching for me.

To my dismay William shook his head. 'How could we,' he said, 'with you being a rich man's daughter? We would not be allowed to speak to each other, let alone spend the day unchaperoned.'

'But – but I must – I truly must see you again,' I said pleadingly, and felt my face redden once more. I had no shame, no pride – I just knew that my life would only be bearable if I could sometimes see William.

'Perhaps, my little love ...' was all he said, as he kissed me for the last time. Then he fetched his horse and put the rug in front of the saddle.

'Perhaps? Perhaps!' I cried in anguish.

'Some day, then,' he amended. 'Some day the time will be right for us,' and with that he climbed on his horse.

'Farewell, sweetheart!' he called as he rode away, and I

could do no more than burst into tears and make my lonely way home.

It was a very different girl indeed who walked back to her father's house that evening. I'd got over my tears at William leaving me so abruptly, for I felt I'd learned a lot about him that day. Remembering his kisses and his whispered endearments, I felt sure he truly cared for me. Somehow, some day, he'd find a way for us to meet. I didn't care that he was a peasant; I loved him, and with love I knew anything was possible.

Two weeks after that I was in despair. William hadn't been in touch – yet he knew where I lived, what my name was, and it would have been easy for him to have sent a message through one of the maids.

Could I have been mistaken about him, then? Could I, with my lack of experience, have been taken in by his honeyed words and sweet kisses? I went over and over the things he'd said to me and tossed and turned in my bed at night. No! I believed in him, trusted him. Everything he'd said to me that day he'd truly meant.

He must be ill, then. Or busy working in the fields. I made expeditions down to the village with one or other of the maids. I looked in the market square, in the shops and ale houses. I made discreet enquiries about a young farm hand called William, but there was no trace of him.

I tried further afield: I rode miles on Polly, visiting the villages nearby, but each visit began with loving optimism and ended in despair. It was as if he'd never existed!

Throughout all this, at home in front of my mother and father, I remained a passive, dutiful daughter. I said no more about the young dandy my father would have me marry, for I'd made up my mind to go along with things for the time being. When I met him, then I'd declare that I could never marry him *to his face*. An insult like that could never be tolerated and that would be an end to it.

Thinking my silence meant agreement, my parents began to arrange a ball at which my future husband would be presented to me.

'If all goes well between the young folk then the engagement may be announced the following weekend,' my father said, rubbing his hands. ·

'And they can be married at the end of the summer,' my mother said, pleased, for she loved arranging things.

I hid a shudder and looked out of the window, seeing only a river bank and two lovers sitting on it, kissing.

'You must be properly dressed for the ball,' my mother said firmly. 'None of your ringlets and lace caps – we'll get a dresser down from London to arrange your hair in the latest fashion. We'll engage dressmakers, too, so they can make you a fine ball gown and start on some garments for your trousseau.'

'Whatever you wish, Mother,' I said, and I dropped a curtsey and went to my room. Once there I pulled the curtains around my bed to hide myself from the world and cried and cried. Oh, William! When would he come for me? How could he leave me like this?

The ball was held a month after I'd first heard the news that I was to marry – and a month to the day, of course, that I'd met William.

I put up with the tortuous hair styling, with the pinning and primping and standing for hours in front of the mirrors while dressmakers attended to me, for I felt sure that any day William would come riding by and send a message for me to meet him by the river.

The message never came, though, and the moment arrived when I stood before the glass, white-faced and heavy-hearted, while my face, my hair and my dress were being given final adjustments by the maids before I was to go and join the guests gathered downstairs.

'You look wonderful, Miss Charlotte!' Maud said, and I looked at my reflection in the mirror and gasped at the awful splendour of my wig and stiff pannier skirts.

'I don't look like me at all,' I said, my face feeling hot under the powder and patches.

'No, indeed!' the hairdresser remarked admiringly, thinking she was paying me a great compliment.

I felt nervous prickles of anticipation run down my spine: soon ... soon I would meet him and then my time would come. I would laugh openly, pour scorn on his foppish face and affected manner, tell him that I'd rather stay a spinster all my life than marry such as he. *Then* my father would see that he couldn't make me marry someone I didn't love.

I walked downstairs, trying to hold my head high in spite of the great weight upon it, and my father began introducing me to some of his business friends I didn't know. There were cousins to greet next, and aunts and uncles only seen at Christmas, and it was some half an hour or so before I was told that our guests of honour had arrived and I was to go into the library and meet my future husband.

'Now, remember your society manners, Charlotte,' my father said, escorting me down the hall. 'All hangs on this meeting – we don't want the young man to think you're just a simple country girl with nothing to say for herself. Don't forget he is accustomed to moving in Court circles among people of fashion.'

I smiled a secret smile. Oh, I had plenty to say for myself; my father need not fear about that!

'I'll leave you young people alone to greet each other,' he went on, one hand on the library door, 'and then perhaps you'll come out and lead the first dance together.'

'Perhaps, Father,' I said demurely.

The library door was opened. I went in and there he was, standing by the big oak table affecting an elegant air, tapping the table with his cane.

I sank into a curtsey. 'Sir ...' I murmured with downcast eyes.

He approached; I saw his shoes with silver buckles and high heels in front of me.

'Do get up, Charlotte,' he said, 'or do I have to give you a helping hand again?'

Forgetting my pretty manners, I let out a squeal of astonishment. I looked closely, with mounting amazement, for beneath the wig and patches and powder – it was William!

I stared at him, stunned. I might have fallen over if it hadn't been for the petticoats with all the padding holding me up.

He laughed and began to peel off the patches on his face. 'Merely accessories,' he said, 'for my father's pleasure mostly – he likes to think of me as a fashionable young buck. It's not to my taste. It was he who insisted on me having my portrait painted looking as if I were being presented at Court.'

I was still speechless, unable to believe what it all meant; how my life had been transformed in a moment.

'And you – tonight you don't look like the simple country girl who loathes the fashions of high society,' he said with a smile.

'I – my father ... I just don't understand,' I began.

'It's really very simple,' he said. 'My father has bought a country house in this area and I happened to be visiting it the day you took a tumble in the river. I ... er ... followed you, actually. I knew my father had made a certain arrangement with the daughter of his business friend and I was anxious to see what she was like.'

'Oh!' I cried in outrage.

He reached for my hand and kissed it. 'I had the advantage

of you there. Do you forgive me?'

'Certainly not!' I said. 'Not – not straight away, anyhow. And I certainly don't forgive you for giving me a month of anguish.'

'Absence makes the heart grow fonder," he said, and he kissed my other hand and drew me closer. 'My little sweetheart; when we're married we'll have no more deception between us. We'll live a simple life here in the country and just be ourselves.'

I melted then at the thought of all the happiness ahead, and allowed him to kiss me. My father came in and gave a very discreet cough so that we broke apart after only a moment.

'Such haste – such haste,' he said, looking shocked at our wanton behaviour, but he drew me to one side as we went out of the door to lead the dance.

'Didn't I tell you all along that I knew best?' he said complacently – but I just squeezed William's hand and said nothing, for I was too full of happiness to speak.

PERILOUS JOURNEY

Barbara Hope

SHE HATED HIM, HATED HIM, HATED HIM! Gwendolen de Beauchamp gazed scornfully at the tall, commanding figure who sat astride his horse staring grimly at the curtain of snow which swept across the valley in front of him.

She shivered, though it was not through the cold, for her cloak was thick and lined with fur, her clothes all artfully woven from good Welsh wool, and her boots were of stout leather. She shivered with anger and frustration – as what strong-minded girl would not, who found herself a captive, an innocent pawn in the power play between rival kings and empresses?

Gwendolen shifted slightly in the saddle, then turned and gazed over her shoulder. Behind, in the courtyard, leather-jerkined soldiers on foot held blazing torches to light the eerie scene and men in cloaks huddled over braziers of glowing coals; above them the mighty edifice of Ludlow Castle reared up and disappeared into the snow-swept darkness. Horses stamped and pawed at the icy ground, fretful and eager to be away. Wind howled around the unseen towers and turrets, the mournful, keening sound reminding her that wolves had been seen in the Clee Forest west of the town, ravenous refugees from the bleak bare hills of Wales in this bitter winter of 1139.

She turned back with a shudder to watch as the stout castellan of Ludlow, Bergac de Fontenoy, his massive figure swathed in an ermine-lined cloak, stumped towards the young man who commanded the party of riders – the *hated* young man – the *hated* Sir Ivo FitzAlan, who for the moment was the master of her fate, the lord of her destiny.

How she hated him! And how she loathed herself! For before the dread tide of civil war had surged over England only three years before, there had been a time when the very thought of Ivo FitzAlan had set her heart trembling, her whole being quivering with eager delight. So tall, so strong, so brave; so like a hero from the legends of old. How could she have been so foolish? She decided that it must have been because she had been young and immature. It seemed to her that there was a vast gulf of years between herself at the age of fifteen and at eighteen, and during that time her eyes had been opened to Ivo FitzAlan's true character.

When he was seventeen he had seemed to Gwendolen like a young eagle, but now he was twenty he was simply a heartless monster. That aquiline profile which had seemed so noble was now seen to be hard with arrogance, carved out of cold stone. That open smile that once had set her blood racing was a mask behind which lurked dark thoughts and treacherous intentions.

Her bitter thoughts – as bitter and as bleak as the biting wind that swept around the courtyard and caused the blazing torch flames to writhe and leap in agitation, setting the shadows cavorting in a crazy dance – were interrupted by the spiteful tones of Bergac de Fontenoy who, unnoticed by Gwendolen, had stridden across to her horse.

'A fine catch!' jeered the massive custodian of Ludlow Castle, gazing up at her, his arms akimbo. He turned and shouted back to Ivo FitzAlan. 'Eh, Sir Ivo? She makes our hand a strong one in the bargaining! Fulke Greville is as good as a freed man already.' He stared up at Gwendolen again, his tiny, pig-like eyes gleaming with malice. With the back of his hand he wiped snow off his heavy moustache and cackled with laughter, a sound as chilling as the freezing wind.

'Oh yes! Under normal conditions, the Lady Gwendolen de Beauchamp would not perhaps have been considered a suitable exchange for so powerful a Baron as Fulke Greville – but these are hardly normal times, eh, girl? We have you – and that traitor who calls himself King, the thrice-accursed Stephen, has Greville. And if we don't get Greville back then it'll be the headsman for Gwendolen!' He laughed again, a bellow of malicious mirth that seemed to set his whole body shaking.

'Let her be!'

Sir Ivo FitzAlan jerked at the reins and sent his horse clumping through the snow towards Gwendolen. He seemed to be angry. His brow was dark and his eyes were narrowed; his mouth was a firm-set line.

For a moment she thought she could detect genuine anger there – and, too, genuine discomfort at de Fontenoy's jeering tones. Then she rejected the thought scornfully. Ivo FitzAlan and his family had sided with the traitor Empress Maud while her own father had taken up arms for Stephen. Her father, Roderic de Beauchamp, had been killed at the terrible seige of Wallingford Castle, less than three months ago, and Sir Guy FitzAlan, Ivo's father – and once Roderic de Beauchamp's firm friend – had been at the same seige, though on the opposing side. Like father like son, Gwendolen thought bitterly; both as bad as each other.

And now she was a captive and, as luck – ill-luck, indeed – would have it, her captor and escort was her childhood friend, the youth she once had thought a princely knight in shining armour. How wrong she had been!

And if he *did* speak harshly to the gross and brutish de Fontenoy, it was clearly because he wanted to be away from here, away from cold Ludlow Castle, and on the road to Chester, stronghold of the Empress Maud – sixty miles as the crow flew, through forest and across heath and snowy waste, in the bleakest of mid-winters England had seen for generations.

'Gwendolen.'

Ivo FitzAlan's voice was low. He gazed at her entreatingly, his blue eyes like soft stars, like ... Angrily, she brushed the image aside.

'We have a long road in front of us. It will be a perilous journey and an uncomfortable one. Would that we could spare a wagon, but ...'

'But you cannot,' she interrupted him, her voice as chill as the driving sleet that hurled itself at the looming castle walls. 'For it would be too slow to escort a wagon, and you are fearful, and rightly so, that friends would hear of our passage and would pursue you from loyal Shrewsbury. You fear, in short, for your own skin, sir.'

Anger flickered across his face like winter lightning; those soft blue eyes turned to chips of ice.

'I fear, my lady, not for myself, but for you! To me you are no mere piece of merchandise to be bartered, but a friend of childhood and thus a precious jewel to be protected!'

For an instant a wild delight surged through Gwendolen de Beauchamp – yet it was a delight that seemed as sharp as a fang sinking into her heart. Then she drew herself up, a haughty expression on her pale young face, masking all feeling.

'Fie, Sir Ivo! Would you seek to placate me with dreary old tales of the long ago?'

His right hand shot out and steel-strong fingers gripped her shoulder through the thick cloak.

'And it is not your friends at Shrewsbury I fear, either! With all England in a turmoil no road is safe. Bands of the dispossessed roam the forests – and outlaws too. Rogues with nothing to lose and all to gain – who think nothing of attacking our party, strong as it is, to capture such a high-born prize as you! Aye, and not only human rogues, but also wolves. Have you not heard their hungry howls in the long nights?' He jerked his hand away, as though suddenly ashamed of his rough action. Gwendolen's shoulder throbbed.

FitzAlan turned to Robert Blois, his burly sergeant. 'Let's away,' he growled. 'Doubt it not, the Empress has spies here, to send word of our passing.'

The horsemen, with Gwendolen de Beauchamp, cloaked and furred, in their midst, thudded out of the castle's high gateway and headed down through cobbled streets towards the ice-bound river.

Disaster struck only ten miles out of Ludlow as the storms relented at last and died to a mere flurry of snowflakes tossed by a calmer wind than had blown for many a day.

Yet if Ivo and his men could now see more clearly, then they could more clearly be seen. And so it was. A party of armed men suddenly appeared at the top of a wooded slope and thundered down the hill towards them.

'Outlaws?' Ivo FitzAlan reined in his horse.

'No!' snapped Robert Blois. 'Stephen's men! I recognise their leader, Gilbert de Forres, one of Ranulf of Shrewsbury's lackeys. They must have had wind of us.'

'Then ride!' roared Ivo.

Gwendolen was aware that she could do nothing rash for she was surrounded on all sides, with burly Robert Blois on her right, ready for any attempt at escape.

'We can outpace them,' began Ivo – but the words died in his throat as more riders appeared high on the slope ahead.

Ivo had forty men as escort. On a swift reckoning there were at least thirty careering down the slope towards them, in long line abreast. Without Gwendolen it would have been a simple matter to wheel round and charge them at the bottom of the slope — hit them at speed, destroy their impetus and despatch them. But with Gwendolen there were no options, no choices at all. Only one thing could be done, and must be done.

Ivo FitzAlan, bleak-faced and sick at heart, bellowed his orders – and twenty of his men thundered off to the right in a mad charge at those who hurtled down toward them, while Ivo and his whittled-down party wheeled to the left and careered off into the suddenly worsening storm.

'Twenty men, and you and me,' muttered Ivo FitzAlan, crouching down and thrusting his hands towards the flames that crackled up from the small fire.

For a second Gwendolen, her cloak wrapped tightly around her and huddling as near to the fire as possible this chilly night, thought that he was talking to Robert Blois, but the burly sergeant was speaking in low tones to the rest of the men, crouched beside the second fire, as small as this one. No mighty blaze to warm the blood at this stark camp site, for fear of watching marauders and roving outlaw bands.

Ivo glanced across at her, a tentative smile on his lean, strong features.

'All this . . .' he gestured around at the forest clearing – the horses tied close together near to the fire, the travel-stained men, grim-faced and weary, the lower branches of the trees sagging under their heavy load of snow: all illumined weakly by the two fires. ''Tis like nothing I ever imagined when we two played and gambolled the time away as children, free of cares and with no thought of the future.'

Her heart went out to him, not quickly but grudgingly. And then the full ache of her feelings came as she too recalled those happy times, so different to the present when the spectre of war and famine stalked the land, and family fought against family, brother against brother, son against father – and friend against friend.

Suddenly she was confused. Did she still love him, even though he was her enemy? Was he truly her enemy? She could not tell. Neither could she tell whether his overtures were genuine. She watched him as he stared bleakly at the dancing flames, the flickering light throwing his face into strong relief.

'Can it be right?' His voice was low, a murmur that she could only just catch. 'Can it be an honest action to treat a helpless girl so harshly, as though she were nothing but a bolt of valuable cloth?' His furrowed brow told of a conflict of emotions that raged inside his mind. 'Nor just any girl, either, but a friend – aye, and more than that once . . .' He glanced up at her again, but his gaze was abstracted. It was as though he did not even see her. 'Where does loyalty lie – to those with the power to rule this sorely troubled land, or . . .?'

He did not finish, for at that moment there was a hissing sound through the air and an arrow thudded into the crackling logs, scattering the fire across the slushy, melted snow.

Instantly Ivo was on his feet, his sword gripped in both hands, and suddenly the night silence was split apart by howls and yells. A shower of arrows pattered through bushes and snow-cloaked trees and all at once figures were swaying and thrashing about on the edges of the clearing, nightmarish in the light of the fires.

Ivo struck out at a raggedly clothed figure who, snarling, leapt at him, then turned swiftly as he heard Gwendolen cry out. A man was looming menacingly beside her, and Ivo's heart was struck chill. He plunged to her side, heaving the man away, then dragged her to the whinnying horses, yelling orders to Robert Blois.

'Hold them off, then follow!'

Then Gwendolen was scrambling on to her horse and, with

He stood where he was, facing the onrushing tide of snarling grey.

Ivo riding by her side, galloping madly through the milling figures into the darkness of the forest.

With the dawn came a new peril – more terrible in its way than any that yet had confronted them.

Wolves.

Gwendolen cast a glance behind her as she rode, catching brief glimpses of the lean, grey-furred creatures as they loped easily along, matching the speed of the two horses. Her eyes widened with fear as she counted at least a dozen, perhaps more. It was hard to tell. So far they had kept to the trees, so that she saw only blurred streaks of grey against the white of the snow.

Suddenly two wolves, ahead of the pack, raced out of cover and sprang at Ivo's horse, and she saw with a cold chill that somehow the steed must have been wounded in the melée round the camp fires. There was blood flecking its flanks, as though from a sword cut.

Ivo had already unleashed his sword, and now it whistled through the air as he struck downwards at the snarling beasts. Gwendolen crouched low in her saddle, turning her eyes away as she urged her own horse faster. And as she did so, she heard Ivo's startled cry.

She turned in horror and reined in her horse. Ivo had despatched the two wolves, but his horse, now clearly exhausted, had stumbled, throwing him to the ground. Already he was scrambling to his feet in the churned snow and mud – and already, too, the wolves in the wood, now scenting blood, were howling with triumph and surging out from the shelter of the trees.

Her mind was in a turmoil. She suddenly realised that she was at last free! Her captor – her *hated* captor! – was as helpless as she, and worse, for he had no horse; his mount, now riderless, was careering off to the north.

The north! There lay Shrewsbury, held for King Stephen –

rightful ruler of England – by its strong sheriff Gilbert Prestcote. There lay sanctuary. And now that Ivo FitzAlan was without a horse, one man with a sword against a half-score of ravening wolves, her way was clear. Ride off, without a backward glance, without so much as a passing thought – and hasten to Shrewsbury town and safety.

Ivo FitzAlan cast one glance at her, then turned away. There was nothing censorious in it, no anger, no wild pleading. It was a glance that said 'So be it. I understand.' He stood where he was, sword gripped in both hands, facing the onrushing tide of snarling grey, his hair tousled in the chill breeze, firm and upright, facing his fate. No knight in shining armour, for his clothes and mail were dirty and travel-stained, yet there seemed to Gwendolen a radiance about him at that moment that shone in the dreary morning light, almost dazzling her.

She pulled at the reins of her horse, wheeling round in the snow, then galloped towards that lone figure.

'Swiftly, Ivo! Leap for my horse!'

A wolf, the leader of the pack, sprang at him and was hurled away by a flashing stroke of the sword. Then Ivo jumped at the horse as it careered by, clutched at its flying mane with one hand and scrambled up behind her. His strong hands reached around her and took the reins, his boots dug hard into the horse's flanks. The animal thundered through the snow away from the yelling pack, which had briefly paused to fall upon their stricken comrades.

They galloped on without a word, and then Gwendolen realised they were still heading north, not west. North – to Shrewsbury!

As if he had heard her unspoken thought, Ivo leaned forward, his lips brushing her wind-tossed hair.

'Shrewsbury is not so far,' he said. 'To deliver you to your enemies is suddenly too hateful a task. I know now that no ties to kings and empresses are as strong as the ties that bind my heart.'

'Ivo ...' She half-turned her face up to his, her voice unsteady. And as their lips met she felt a fierce shaft of purest joy surge through her wildly beating heart.

Above, the early morning sun conquered the thinning snow clouds, shining warmly down on the two figures who seemed now as one, as they raced together across the fields of white.

A DEBT OF HONOUR

Angus Allan

'SAIL DEAD TO WINDWARD, on the port bow!' The lookout's hail came at the very moment that Mary Dalton emerged on deck of the merchantman *Fair Maid*, driven to seek the fresh breeze by the close, oppressive atmosphere of the cramped passenger accommodation. The scantily armed brig was just three hours out of Guernsey, bound for Plymouth, and it was high summer in the year 1810, when Great Britain stood virtually alone against the hostile might of a Europe dominated by the Emperor Napoleon Bonaparte.

Mary Dalton – just seventeen – was on her way to begin a new life as a maidservant in the home of her stepfather's brother, Caleb Doyle. She knew it would be a hard existence, but it couldn't possibly be worse than the misery she had endured since her own true father had died. Long hours of drudgery under the harsh discipline of the man who had married her weak, foolish and totally uncaring widowed mother. The welcome wind played havoc with her long, dark hair, and she felt the *Fair Maid* heave beneath her feet as hands ran to the sheets and the towering canvas volleyed like a rattle of musketry.

'Is something amiss?' She plucked at the sleeve of the brig's captain, Ronaldson, and was shaken off angrily.

'Get below, girl! We're in for a fight, and this is no place for you!'

Mary shrank back against the bitts of the mizzen mast, hearing the captain's curses as he realised that his ship couldn't possibly outrun the sleek, beautiful lugger that bore down relentlessly towards them out of the wind's eye.

'Damned French privateer! Crammed with men, and all hungry for the pickings of my cargo, blast 'em! Run out the guns! We'll show 'em we don't yield without snapping our teeth!'

Ronaldson had no time to be bothered whether Mary had obeyed his order or not. He knew that his fate was inevitable. Death, if he was lucky. If not, then capture, the loss of his vessel, and years spent rotting in a stinking French jail. Manfully, his men – but they were no Royal Naval seamen – loaded, rammed and ran out the feeble pop-gun cannons that were the brig's pathetic armament, and sent a ragged broadside into the wide blue yonder. Mary could actually hear the roar of derision from the crew of the enemy lugger.

The ringing crash as hull struck hull made her reel, grasping for the support of the mizzen ratlines, and then leaping Frenchmen were pouring over the *Fair Maid*'s gunwales, for all the world like pirates in their rag-tag miscellany of improvised uniforms, knives between their teeth and cutlasses in their hands. Mary flinched and covered her ears with her hands. The din was like that of a hundred tinkers, mending kettles. So much for the poetic notions of 'the noble clash of steel on steel . . .'

Crouching, she saw Ronaldson go down. The flashing bang of the pistol fired by the man at the wheel was drowned by his own mortal yell as a French boarding-pike found its mark. A body, toppling from the main yard, bounced from the backstay and landed sickeningly at her feet.

Now a wolfish Frenchman with a broad black moustache, eyes red with the blood-lust of battle, seized her by the shoulder and hauled her upright. 'A prime chicken for Gaspard's larder,' he bellowed, his thick lips dribbling spittle. 'I'm in luck – the spoils of war have never been so good!'

Shrieking, Mary lashed out with fist and foot, and the man's gloating grimace turned to one of agony. All around them, the heaving conflict seemed no more than a blur, as Mary tripped, fell headlong, and saw her enraged captor swing his cutlass high!

The vengeful blow never fell. The big sailor's wrist was caught by a slim young man in immaculate dark-hued broadcloth, the waist girdled by a sash of red, white and blue. Mary saw the flash of white, even teeth in the handsome, tanned face. Saw Gaspard – if such was his name – whirled round and felled with a straight-armed blow to the jaw!

She gasped as the young man swept his arm around her waist, turned like a dancer in the same movement, and with an agile leap, carried her bodily across the bulwarks to set her down as lightly as a feather on the lugger's deck.

Speechless, she caught the brief bow, and heard his ringing apology, shouted over the incredible din.

'A thousand pardons, Mam'selle! I beg you — stay here and make no move. I guarantee your safety!'

He whirled, as if to return to the brig, but there was no need. A French voice bellowed, 'It is all secure, *mon Capitain*! She is ours!'

Mary's rescuer waved an expressive hand. '*Bien*,' he said. 'A most profitable interlude.' Again he turned his dazzling smile on the girl. 'Ah, but I fear this has been a most distressing experience for you, Mam'selle ... uh ...'

'Dalton,' Mary offered. 'Mary Dalton.'

'*Enchanté*.' He bowed again, and Mary felt her hand taken, and lightly brushed with his lips. She blushed furiously, inwardly furious with herself for doing so.

The eyes twinkled. 'Allow me to present myself, Mary.' It came out as 'may-ree', and she realised, incongruously, that it sounded nice. 'Captain Jacques Dumont, of His Imperial Majesty's privateer *Quatre Vents*. It rhymes, *oui*? Dumont –

She gasped as the young man swept his arm around her waist and with an agile leap, carried her bodily across the bulwarks.

Quatre Vents. But there is surely no poetry on earth to compare with such a charming young lady.'

Mary's mind was whirling. She knew she was blushing again. She stammered something – she didn't know what – in clumsy reply.

'I fear that my little exploit has discommoded you somewhat,' said Dumont, keeping hold of her hand and leading her away from the crowd of French seamen who were busily transferring plunder from the brig to the lugger. 'May I ask what you were doing aboard the *Fair Maid*?'

She told him, and he clucked his tongue sympathetically.

'We do not, of course, make war upon ladies,' he said. 'And I imagine you would not be happy if I took you back with me to France, to be among those you so reasonably would call your enemies ...'

'Is – is there an alternative, Monsieur?' faltered Mary.

'But of course!' He laughed, and it was a pleasant sort of laugh. 'You will be my cabin guest for supper tonight. And then, under cover of darkness, I will take *Quatre Vents* inshore, not far from Plymouth. I will have some of my crew – they are not all like that idiot Gaspard, you understand – land you in a small boat.'

'You are not jesting with me, Captain Dumont?' Mary searched his eyes.

He smiled. 'I admit, it will be hard to part with such a beautiful girl,' he said. 'But no. I do not joke.' He thought for a moment. 'I remember once, when I was a boy. My brother and I found a magnificent butterfly resting on the mimosa at our home in the south. He wished to kill and take it. To keep for ever. But I said that such a precious thing should be allowed to go free. To enchant others who saw it ...'

Mary gulped. Her heart went out to this strange young man who combined such consideration, such gallantry, with his chosen profession of – she could think of no other term –

bloodthirsty piracy in the name of his Emperor. For privateers though they claimed to be, Napoleon's free-ranging irregular captains, not of the full-time French navy, *were* regarded as pirates in England.

'You can't risk yourself by sending me home,' she said at length. 'You know the strength of our coastal fleet. There are guard-boats, launches and cutters. One sniff of your presence, and militiamen by the score would put out to attack you.'

'Your concern touches me, Mary,' he said. 'But I snap my fingers – so – at the English militia. I am,' he continued grandly, 'Captain Jacques Dumont – a legend in his own lifetime!'

He winked, seeing Mary's eyes widen, and leaned closer to whisper in her ear. 'Excuse my act. For my men, you understand. They are impressed by such theatrical poses!' And Mary was suddenly aware that they were surrounded by grinning, listening Frenchmen, all nudging each other and admiring their leader's pretty prize!

Dumont was as good as his word. The supper – it was the finest Mary had ever eaten – passed far too quickly. In the surprisingly comfortable stern cabin beneath the afterdeck, she ate lobster, drank wine, and listened to Jacques tell stories of his boyhood in Grasse, during the heady, turbulent days of Napoleon's rise to power. She knew it was foolish and hopeless, but already she was in love. In love as she had never, in her brief and cheerless life, been before.

It was with tears in her eyes that she at last took her leave of her handsome captain in the soft moonlight, with the loom of the Devon coastline no more than half a mile from the ship.

'Perhaps,' he whispered to her. 'When this insane war is over ...'

They rowed her ashore, and Dumont's sturdy coxwain, at his chief's orders, risked his life to the full by actually escorting her on the lonely highway to the outskirts of Plymouth itself.

Her mind in a turmoil, Mary sought out the big house where the merchant, Caleb Doyle, held sway.

To say that Mary was welcomed would be an overstatement. Caleb Doyle was as harsh and soulless a man as his brother, her stepfather. He made it perfectly clear that she was in his employ under sufferance and that she would have to work like a slave to earn her keep. There was not even anyone of her own age to lighten her heavy heart – only a wizened old butler, deaf and crotchety, and a housekeeper with a rat-trap face who called her 'girl', and eyed her with clear disfavour.

Mary said nothing of her adventure. Little concerned with military or naval affairs, not a soul in the house would have been interested. It would be unlikely that any of them would ever learn at all of the unfortunate fate of the *Fair Maid.*

That night, in her lonely garret, Mary cried herself to sleep. A sleep confused with chaotic dreams of sea battles, of grinning, pot-mending tinkers with faces slashed by gloating black moustaches, of billowing sails and struggling men. And always the nebulous, half-seen figure of Jacques Dumont, who despairingly would fade away, even as she stretched her arms out to him for comfort.

She awakened early. Had the banging on the main door of the house been part of her nightmare? No – there it was again. And she could hear raised, excited voices down in the hallway. Mary dressed herself and tiptoed to the gallery beneath the back stairs of the attic. From there she could look down into the room below without being seen.

Caleb Doyle was there, speaking to a fat, florid man in the over-ornate uniform of a militia colonel, who gobbled as he spoke, as if his mouth were full of hot boiled potatoes.

'You're a magistrate, Doyle,' he was saying. 'It's your duty to attend the hearing, man! Frankly, I can hardly believe our luck. Calm sea, little wind, and dash my wig if the coastguard

96

cutter didn't catch a frog lugger trying to claw off shore! What the devil they were doing so close, I can't begin to imagine!'

Mary listened with mounting horror as the bloated soldier continued.

'The frogs tried to run, of course. But they bargained without the wreck of the frigate last week's storm drove into the shoals. Ran full tilt into it. Bang went the masts!'

'I wish you'd get to the point, Colonel,' said Doyle, clearly suffering from early morning irritability.

'Hmmf. Lugger went down like a stone. Full of men. Those that weren't drowned were given a bellyful from the coast-guard's swivel-guns. Except that one feller swam ashore. And ran straight into one of my patrols. We've got him in the town lock-up right now. The Captain, no less!'

'I see,' said Doyle. 'You're going to hang him, but you need me to pronounce sentence and make it official.'

'Exactly. The poltroon knows it, too. Keeps waving his arms and insisting he should be treated like a prisoner of war.'

Mary had to clutch at the banisters to stop herself falling. Her head was swimming. She felt sick. She heard Caleb Doyle's voice again, a cautious note in it.

'You're sure he *isn't* one of Boney's navy?'

'Sure?' blared the Colonel. 'Of course I'm sure! Why, the man's blabbering about letters of marque. Actually *confesses* himself to be a privateer! Hah! Privateer! Fancy frog name for an out-and-out pirate, and won't it be a feather in our caps when we've got him dangling from the Plymouth gallows!'

Mary stole back to her room. Jacques — *her* Jacques – was at that moment languishing in a stinking Plymouth guard-room, facing the certainty of a hempen noose after what could only be the travesty of a trial. He would be alone, bewildered, ashamed of the loss of his ship. He would be totally without hope ...

She wrung her hands. Yes, he was an enemy of her own

country. But he had saved her life. Whatever the allegiance of her blood, she owed him everything. She drew in her breath, and came to a wild and bold decision, her heart telling her that there was no contest. After all, what did she owe to anyone *else*? To her bullying stepfather or his surly brother? She recalled her own kindly father, and knew that somewhere, somehow, his spirit was urging her on, trying to tell her that she was right ...

Mary had no difficulty at all in slipping down to Caleb Doyle's study. The man had gone off with the Colonel.

She found what she was looking for – a heavy horse pistol, in a drawer of his bureau, and checking to see that it was primed and loaded, she thrust it beneath the cloak she had flung over her gown. Then, silently, she slipped out the back way and headed for the town.

People took scant notice of the girl as she hurried along the back roads and byways. There was no mistaking the militia headquarters, for a milling crowd of uniformed soldiers thronged the street outside, being addressed by their fat colonel and her step-uncle. Her heart quickened. Jacques was not there. He must still be inside.

Mary disturbed nothing more than a scavenging cat and a brood of nervous hens as she made her way round to the back of the building. Typical of the militia – part-time amateurs more used to the plough than to the rifle, they had left no one on guard in the rear.

She used the barrel of her pistol to force the feeble padlock on the rear door, and stepped inside. One man – a sergeant who was more usually a local dairyman – half rose to his feet, a shout forming on his lips.

'I'll use this,' said Mary, and felt that she meant it. The soldier stared down the muzzle of the heavy weapon and sat down again, his jaw closing with an audible snap.

'*Mary*!' Jacques Dumont, bedraggled and far from the

smart figure he'd cut on the deck of *Quatre Vents*, gaped at the girl, his knuckles white on the bars of the cell that imprisoned him.

'You,' Mary snapped at the soldier, gesturing with the pistol. 'Open it.' Ashen-faced, the sergeant did as he was bid.

'Better tie and gag him, Jacques,' whispered Mary. 'If we're to get away with this, there isn't a second to lose!'

'My brave Mary,' said Jacques. 'Ah, you are *magnifique*! But we haven't a chance!'

Mary felt stronger, more confident than she'd ever done before. She kissed him quickly, glowing with pride at the admiration in his eyes.

'Don't be so sure, my love,' she said. 'The men have their horses out at the back. But there's only one simpleton with them, and he's asleep!'

The girl could hear the loud, blaring tones of Caleb Doyle at the front, telling the grouped militia just how much of an example he was going to make of the French prisoner. She could hardly suppress a giggle of excited laughter.

The guard by the horse lines awoke as they untied a pair of sturdy bays – and Mary was thankful that it was Jacques who dealt him a clench-fisted blow behind the ear that sent him back to his slumbers. The mounts were unsaddled, but that didn't matter. In an instant, the two were off, bareback – and not a soul saw them go. They had locked the sergeant in his own cell, and his cries went unheard against the sound of Doyle's hoarse-voiced ranting.

Five miles out of Plymouth, they drew to a halt. Mary and Jacques looked at each other, their hands clasped. The horses stood patiently, as if not wishing to disturb the lovers' moment.

'What do we do now, *chérie*?' The Frenchman's eyes were deep with emotion. 'You have returned my feeble favour a thousandfold – and yet, what hope can there be for us? I am virtually a condemned man, and now in the eyes of your countrymen you are – forgive me – a traitor.'

'I can live with that, Jacques,' said Mary. 'Besides, I don't think you can take up arms for France again. From what I know, your Emperor is not the sort to forgive a captain – even one who is a legend in his own lifetime –' she smiled to show she was joking 'for losing his ship for the sake of a girl.'

Jacques nodded soberly. 'I fear you are right,' he said.

All that day, they hid in a wooded combe, and at nightfall, they stole a rowing boat from a lonely cove. They left the coast of Devon behind, heading they knew not where, hopeful only in the kindly fate that always seems to smile gently on those in love.

And smile it did. Scarcely had dawn broken than they were sighted and picked up by a ship in mid-channel. Not, thankfully, a British frigate. Neither, equally happily, by a French vessel. She was the trader *Cyrus*, and she flew the neutral ensign of the United States of America.

Closely, their arms around one another, Mary Dalton and Jacques Dumont stood against the quarterdeck railings. They did not speak. There was no need. Somewhere in the New World there was another life for them both. They would be married. Have children. Become Americans – just like the grinning skipper who shot, from time to time, an amused glance at them from his discreet place alongside the helmsman. The sun was high, high in the sky, and quite suddenly, the whole European war seemed very far away.

FOREVER IS A LONG TIME

Mary Hooper

'Are you sure that's everything, Mother?' Caroline said. 'I wouldn't want to get to Brighton and find I'd left something absolutely essential behind.'

Mrs Smythson paused and laid another layer of tissue paper in the travelling box. 'I'm quite sure I've packed all you'll need,' she said, 'but you and your cousin Netty are a size so if you find yourself lacking anything she'd be sure to lend it to you.' She straightened up and frowned slightly. 'Daisy should be doing this but I really can't trust her with packing. She leaves out anything she can't manage to fold neatly.'

Caroline got up off her curtained bed and walked to the window, scarcely able to contain her excitement. It would be the first time she had travelled on the stage coach by herself, the first time she had stopped overnight at an inn completely alone – and also the first time she'd been asked to be a bridesmaid.

'Do you think it will be a fashionable wedding?' she asked eagerly now. 'Do you think Netty got her designs from Paris? I hear the Prince Regent himself is at Brighton most weekends, just suppose he ...'

'It won't be *that* fashionable,' her mother interrupted, 'at least, not enough for the Prince to attend. Your Aunt Alice tells me that the church is a small country one and that Netty's fiancé is an old family friend – he and Netty grew up together so both families know each other very well.'

'Oh,' Caroline said, disappointed, 'but maybe I'll see the Prince anyway. I hear he goes sea-bathing and that a special machine for bathing has been constructed for him – royal blue with a gold crown on top!'

Her mother placed a silk chemise on top of the box and smoothed it down. 'I don't know about that,' she said, and shuddered delicately. '*Sea* bathing. Whatever next?'

A lace-edged camisole went in next, then silk stockings, three pairs, and two cotton night shifts.

'I really think we're packing too many things,' Mrs Smythson said, shaking her head. 'You're only there for three days.'

'But Brighton's such an elegant resort,' Caroline said. 'I hear they change their clothes several times a day. I don't want to seem dowdy, do I – Netty's dowdy country cousin.'

Her mother straightened up from her packing. 'It's really most kind of Netty to ask you to be a bridesmaid at all,' she said. 'We scarcely see them these days what with the roads being so potholed and the journey so tedious, with the risk of highway robbers, too ...'

'Really, Mother,' Caroline said hastily, before her mother could change her mind about her going at all, 'it's not nearly as bad as you think. I shall be perfectly all right.'

'I only wish I could go with you to chaperone you on the journey. I daren't leave your father in his present ill health, though.'

'Of course not. You mustn't dream of it,' Caroline answered even more hastily.

'That's all, then.' The box was shut with a click. 'Now, young Toby will go with you to the coaching inn, then you must ascertain the correct coach and ask for an inside window seat.'

'I'll remember all that, Mother, and I'll be perfectly all right, really I will.' Caroline's satin-slippered feet walked eagerly to the bed and back and her hands fluttered like excited birds. 'I can't wait to meet her beau. Will he be handsome, do you think? Will they be very much in love? Oh, it's all so romantic!'

At the coaching inn Toby was tipped and went away well pleased, bidding Miss Caroline a pleasant journey. Alone at last, she gazed around at the busy cobbled street, the horses and the people, and felt excitement mounting again. She was free! For five whole days she wasn't merely someone's daughter – a child to be taken out to tea-parties, expected to play the piano for the amusement of her mother's friends – but a young lady of quality travelling to a fashionable resort. Why, any kind of adventure could befall her.

Caroline's coach was located, her box was stowed on top and she climbed in. She nodded her head slightly at her two travelling companions, trying to hide her disappointment, for neither of them looked exciting nor fashionable, nor the sort to make interesting a long journey. One was a portly man who, hands across his stomach, was already half asleep, and the other was a woman, clearly his wife, dressed in a red serge dress, on her head a particularly unbecoming felt hat with a large feather.

The coachman climbed aloft and Caroline peered out of the window, anxious to be away.

'I say! Is this the coach for Brighton?' a voice called somewhere outside, and the coachman replied that it was.

'I'm just in time, then,' the same voice exclaimed, and the coach swayed slightly as someone opened the door and climbed in.

'A good morning to you all!' the young man said. 'I trust I have not held you up.'

Caroline smiled because his manner and his grin were infectious.

'Thomas Wainwright at your service,' he said, sitting in the corner opposite Caroline. 'With whom have I the pleasure of travelling?'

The couple gave their names reluctantly and then the large man promptly closed his eyes and seemed to go back to sleep again.

'And I'm Caroline Smythson.'

'Caroline. What a charming name. I believe it's my favourite!' the young man – Thomas – said, and he picked up one of Caroline's hands and kissed it.

Caroline smiled again and blushed.

'You may think me forward,' he said, 'but I like to get acquainted with my companions on a long journey. It makes things so much less tedious.'

Caroline lowered her eyes and removed her hand, wondering why her heart was beating fast and there was a sudden dryness in her mouth.

Ages later she described how she had felt to her great friend, Milly, who was more experienced in these things.

'Why, you fell in love at first sight,' Milly said wonderingly when she'd finished telling her tale. '*That's* why your heart was beating so loudly and your throat was tight and you wanted to laugh and cry at the same time. Love at first sight...' Milly breathed out with a sigh, 'I've only read about it. I wish it would happen to me.'

And this was exactly what *had* happened, though Caroline didn't realise it then, but put it down to the stuffiness of the carriage and the excitement of the forthcoming journey.

By nightfall Caroline was tired and she felt that every bone in her body ached. The journey across London had been relatively smooth and the road even, but once the outskirts of the city were reached the road was pitted with vast potholes and in places was deep in mud, so the going was hard.

The large man and his wife had got off at Barnes to be

replaced by two clerics and a woman with a dog. Thomas had moved to sit next to Caroline. 'All the better to talk and point out items of interest,' he said, adding that he knew the road well.

When they stopped for the night at a coaching inn he asked Caroline to dine with him and, delighted, she agreed, for she had thought she'd be forced just to retire and dine in her room, it not being seemly for a young woman to dine alone in mixed company.

Over the meal, between the fish and the roast venison, Caroline realised how she felt about the young man sitting opposite her. It happened when they were each lifting a glass of wine to their lips.

'Let us drink a toast of friendship!' Thomas said, and he twined his arm through hers before lifting the glass to his lips. They paused, their eyes met, and for a short enchanted moment it was as if they were the only two people in the world. Caroline had the feeling that even if someone had rushed up to their table shouting 'Fire!' neither of them would have noticed.

'A . . . a toast of friendship,' Caroline whispered a moment later, trying to pull herself together, and they drank deeply, still unable to tear their eyes away from each other.

Caroline could not sleep that night, yet it wasn't the strangeness of the room or the soft feather mattress which was at fault, for she scarcely lay down upon it. Whenever she did she was filled with a great impatience and excitement, as if she wanted to run round the room and shout how she felt across the fields. She spent most of the night sitting at the window seat looking at the moon and wondering what had happened to her. It felt like the most wonderfully romantic thing in the world . . . to be travelling alone for the first time – and to a wedding, too – and to fall in love along the way. Oh, just let him feel the same way, let him ask to call upon her at home –

let him, too, be staring at the moon and finding it impossible to sleep.

And in his smaller room on the next landing Thomas was indeed doing just that – but he had an altogether more troublesome reason for his sleeplessness than Caroline had.

The next day both Caroline and Thomas seemed happy and, at first glance at least, rested and composed. If the two clerical gentlemen had looked closely, though, they might have seen the lilac shadows of sleeplessness under Caroline's eyes and noticed that Thomas's face looked drawn and pale.

Brighton drew nearer. Thomas pointed out the fine buildings and architecture and, trying to make her laugh, told her something of the scandals of Prince George, the Regent, which were open secrets across Brighton. They neared the great Pavilion and Caroline gasped aloud at the golden domes and minarets, for with its many glass windows sparkling under the sun it looked like a magic palace from a fairytale.

'It's beautiful,' she breathed.

'And also wasteful and extravagant!' Thomas said. 'It seems that our Prince can do little except spend money on impossibly expensive things like his onion palace!'

'But it's so lovely ... surely it's worthwhile building something so beautiful?'

'They say that beauty lies in the eye of the beholder,' Thomas said, his voice growing serious. He picked up Caroline's hand. 'But I have seen no more beautiful sight than the one sitting next to me today.'

Caroline blushed but saw her opportunity and seized it. 'Then ... then you mean we shall meet again?' she said. 'Perhaps you could visit me at my aunt's house.'

Thomas's hand trembled slightly in hers. 'I fear not,' he said huskily.

'But *why*?' In her anxiety Caroline forgot that it wasn't mannerly to persist with such a question.

He shook his head. 'I have prior commitments,' he said formally, and Caroline withdrew her hand sharply and put it to her lips, aghast.

'Then ... then are you married, sir?'

He shook his head and his mouth set in a firm line. 'I can – I must say no more, save that I didn't mean this to happen, this attraction between us. I've acted in an ungentlemanly manner. Please forgive me.'

Feeling as if her heart were breaking, Caroline looked out of the carriage window and as the Pavilion disappeared into the distance she fancied it shimmered mistily, and she knew her eyes were full of tears. If only she could keep from crying openly until her journey ended ...

Her stop came, and she dismounted as if in a dream. The coachman handed her box down. She looked round for Netty but she was nowhere to be seen.

The driver whipped the horses to be off and Thomas leaned out of the carriage window. 'Please – I cannot bear to leave you so,' he said desperately, but Caroline resolutely turned away from him.

'Caroline ...' his voice pleaded as the carriage drove off, but she hardened her heart and would not look at him. Oh, she had been so foolish. Her first excursion into society alone and she'd fallen in love with someone who wasn't free to return her affections.

Netty didn't appear for half an hour, then she drove up in a little gig full of apologies and giggles, saying that she'd started off in good time, really she had, but the dressmaker and caterer and vicar who would conduct the wedding had all conspired to stop her.

'You look terrible!' she said cheerfully, hauling Caroline's box on board. 'The journey could not have agreed with you.'

'Indeed it didn't,' Caroline said, sighing.

Netty's mop of blonde curls shook. 'You'll have a marvellous time here, Caro, that'll make up for it. We'll try and find a nice young man to escort you around Brighton while I'm busy.'

'But I shall be perfectly content just being your companion,' Caroline protested, not wanting any sort of man thrust upon her. 'That's what I'm here for, isn't it? I'm to be the bride's maid.'

'But while you're being one how much more delicious if you can meet a fine young beau at the same time!' Netty said mischievously.

Caroline felt her eyes fill with tears again but she blinked hard and made them go away. Time enough to cry and go over exactly what had happened when she got back home. Until then she would give Netty her undivided attention and try and wipe it from her mind, for only that way could she get through the next few days.

The day passed quickly. Caroline met her Aunt Alice again and her little cousins, paid a visit to a neighbour's house and was shown Netty's beautiful wedding finery.

'I'm so excited about everything!' Netty said that afternoon. 'Mother has hired the finest caterers in Brighton – they cook for the Prince Regent's parties – and the silver plates they serve from are replicas of those used in the royal palaces. Imagine that!'

Caroline smiled. Netty was entranced by the ceremonials and trappings of the wedding but hadn't so much as mentioned her fiancé!

'Aunt Alice says your fiancé is a local man,' she ventured.

'To be sure. We were childhood sweethearts,' Netty said. 'At least, that's what Mother keeps telling people.'

'And what is his business?'

Netty ran to the window. 'You'll be able to ask him yourself, Caro, for here he is.'

They waited while one of the maids answered the door. 'He's been away for a whole week,' Netty said, pouting so that her pretty face didn't look nearly as pretty. 'I feel quite neglected. I shall just tell Thomas when I see him that . . .'

At that moment the maid announced him and Caroline felt the room spin about her. For a split second she wondered if there had possibly been some mistake, that her Thomas on the coach had had a change of heart and somehow found out where she was staying. Then as if from a long way away she heard Netty declare, 'Here he is, Caro – Thomas Wainwright, my fiancé; Thomas, this is Miss Caroline Smythson, my bridesmaid and one of my dearest friends,' and somehow Caroline managed to offer him her trembling hand.

Thomas gave her one anguished, puzzled, pain-filled look and then he kissed her hand and immediately turned away. 'How do you do, Miss Smythson,' he said stiffly, and Caroline felt as if she was going to faint.

Netty passed between them, prattling away about the bridesmaids and the champagne and her wedding dress, completely oblivious of the pale, sad faces of her two companions. Caroline realised, wonderingly, that she didn't notice anything was amiss, that she saw nothing of the pain on Thomas's face and that, if the truth be known, she didn't love Thomas with the great depth of feeling that Caroline did.

'If you'll excuse me,' she murmured when a decent interval had passed, 'I'm sure you'd like to be alone together.' And she hurried from the room before Netty could protest, for she felt she couldn't bear to be in their company for another second. Oh, that such an awful thing could happen . . .

She ran into the gardens surrounding the house, down to where the bushes grew thick and she could hide. Once there, decently hidden, she allowed herself to cry, tears cascading down her cheeks in never-ending streams, unable to believe that fate could be so cruel.

A few moments later she heard Thomas calling her name.

'Caroline!' he said, his voice worried and urgent. 'Caroline, I know you're there somewhere. Netty has sent me to find you. She wants to discuss some outfit or other.'

Caroline stiffened, lay perfectly still. She wouldn't come out; she wouldn't let him see her in such a state.

'Caroline! Where are you, sweetheart?'

Caroline let out a sob at the tenderness in his voice and Thomas found her and, kneeling on the ground, gathered her in his arms and rocked her gently to try and stop her crying, though it was all he could do not to cry himself.

'I know . . .' he said brokenly, 'it's monstrous; fate dealing us the wickedest hand in the world. I wouldn't have had this happen for anything. Hush, darling, now though, for I want to tell you something.'

And Caroline, worn out from crying, at last hushed.

'Netty and I – well, we've known each other from infancy. Our two families have always hoped we'd marry and because Netty is a sweet girl I thought that if we were fond of each other that would be enough.'

Caroline drew in her breath in a shuddering sigh, staring all the while at his white face.

'When I met you on the coach I realised that there was more to loving someone than I'd thought. I fell in love with you so deeply and completely that every bone in my body ached to touch you. I'm tormented by thoughts of you; I love you and I'll go on loving you until the day I die.'

'No!' Caroline said hoarsely. 'You cannot. You must not!'

'But I do – and it is not too late. All we need is courage. There *is* a way for us to be together.'

'No!' Caroline said again, shaking her head in horror. 'It cannot be. We can never be together! The . . . the scandal . . .

*Thomas found her and, kneeling on the ground gathered her in his
arms and rocked her gently to try and stop her crying.*

the shame and misery it would bring upon me and upon Netty and all the family would be more than I could bear. Netty loves you; she's my friend. I could not wreck another girl's life.'

'Then you would wreck your own. And mine.'

'Then let it be so!' Caroline said, tears spilling from her eyes again.

'But sweetheart!' Thomas said despairingly, and he caught hold of her wrist, pulled her to him and kissed her passionately, desperately, knowing that it was to be for the first and last time. Caroline responded for a brief, sweet moment and then she pulled away and began to run as fast as she could towards the house.

'Don't follow me! I beg you let me be!' she called despairingly behind her.

Two days later the small church was filled to capacity and bright with yellow roses as Netty and Thomas vowed to love, forsaking all others, until death did them part.

Caroline, standing behind them in pink silk, trembled slightly when she heard the words of the solemn vows and bit her lip very hard to stop herself crying out.

A moment later Thomas bent to kiss his new bride and turned slightly for one last, anguished look at Caroline, but her eyes were brimming with tears and she didn't see him.

Only a distant relative sitting in a pew nearby saw the look and, glancing at Caroline, wondered to himself why a single diamond-bright tear fell from her eye and landed on the petals of her bridesmaid's bouquet ...

A YEAR AND A DAY

Joyce Wilson

WHEN SIR GILES FOUNTAIN RETURNED from fighting the French at Crecy he spent the stormy channel crossing boasting of the English archery that had won the day, and grumbling at the nagging rheumatism he had contracted in the endless rain that had beset the English campaign.

Behind him on his horse, as they rode later through the great forests of the south to Fountain Castle, sat a young Burgundian whose father Sir Giles himself had killed only a month before in battle. It was the custom, part of the code of chivalry in the enlightened fourteenth century that governed even the bloodiest of wars. A victorious knight would adopt a child he had orphaned in battle, and rear him as his own in the peace that followed.

It was even more natural that Sir Giles, himself a dark-haired, burly descendant of a Norman who had conquered England almost four centuries ago, should bring a French child home. Pierre de Byron, the boy who rode so proudly and silently behind him, could easily have passed for brother to the three children who ran to greet their father as his horsemen broke from canter to a jangling trot and rattled over the drawbridge into the castle courtyard.

In the airless, low-built cottages that clustered outside the castle walls the news that Sir Giles was home again brought no joy. He came on the heels of a bad harvest, and would be demanding more than his usual share of their grain and their salted meats to survive the winter. In his absence at least two of his bonded serfs had married their childhood sweethearts without his permission, and would now face his wrath – plus a heavy fine which might take a lifetime to repay.

The knight who could afford to be generous in victory to Pierre de Byron would show no leniency to the impoverished villagers whose families had lost fathers in that victory.

In one of the houses, at a distance from the castle, a young fair-haired girl sat beside the deep hearth of the single room where the hens scratched the packed earthen floor, facing a small boy whose eyes were filled with fear and who was plying her with questions.

'Shall we lose our home now? Will Sir Giles tell us how father died? I know he died bravely, Veronica.'

'He should never have gone to the wars, brother Daniel.' The girl's voice was low with anger and grief. 'His skill with growing crops was of more value to Sir Giles than his skill with the bow. Perhaps that will save us. I have learnt from Father all that is needed to keep our strips of land in good heart.'

'I could help. I am old enough,' her brother said eagerly.

'And old enough, soon, to become our lord and master's slave for life. I'll not have that for you, Daniel. One day we must leave this place, now that both Father and Mother are dead. Then, if you can only stay at liberty for a year and a day, if we could only find somewhere to hide, the law of the land says you will become a free man. It is what I want for you, brother.'

The boy's reply was silenced by a babble of voices from the street, and with a clash of spurs and a gleam of swords the single room was suddenly alive with intruders.

'Veronica, maid of this village, daughter of Daniel the ploughman dead in the war in France?' A man in the blue and green tunic of Sir Giles's colours stood silhouetted against the narrow doorway. Veronica got to her feet, and placed a protective arm round her brother's shoulders.

'I am Veronica, daughter of a brave soldier who should not have gone from this land.'

'Enough of that talk. Where you and the boy are going now you'll learn to hold your tongue.'

'Going? Where should we go?' Her brother clung to her, and she shook her long fair hair back from shoulders that had begun to tremble.

'And tuck that mane of gold under your coif, girl, before we leave for the castle. You know there are no fair heads in this district – unless they be witches come from far.'

At the mention of the castle Veronica felt slightly less afraid. If she and Daniel were to be thrown out of their home, then at least shelter of a better kind was to be offered, it seemed. She looked round the room for the white coif she wore whenever she left the house. She knew it was true, that fair hair bred suspicion in the region. It was a strange beauty she had inherited from a grandmother who had practised herbal medicine, but had certainly been no witch. The villagers had loved and respected her for her healing powers.

'We'll take the hens, too. All chattels go with you.'

Veronica and her brother watched helplessly as a young soldier began to chase the hens about the room, and it seemed an eternity before they found themselves out in the cool, rain-touched air, walking behind the horses on the track that led to the castle.

At last, as the drawbridge closed behind them and she stood with Daniel in the castle's courtyard, Veronica felt that if she lowered her guard for a single moment she and her brother would become prisoners for life in this strange new world. Then, as she scanned the high stone walls as if already seeking a means of flight, her eyes met those of a dark-haired boy who was watching her from a narrow window.

Her heart beat faster. There was something in the proud, silent gaze of the watcher that gave her the feeling that all was not hopeless. But as quickly as their eyes had met, the boy disappeared.

'Wait here.' Sir Giles's sergeant marched away and disappeared through an arched doorway. After a few moments a serving woman walked into the courtyard and beckoned to the new arrivals. They followed her into a high-ceilinged kitchen hung with well-scoured pans and rich with smells of cooking such as they had never known.

'My name is Abigail. Head of the kitchens. The boy will turn the spit. You, my girl, will be set to learn to sew for the master's children. Embroider, too. You'll learn a stitch or two before you leave here. That is if you ever leave,' she added with a snigger.

Veronica's heart sank. 'Will my brother and I be parted, then? He is so young. Our father died for Sir Giles in France.'

'He was not the only one to die.' The woman's voice softened. 'After dark, you can both sleep down here on the straw with the others. You'll find it warm enough.'

She took Daniel by the arm and led him to the centre of the room where a boy half his age crouched over a fire working a set of bellows almost as big as he was himself. He gave Daniel a conspirator's wink as Abigail deftly slung a whole deer's carcase on to the iron hooks of the spit above the embers.

'There's a half day's work for you, lad, turning that creature in time for Sir Giles's banquet tonight,' she said.

An hour later Veronica herself was at work, wearing a hand-me-down gown that was costlier than any she had ever seen, and stitching the plain background in the embroidery picture that some more privileged mortal would decorate with a hunting scene.

She was becoming bored with her task, and longing to see her brother again, when one of Sir Giles's children ran noisily into the room and stood looking over her shoulder, lips curled at the clumsy attempt Veronica had made.

'I'll not embroider today, Mama,' the girl said to the woman who had followed her into the room. 'I'll leave it to my father's serf.'

'Then you shall speak French, beloved, with the new-comer, Pierre de Byron. When you go to Court at Richmond it will help you find a husband of rank.'

'I do not like the French boy.'

Ignoring the protest, Lady Fountain clapped her hands for a servant, and moments later a steward in blue and green ushered in the dark-eyed boy whom Veronica had seen at the window in the courtyard. Without seeming to neglect her row of stitches, she managed to study him further, and saw that his eyes were brown, and that his manners were those of a nobleman. He too was careful not to seem to notice her, but she knew he was aware of her presence, and she was suddenly conscious of her hand-me-down clothes and her rough hands, worn from her struggle to keep up the work on her father's land.

Listening to the strange language in which Pierre de Byron spoke with Sir Giles's daughter, Veronica felt more of an outcast than ever. Not until Lady Fountain left them to walk in her private garden did she dare to look up – to find the French boy smiling in her direction.

'You have the most beautiful hair, I think,' he said in rather stilted but very correct English.

'Well!' The Fountain girl gasped her displeasure. 'I'll tell my father the moment I see him that you spend your time speaking to serfs and not to me, Pierre de Byron.'

'This young lady is no serf, Mademoiselle, if her bearing is anything to go by. She has the appearance of a free-born woman. She is my equal in other ways, too. We are both, after all, here against our will.'

The admiration on the French boy's face as he talked of her sent Veronica's pulse racing. But she kept her eyes on her work. He did not know the wrath of the Fountain family the way she and the people of the village did. This proud young rebel went too fast for their good. For the time being all she wanted was to find her brother again that night and make sure that he had survived the first day at the castle.

But she could not deny that Pierre de Byron was the most interesting young man she had ever encountered, and that something in the arrogance of his manner aroused an echo in her own rebellious heart.

The tallows fixed in their brackets on the stone walls were flickering feebly and the sound of the last revels had died away after the banquet when Veronica at last crept to the straw where she and the servant children were allowed to sleep. She found Daniel curled up in a ball, in an exhausted sleep. It was almost dawn when he stirred, and muttered to her. An older serving boy told them to hush, but Veronica hugged her brother to her, telling him everything she had seen in the rooms above. He told her in his turn of the tiring, boring work, the dozens of serfs employed for no payment but a scrap of food at the day's end.

'I cannot stay here, sister. I will die in the smoke. If I could just breathe the sweet air for a moment, it would help me through today ...'

Veronica raised herself carefully on one elbow, making sure the others slept on. 'Move slowly, and keep low,' she whispered.

Moments later they stood in a corridor of the slumbering castle, watching a sleeping guard with bated breath, then, their bare feet making no sound on the wide stone flags, brother and sister began to run. They ran blindly, through endless bleak passages, past endless closed doors, until at last they came to a door half open which led on to a cloister. They found themselves in a garden that shone with the white of lilies and was alive with the twittering sounds of waking birds.

They began to run about in the grass, in silent delight at the chill dew on their feet, till at last they sank breathlessly to the ground, breathing in the air with great thankful sighs. When Veronica looked up again it was to find Pierre de Byron's dark eyes upon her.

'So we really do think alike, you and I,' the Frenchman said. 'I think I shall never sleep in this place.'

'*I* slept.' Daniel eyed the stranger doubtfully.

'Daniel,' Veronica reassured him, 'I believe this is a friend.'

'Yes. I am your friend. And as three friends in an unfriendly place we must of course escape,' Pierre said.

'Escape?' Veronica frowned. 'You do not know our harsh laws. It would mean a branding, if we were caught. My brother and I are as good as slaves, Pierre.'

'With me you would not be caught.' He took her hand and, responding instinctively, she held it tight. He went on, 'In France I could not attempt to flee because Sir Giles watched me himself, day and night. It was a matter of honour to bring back a captive and rear him as a son. But now – he does nothing but drink and sleep.' He shrugged expressively. 'In this place I am no longer watched so closely.'

'It is no good unless Daniel can stay at liberty for a year and a day,' Veronica explained. 'Our laws say he will then be a free man. Where could we hope to hide for so long?'

'There are people who would help you,' Pierre assured her. 'A singer at the French King's court fled here, and sings now of rebellion to those who will listen. Gervaise the troubadour. I knew him. And I know the code word that would lead us to him or his friends.'

Veronica shook her head, and yet his words gave her hope. She had heard of such men, too, when the villagers dared talk freely.

'But how? Will it ever be safe to leave?'

'One knows these things. Just as you and I knew, the moment we met,' Pierre said very quietly.

Veronica blushed slightly. It was true. She had been drawn to him from the first moment. 'When would we leave?'

'After the full moon dies. We walk at night, and trust ourselves only to darkness. Agreed?'

'Agreed.'

It was a week later, after yet another banquet in honour of the exploits of the English in France, that the three of them made their escape. Pierre managed to steal three warm cloaks from the guardroom while Veronica took from the kitchen what scraps of food and provisions she could conceal in her kerchief. They hid in a washroom until an hour after midnight, when they climbed perilously on iron rungs down the dripping walls of the castle latrines to the stagnant waters of the moat. Half drowning, half swimming, they reached the outer bank, and began their long, stumbling journey to freedom.

By dawn they had covered almost twenty miles. Another day and they would have cleared Sir Giles's territory. They took a well-earned rest in the lee of an arched bridge, taking turns to sleep. Once, while Daniel slept, Pierre took Veronica gently in his arms and cradled her head in the curve of his shoulder. It was the first peace and happiness she had known since her childhood.

At dawn next day they hid again, in a wide ditch only yards from the rough road, while the familiar blue and green livery of the Fountain household bobbed by. This was a search party led by Sir Giles himself, cursing loudly against his enemies, his serfs, and his aching bones.

'He'll not keep going long at that rate,' Pierre said with a grin. 'Even I am not worth so much discomfort.'

Veronica smiled in spite of her fear of discovery. Her heart was lighter than it had been since her father's death, and the

At dawn they hid again, in a wide ditch only yards from the rough road, while the familiar blue and green livery of the Fountain household bobbed by.

next night she walked sure footed through the dark, her hand firmly in Pierre's.

On the fifth day their hunger got the better of them. The few provisions they had brought were gone and they had found nothing else but some turnips on the second day scattered wastefully in a field for pigs to scavenge. They had waited until nightfall to join the scavengers. Now there was nothing for it but to find real food, or they could not go on for much longer.

It was Daniel who then came into his own. Smaller than the others, and agile as an eel, he crept through the fence round a large dwelling and braved the dogs that bayed at his approach. Where there were dogs there would be food thrown on the ground.

As they waited anxiously for him under cover of the trees that edged the fence Pierre and Veronica talked of freedom. Veronica wanted land, to work the soil as her father had taught her. Pierre wanted to find a ship, and the freedom of the sea.

'We could sail for France,' he told her. 'The land is rich. We could find the place where your father fell in battle. Would that not give you comfort?'

'Would you do that for me?' She gazed into his face, her eyes alight with joy that someone could know so much of her innermost feelings without being told. There was a moment in which all the great forests of the south through which they fled seemed locked in silence as Pierre leaned forward and kissed her softly on the lips.

'It is the place where my father also died,' he told her. 'We have so much to bind us together, you and I.'

As Daniel reappeared, running low, his arms clutching an odd collection of bread and meat and half-eaten apples, Pierre took Veronica's hand, and kissed her fingertips, and this time she knew that the roughness of her skin was of no importance. All that mattered to her now was that they were together.

They fell on the scraps of food and ate hungrily. Later they walked fast through the night, until, as dawn was breaking, ahead of them they saw a trio of men walking in the middle of the road, and on the still air the sound of singing reached them.

Pierre quickened his pace. 'I know that song. If I try the code word perhaps by a miracle these men could turn out to be the very band we are seeking!'

He was almost right. As soon as they heard the code word the men shook him warmly by the hand. He told them that he knew Gervaise the troubadour. They explained that one of their number was a Frenchman who had been taken prisoner at Poitiers and was too important a rebel to be left to the mercy of the English.

'We should be in Hastings two days from now. A boat waits for us there. It is the shortest crossing.'

'Do we take it?' Pierre looked at his companions. Daniel shrugged, and waited for Veronica to speak.

'You have everything to gain,' Pierre said, putting an arm about her shoulders.

She looked up at him with troubled eyes. 'But how shall we live?' she asked. 'I do not speak the language, and I have no skill in sewing.'

Pierre laughed. 'You will grow vines, little peasant. And we will make wine as golden as your hair.'

She shook her hair free of its covering. 'That is a crop my father never knew. I don't know how ...'

Not caring who saw him, Pierre reached out and touched the long, golden strands that fell about her shoulders. 'You will be back home with me in time for the wine harvest. *Le grand travail.* You will learn the hard way – but then, I think you are used to that.'

'And in a year,' Daniel said brightly, 'you will have learned it all. And I can come home again.'

'In a year,' Pierre added softly, 'who knows?'

Veronica put an arm round her brother and held him close, smiling at Pierre above the small boy's head.

'A year and a day, little brother,' she said. 'I think I'd like to stay in France a year and a day at the very least . . .'

HIGHWAY TO HAPPINESS

Barbara Hope

'STAND! STAND AND DELIVER!'

Young Emma St Aubyn, huddled in the corner of the swaying, creaking coach as it lurched and jolted over pot-holes and splashed through wide puddles, silently groaned in utter misery. A highwayman! Was she to be spared no humiliation?

She still felt ill from the vile potion Mrs Grabbidge had forced down her throat, and her head was swimming. The odious concoction had been meant to put her soundly to sleep, but either the mixture had been too weak or she had not been given enough of it. Whatever the reason, it had not worked as it ought to have done, but had merely made her drowsy and queasy. She had felt just so when Papa had once taken her for a jaunt on a sailing smack from the port of Brighthelmstone. It had not been at all enjoyable, although Papa had derived a good deal of amusement from her wretched state. Dear Papa: sometimes his humour had been a mite too boisterous.

A tear welled up in her eye and she fought hard to hold it back. She did not wish to draw attention to herself, for she had thus far successfully feigned unconsciousness, even uttering an occasional sleepy mumble, so that Mrs Grabbidge and Silas Starker would leave her alone.

And now this. A highwayman! Would she be dragged out of the coach by the ruffian, in his search for rich pickings? And when he found nothing – as indeed he would, for Silas had stripped her of her most cherished belongings and all she had now were the clothes she stood up in – might he not be so enraged that he would strike her down, hurl her into the muddy road in his anger? It seemed very likely. On the other hand ...

Emma gritted her small white teeth. On the *other* hand, would that not be the perfect moment to escape? Surely in the darkness and the wind and the spattering rain, she might elude her captors?

To be sure, she had nowhere to go to in the immediate vicinity, for who would believe her tale of the rascally Silas and his wicked plot to steal her inheritance, her lands and possessions? Even kindly Squire Renton of Foxcombe Farm, her nearest neighbour, would find it difficult to credit that Silas Starker, the eminent lawyer of Charnleigh, had, on finding no will amongst poor Papa's papers, forged one himself, making sure that all was left to him.

All! Not one jot nor tittle had the scoundrelly lawyer let her keep. Even the puzzling mystery of where Papa's missing will had disappeared to – ''Tis somewhere safe,' he used to say, with a gleeful smile, 'writ on something valuable, m'dear!' – could not take her mind from the thought of Silas Starker's black treachery. For not only had he dispossessed her entirely, but was now (indeed, at this very moment!) on the way to deposit her in the private asylum owned by a rascally friend of his own, where, it was rumoured, members of the aristocracy shut away their crazed or merely troublesome daughters and sons.

She *must* escape. This could be her only chance.

'Hold, coachman! Off your box and down on the road, else this pistol I'm holding will blow you off it!'

The coach had now rumbled to a halt and the horses were whinnying and moving restlessly in their jingling harnesses. Emma risked a narrow-eyed glance across the carriage and saw fat Mrs Grabbidge clutching her cloak to her in horror, while Silas himself was scrabbling around like an old crab and gibbering hoarsely. Indeed, to Emma, he seemed nigh on the verge of a fit of apoplexy.

'These plaguy highway dogs!' he swore. 'A curse on them and all their breed!'

'Ho! Methinks I hear the dulcet tones of Lawyer Starker!' a voice cried. 'Out you come, Silas – or shall I drag you out bodily, you old bag o' bones?'

Emma's eyes widened. So it seemed that the unseen highwayman knew Silas. She cast a swift glance at the lawyer and saw that he had blanched and was now clutching at his neckband as though it were choking him. He struggled to his feet and a look of rage flushed his thin, bony features. He stuck his head out of the window.

'Why, 'tis indeed that brass-browed rascal! Popping his head out like the demon in a pantomime! Out, I say!'

The door was suddenly tugged open and Silas was jerked forward. He disappeared from view with a wild yell. A shadow fell across the doorway, blocking off the moonlight that streamed down from a cloud-wracked sky. A tall man in a tricorne hat and long cloak, holding a solid-looking horse pistol, appeared. Over his eyes was a mask of dark blue velvet and Emma noted a devil-may-care sparkle in those same eyes that now surveyed the coach's interior.

'Egad! Who's this monstrous fat beldame a-quivering in one corner?'

'How dare you, wretch!' Mrs Grabbidge's voice, never an attractive one, was now a hoarse shriek.

'Aha! 'Tis the delectable Widow Grabbidge, a partner in crime and fellow plotter in all Starker's schemes. And here . . .' the highwayman's tone suddenly changed as he noticed Emma. 'A thousand pardons, ma'am, for the roughness of my speech. I was not to know that a fair flower resided in such a jungle of noxious weeds!' With a flourish he doffed his hat and bowed low. 'Captain Tom Mennard, offering you his most humble services, ma'am – and truth to tell,' again his voice altered, so that his tone was now cool and incisive, 'it would seem you need them!'

He reached forward and helped Emma down from the coach, gazing at her with narrowed eyes. Emma, her heart a-flutter – and not simply as a result of her recent misfortunes – leaned weakly against the side of the vehicle.

Mennard swung round on Silas Starker and thrust the huge pistol at him.

'What's your game, Starker? I know you for a sharking, mercenary, infamous rogue, but now methinks you've gone into the abduction business.'

Starker, now dripping wet and smeared with mud from his descent into a puddle, seemed bereft of speech. All he could do was shake his skinny fists and gobble with rage.

'They ... they were taking me to Crookham Asylum,' stammered Emma. ''Tis all a most monstrous plot, sir ...'

'Hold your tongue, hussy!' screeched Mrs Grabbidge, her many chins wobbling like a turkey's wattles. ''Tis but a witless serving wench. A thieving ingrate who needs a lesson!'

'Cease your lies, madam,' snapped Mennard, waving the pistol under her beak of a nose. 'If she's a serving wench, I'm King George! Crookham Asylum, eh? This is a wicked business indeed, Starker, if you are scheming to throw her into that pesthole! Egad, I've a mind to ...'

But what he intended Emma was never to know, for at that moment, borne from afar on the night wind, there came the sound of galloping hooves.

'The Redbreasts!' cried the coachman, 'We're saved!'

Throwing caution to the winds he leapt at Mennard, but the highwayman, with a light laugh, stepped aside and put out his booted leg. The coachman tripped and yelped. His momentum carried him forward into Lawyer Starker who, cursing savagely, spun round and pitched into Mrs Grabbidge. All three, arms waving wildly, crashed to the muddy road, Mrs Grabbidge breaking the falls of the other two – although, Emma noted, this consideration on her part seemed not be appreciated either by the coachman or by Silas himself. She shut her ears to the bellowed imprecations that arose from the kicking, threshing tangle on the ground.

She gazed up the road. Revealed in the moonlight as they rounded the bend, though still some way off, thundered a group of horsemen.

'Egad, 'tis the Runners indeed,' muttered the highwayman. 'Methought I'd lost those rascals the other side of Fleet.'

The Bow Street runners – called the 'Robin Redbreasts' by all and sundry for their habit of wearing scarlet – had seen the coach and now their leader threw up an arm. There was a flash and a cracking report, and a pistol ball whined off into the night.

With a reckless laugh that thrilled Emma to the very core of her being, Captain Tom sprang on his horse and reached down for her.

'Come, m'lady. I have a better-class hostelry in mind for you than Crookham Asylum.'

He hauled Emma up on to the horse, then, catching hold of the traces of the coach, whipped the horses into a gallop so that the heavy vehicle lurched and swayed behind them, blocking the road. The highwayman set spur to shank and galloped away.

'Silas Starker is the most perfect compendium of impudence and wickedness I've come across, depend upon it!'

Tom Mennard strode across the sunlit sitting-room of the old cottage, a frown lining his brow. Emma, seated beside the window, turned her head from the diamond-leaded panels, beyond which was revealed a profusion of roses, hollyhocks,

With a reckless laugh that thrilled Emma to the very core of her being, Captain Tom sprang on his horse and reached down for her.

campanulas and geraniums, and gazed at the highwayman's lean, darkly handsome profile as he prowled around the little room.

'Now, Tom – there's good in all men.'

Captain Tom chuckled and laid a hand lovingly on the white head of the motherly, russet-cheeked old lady – so different, thought Emma, from the odious Mrs Grabbidge – who sat placidly embroidering beside the fireplace.

'A just reproof, Aunt Priscilla. And yet, as you know, the rascal's filched my own good name, and done far worse to sweet Emma here.'

Emma modestly lowered her eyes and strove to hide the blush that threatened to steal across her cheeks. Already, after only a week, she found that the dashing Captain Tom Mennard occupied her thoughts far more than she would have thought possible. And not only because he too had fallen foul of the rascally Lawyer Starker and had been forced to take to the road because of the man's villainy. Silas had been attorney to Tom's father too, and when old Colonel Mennard died it was discovered that most of his vast wealth had vanished. Clearly Silas had plundered it, yet the scoundrel had cunningly concocted evidence to prove that it was Tom who had been stealing from his own father.

'Perhaps you're right, dear,' admitted Aunt Priscilla with a sigh.

'Why, the effrontery of the rogue! Openly forging the will, relying on the helplessness of his victim – for who would listen to a complaint by young Miss St Aubyn against that much-respected Lawyer Starker of Charnleigh? Egad, 'tis monstrous!'

'I believe,' said Emma, 'that I would not mind so much about dear Papa's house and lands, if only Silas had let me take my father's most precious possession – and one which Silas himself hated, yet spitefully kept from me – a portrait of myself done two years since by Sir Thomas Gainsborough.'

'And a charming portrait you made, I'll be bound,' murmured Tom, though not so softly that Emma did not hear the compliment. This time, she could do nothing at all to still the blush that rose to her cheeks.

'Hush, Tom, else you'll throw the poor girl into a confusion.' Aunt Priscilla turned to Emma. 'And what d'you think happened to your late father's real will, my dear?'

'I don't know. Silas Starker swore it had vanished, and I suppose it must be so. Papa loved his little jests. I'll warrant he placed it somewhere in the house that can only be tripped upon by accident ...'

'Then by Heaven I'll find it!' said Tom, thumping his fist on an occasional table and causing Aunt Priscilla to drop her embroidery. 'If it is there, in Charnleigh Manor, then I'll pull the house apart until it is revealed!'

'Not 'I'll' but 'we'll,'' Emma said quickly. 'We will go together.'

'I'll not hear of it,' said Tom. 'Why, who knows what dangers there are now Starker has taken possession.'

'You forget, sir,' Emma interjected sharply. 'It was my home, and I know the house well. Besides, I'm not one of your simpering, prissy little featherheads. I *shall* accompany you!'

Tom Mennard jumped back in mock surprise. 'That you are not,' he said with a grin. 'Why then, and so you shall. You have the right on your side. But,' he shook his head slowly, 'I doubt that Melissa will approve.'

Melissa! Who – *who* – was Melissa?

Through all that week, while Emma had been recovering her strength in Aunt Priscilla's charming cottage, no mention had ever been made of any Melissa. And yet that she was very close to Tom Mennard was clear, by the light in his eyes when he'd spoken her name.

The question pounded in Emma's brain throughout the long journey by the light of the stars to Charnleigh Manor in the gig, and kept on pounding as they stealthily entered by a rear window whose catch Emma knew was broken, and searched the lower rooms using a single candle to light their way. *Melissa!* It was like an aching tooth that would not be assuaged.

'Your late father's study,' suddenly whispered Tom, as he opened a door and peered in. 'Now the private sanctum of Silas Starker, scoundrel and rogue.'

Emma shut the door behind them. Tom began quietly to pull open drawers in the large desk as Emma leafed through papers in the pigeon-holes.

'Egad! Bills, bills and more bills!' Tom muttered. 'I swear Silas is being dunned by every tradesman in the kingdom. No wonder the rascal needs to bolster up his lawyer's income with his clients' estates.'

With a snort of irritation he pushed home the final drawer and stood up, hands on hips. He stared around the shadowy room then frowned, peering towards one wall where a small oval portrait in a gilt frame could just be seen, the face of the sitter easily recognisable even in the candlelight.

'Why, here is your Gainsborough portrait. Did you not say that Silas hated it?'

'He does,' said Emma, puzzled. 'I would have thought he'd have destroyed it by now.'

'Ah, 'tis all of a piece with his grasping nature. A valuable little painting, even by so modern a master. Silas would not easily part with something that might yet bring him money.'

Tom strode across and lifted the painting down, gazing at it then casually turning it over to glance at the back. As he did so he gave a mutter of surprise, but Emma was staring at the wall behind him.

'Look!' she said, pointing. 'A small wall safe, cunningly hidden behind the picture.'

Tom looked up and uttered an exclamation of triumph. 'And simple enough to open, I swear.'

Suiting action to word he put the portrait down and began turning a dial on the little safe's door, his fingers delicately feeling their way as he listened for the least response from the mechanism. Suddenly, with a distinct 'click', the door swung open. The highwayman stared at the papers and documents inside and then began to take them out, every now and again exclaiming with astonishment.

'All the evidence we need, egad! Why, the rogue has swindled near every important client in the country. Here – a document actually listing his rascally peculations, including details of how he robbed my own father's estate. This will . . .'

He looked up as Emma gave a startled scream. Standing in the doorway was Silas Starker, a pistol in his hand and a scowl of fury on his sallow face. Tom silently cursed the fact that his own weapon was in the long pocket of his cloak, well out of reach.

'Much good may it do you, you interfering jackanapes,' snarled the lawyer. 'A pistol ball in the heart for you, and then 'tis off to Crookham Asylum for missy here. And who'll believe her ravings, eh?'

He squeezed the trigger of the pistol – but the only sound to be heard was a sputtering fizz. Tom gave a yell of laughter.

'Miserly to the end, you rogue! Too tight-pursed even to keep dry powder for your pistol!'

With a leap he was on top of the cringing lawyer, and in a second had hurled him to the floor. Using the curtain cord to tie his wrists together, Tom bound his prisoner to the table leg with his own belt.

'He'll keep for the Runners, and then it's Reading Gaol for a long, long stretch.' His voice rose with excitement and he pointed to the Gainsborough portrait lying on the table. 'See, my sweet! The rear of the frame opens and you can see the back of the portrait. There are words there, written on the canvas itself! Your father wrote his will on the back of the Gainsborough!'

Emma's brain was whirling with the rush of events – and then her heart did a somersault as Tom crossed the room and crushed her to him, his lips closing over hers with a fierce yet tender passion.

'Why ... why, sir ... what liberties you take!' she said breathlessly. Yet her cheeks burned and her heart pounded in the most surprising and deliciously uncomfortable manner. 'And ... and what of ... Melissa, pray?'

For a moment Tom gazed at her uncomprehendingly. Then his brow cleared and he roared with laughter.

'Melissa? Why, you goose! Are you jealous of Melissa? Yet, come to think on it, how were you to know? Melissa is my little spaniel, kept for me for the moment by my sister in Bath. Though – dare I hope? In a very short while, Melissa may find herself in a new home with the two of us together!'

And Emma could only nod her head, and smile in radiant agreement.

ONLY A DREAM AWAY

Mary Hooper

'Emily!' Cook bellowed. 'Where are you, girl?'

I hurriedly shut the scullery window – I'd been gazing outside into the garden and dreaming – and ran into the kitchen.

'Land sakes, don't you ever hear me the first time I call?' Cook stood there, arms crossed over her chest, red-faced and angry. As she usually was.

'What's with you, girl?' She didn't wait for a reply but went on, 'You'd better watch your step or it's back to the workhouse for you!'

I flinched and she nodded knowingly at the effect her words had on me, the same effect they always had: not for anything would I get myself sent back to the workhouse.

'What was it you wanted?' I asked timidly.

'What *was* it? Have you forgotten that the mistress is entertaining this evening? There's pheasants to pluck, salads to garnish, potatoes to scrape – don't just ask, girl, get on with something!'

I didn't say anything else, just hurried over to the big table where Lucy, one of the other kitchen maids, was slicing beans. She winked at me and nodded towards a mountain of carrots waiting to be scraped and cut into matchstick lengths.

'You should know better than to daydream on a day when Lady Fountney's got a formal dinner party,' she said to me in an undertone. 'Cook's like a great angry bear on days like this.'

I sighed. 'I know,' I said, 'I was just – well, looking out of the window and wishing. It's such a lovely afternoon and the garden's so bright with flowers it almost makes your eyes ache to look at them. I was just thinking what it would be like to be a lady and have nothing more to do than walk along grassy paths and smell the flowers.'

Lucy giggled. 'Looking pretty under the sun and sniffing flowers isn't for the likes of *us*,' she said. 'And think yourself lucky that you've got a job in a great big house and were saved from the workhouse!'

I pulled the knife along the carrot with such force that the tip of it ended up in the palm of my hand and I gave a little squeal of pain. I was forever being reminded of how grateful I should be and it made me so cross!

'I *am* glad to be here,' I said with another sigh, 'but that doesn't stop me wanting more – dreaming that some day I may be ...'

'Was it really terrible in the workhouse?' Lucy interrupted suddenly. 'I can't help but ask. I know you never speak of it – you just go all pale whenever it's mentioned.'

'And I don't want to speak of it now,' I said with a shudder. 'It was an awful place and I never got used to it – no, not even though I was born there.'

'And why were you born in there?' Lucy finished the beans but stood looking at me, head on one side, curious as a cat.

I touched the small gold heart-shaped locket I wore on a chain round my neck. 'I – I don't know much about it,' I said. 'My mother was taken in there when she was expecting me. I was born there, and then she died of fever when I was two years old.'

'And you can't remember her?' Lucy asked sympathetically.

I shook my head. 'Not a thing – though I try so hard to. Sometimes I can conjure up a picture of someone in a long white dress sitting and writing a letter by the light of a candle, but I don't know if that's just something I've dreamt about.'

''Tis right romantic, you know that?' Lucy marvelled. 'But didn't she leave anything for you – any papers to say who you were?'

'She did,' I said, 'and she left me a ring and her clothes, too, but they were all stolen before I was old enough to know anything about it.'

Lucy shook her head slowly. 'So there's just the necklet?'

I touched the gold heart again. 'Even the thieves in there couldn't bring themselves to take a locket from round the neck of a baby.'

'Lucy!' Cook marched in from the servants' hall. 'Haven't you finished those beans yet? I want the parsnips chopped ready for glazing now – be quick about it!'

Lucy went off and I bent my head over the carrots, my hands now stained brown from the carrot juice. Ah well, no one would be looking at my hands except me. Now, if I were one of the young ladies upstairs, one of Lady Fountney's daughters, my hands would be white and smooth, with pink nails like shiny shells and maybe a dainty ring or two on the fingers. Those same hands would be placed lightly on a young gentleman's arm this evening to go in to dinner – the grand dinner which I was helping prepare for now. I stopped scraping, lost in daydreams again. If only ...

'Carrots!' Cook barked. 'Are they ready?' She came over and looked into my enamel bowl, then picked up a few to compare the size of the matchsticks.

'Useless!' she said. 'No pride in your work. You'll never make a cook, girl! You'll be a scullery maid all your life.'

She took the carrots away and returned with a huge bowl of egg whites. 'See if you can whisk the whites for a flummery,' she said. 'You'll need to beat them for at least an hour, mind. No slacking!'

I took up the bowl and whisk wearily. I'd done this job before, whisking and whisking until it felt as if my arm was going to fall off, and the whites still hadn't got crisp enough to please Cook.

A jangling bell rang somewhere upstairs and Cook bristled with indignation. 'Upstairs visitors,' she said, 'and on a day like today!'

'Not for dinner already?' I faltered.

'Silly girl, at four in the afternoon? It's one of Lady Fountney's friends come a-calling. That'll be afternoon tea for four or five, cucumber sandwiches and cream scones – and more than likely the footman to be catered for down here, I'll be bound.' She thumped on the table. 'How they expect me to cook dinner for fourteen as well I don't know!'

She disappeared into the pantry to collect things for afternoon tea, pausing only to shout, 'Get those egg whites in the cool or they'll never stiffen!' to me.

I needed no further invitation to go out of the firing line and into the cool of the scullery with its big open window to the side garden. There were two little chairs in there and I sat down on one and put my feet on the other, enjoying the peace and quiet – but remembering to whisk, of course.

I heard one of the upstairs maids come down with the tea order and Cook complaining, and then the clattering of cups and saucers, and after that everything went quiet for a bit. I thought that Cook had probably gone into her own room with a cup of tea.

I rested my arms for a moment and stared out into the garden that I loved so much. Hollyhocks and lavender, sweet peas and thyme – the smells fought with each other to make themselves known. I gave a big, appreciative sniff, closing my eyes to savour it the more, and when I opened them someone had come into the scullery.

'Oh!' I said, so startled that I almost upset the bowl.

'Sorry,' the young man said, 'I didn't mean to frighten you.'

We stared at each other. He was about my age, I suppose, and wearing a dark suit and shirt with a high collar. He was also very nice looking, with strong white teeth and eyes that looked at me with kind amusement. There was utter silence for a moment and it was – oh, Lucy would have said I was being fanciful again – but it was as if the world had suddenly stopped. All that was left was me and him, him and me, suspended somewhere in time.

After a moment I seemed to come to. I heard people walking about upstairs, birds singing, bees buzzing in the garden. We smiled and it was as if we both knew that something strange had happened to us ...

'I *am* sorry,' he repeated. 'I gave you a fright, didn't I?'

I nodded and sat down again, still shaken – though not by the surprise he'd given me, but by something else. Something I didn't have a name for just then.

'I usually look in down here while the ladies are chatting upstairs,' he said. 'Your cook does a particularly delicious almond cake.'

I laughed. 'She said there'd be a footman to be entertained! Just a moment and I'll see if there's any cake in the larder.'

I left the bowl and whisk and went off and when I came back with two slices of almond cake on a plate the young man was sitting on the other chair whisking away furiously.

'You don't have to do that!' I said.

'I want to. It'll be payment for the cake I'm going to eat.'

I sat down opposite him and watched him cram the cake in his mouth and eat it with relish. 'They can't feed you very well in your house!' I said.

'It's just that our cook isn't such a dab hand at cakes as yours is.' He swallowed the last morsel. 'You're new, aren't you?' he asked curiously.

I nodded. 'I've been here a month.'

'And do you like it?'

'It's nice enough,' I said. 'Cook's frightening but the other maids are kind. I hardly ever get to see Master and Mistress upstairs.'

'All in good time, I suppose,' he said. He put the plate down and stared at me again and I felt a shiver run through me. I touched my hair, smoothed down my apron.

'I . . . I must look a sight,' I said, 'and what would Cook think – me entertaining in the scullery?'

He smiled. 'I think you look very nice. You've got a smudge of flour on your cheek and your hair has escaped from its bun – but you've got the most beautiful brown eyes I've ever seen.'

'Oh!' I was shocked and pleased at the same time. 'Such talk . . . such talk is unseemly.'

'I know,' he said, 'but it's perfectly true.'

I felt myself go pink with pleasure; no young man had ever spoken to me so before. I looked into his eyes and felt myself mesmerised again . . . drowning. I leaned towards him slightly and he leaned towards me. I think – oh, shameless thing that I was – that our lips might have actually touched, but just then Cook opened the door of the scullery.

I jumped up, waiting for the shout of anger. It never came, though. Instead Cook bobbed a curtsey: 'Why, sir, whatever are you doing in my scullery?' she said.

I stared at the young man and blinked several times.

'Sorry, Cook, I was sampling a couple of slices of your delicious almond cake,' he said, cool and calm as anything.

'I'm pleased you like it, sir, but I can't have you a-keeping of my girls from their work!'

I stood up, confused. I didn't know what to say. Who was he and why was she calling him 'sir'?

Cook and he exchanged a look and then Cook nodded in the direction of the larder. 'Egg whites to go into the larder,

Emily, and you can start peeling the apples.'

I scuttled off to do as I was bid, my mind seething with a hundred questions. Lucy stood in the kitchen chattering to Kate; they both burst into giggles as I approached.

'You're a dark horse!' Kate said, 'entertaining in the scullery when no one's about!'

'I was only in there whisking egg whites,' I protested. '*He* came in for some almond cake.'

Kate clutched at Lucy's arm. 'Oh, he came in for some almond cake, did he? Oh, my!'

'Just look at her! Entertaining the gentry in the scullery, bold as brass!'

'I ... I didn't know who he was. I thought he was the footman!' I said, which only served to make them giggle harder. 'Who *is* he, then?'

'Why, he's young Master David Becket-Smythe!' Lucy said. 'The son of the Honourable Mrs Becket-Smythe upstairs.'

'And the heir to thousands of pounds!' Kate put in excitedly. 'It's said that they're one of the richest families in England.'

'Oh!' I felt a chill go through me; he'd just been amusing himself with me, then – playing pretty compliments to a servant girl and no doubt laughing to himself at how she responded. Oh, to think I'd nearly kissed him! I felt myself blush with mortification and embarrassment.

I took the apples into the larder to peel, not wanting him to see me on his way out; not wanting to give him another chance to laugh at me again. How *could* I have believed him to be a footman!

There wasn't much more time for thought that day; the whole of the downstairs staff were whirled into preparing, cooking and producing the grand dinner that evening. In the early hours of the morning, though, when I was tucked up in my hard bed, I thought of him again and found that, even though I knew he'd just been playing with me, it didn't affect my feelings for *him* at all. I just couldn't get him out of my mind! It didn't seem possible . . . but could it be that I was in love?

Three days later I was still in the same confused, melancholy state. I'd heard that falling in love was a beautiful thing – but it was only beautiful, surely, when you knew your love could be returned. For a kitchen maid to love an aristocrat was laughable; ridiculous and pathetic.

Cook was baking that day and the kitchen was hot and steamy, the big pine table full of pies, pastries and cakes. I looked at the fresh almond cake dolefully; I would never be able to see one again without thinking of *him*. I pushed open the door to the garden to try and get a breath of air.

Cook glanced at me. 'I'll give you five minutes out there gathering some herbs,' she shouted across the kitchen, 'and then I want you to start on the washing-up.'

I nodded gratefully. Cook was quite reasonable sometimes – and since the incident a few days before she'd become a little softer towards me. Maybe she, too, had been in love once, I thought sadly. Been in love and known that her love would never be returned . . .

I walked down the path of the kitchen garden and bent over to pick a few sprigs of rosemary. I heard a soft footfall, a cough – and I wheeled round to find myself looking into the eyes I'd done nothing but dream about for the past three days.

'Cook said you were out here,' he said. 'I didn't startle you again, did I?'

I remembered myself and dropped a curtsey but he just laughed.

'You don't have to curtsey to me,' he said, taking my hand.

I wriggled my fingers to try and escape from his firm grasp.

'Don't; it isn't seemly,' I said. 'It's not right to take advantage of a servant girl.'

'Not seemly, no. I've been awake these last two nights thinking of that. Yet I haven't come back to take advantage of you ... I just wanted to see you again.'

'No!' I turned my back on him. 'You mustn't speak with me so, mustn't joke about such things.'

'Emily! I didn't come here to joke with you!' he protested. I felt his hand on my waist and delicious shudders went through me. 'I can't get you out of my mind, don't you understand? You're the loveliest, most delicate little creature I've ever seen. You're so natural ... you're real and honest and true. I *had* to see you again!'

A faint sigh escaped my lips and he turned me round to face him. 'I can hardly believe it ... but I think I love you,' he said gently, and then his lips came down on mine and I could not resist returning his kiss.

'Nothing will ever come of it, you know,' Kate said to me nastily one evening. It was about a month since David and I had first met and incredibly, unbelievably, we still felt the same way about each other. We met whenever we could: the shy and awkward kitchen maid and the rich young sir – and if people thought it strange to see us walking down the street together or driving out in his carriage, they were much too polite to stand and stare or make any comment about our friendship. All except Kate.

'He's just amusing himself with you. Slumming it!'

I said nothing, but turned away so she couldn't see how her words had hurt me, for I was scared in my heart of hearts that they might be true – but the very next day David asked me to marry him!

'You can't mean it!' I said, my eyes filling with tears. 'It doesn't really happen like this. You can't!'

'My darling Emily,' David said, squeezing my hands, 'I've never meant anything so much in my life. I want to marry you whatever anyone else thinks. Of course, my parents will cut me off so I don't see a penny of their fortune but I'd rather live in the workhouse *with* you than in a palace without you.'

I felt my cheeks go pale at the dreaded word again. I'd told David about my background, of course, but no one who hadn't been in a workhouse could understand exactly what the word meant.

He kissed my hands. 'I'll speak to Father tonight – though whatever he says I intend to marry you.'

I clutched at the gold heart at my throat. 'Don't – don't lose your family because of me,' I said. 'Your mother – it would break her heart if you married beneath you.'

'And it would break my heart if I lost you,' David said, kissing me again.

Two days after that David and I stood in the scullery where we'd first met. His arms were tightly round me, his lips touched my hair.

'It's done,' he said. 'My parents have been told and I intend to speak to Lady Fountney today and ask her to release you from service. We can be married whenever you like.'

My eyes widened. 'You mean your – your parents have agreed?'

He shook his head. 'No, my sweet. They haven't agreed, I'm afraid.' He smiled wryly. 'They've gone quite mad, as a matter of fact. Raved and ranted and threatened me with all sorts of dire things.'

'But ...'

'But they haven't made me change my mind – nothing can do that. I want to marry you no matter what. And if they say we shall live in poverty then that's what we'll do!'

'No!' I broke away from him. 'I won't let you! I won't let you give up everything for me – I love you too much! You don't know what real poverty is like – you'd never endure it. I couldn't bear to be the cause of that. I won't marry you!'

I blundered out of the door and left him standing there. I was sobbing as I ran up the back stairs to my room, but I knew my sacrifice was worthwhile. David should never go through what I'd been through; it would not be *me* who brought him disgrace and poverty as a dowry.

My days after that were black. David sent messages – I wouldn't read them. He turned up himself and I locked myself in the pantry and refused to come out until he went away. My eyes were constantly red from weeping.

I suppose things might have gone on like that, with me getting more and more unhappy as the months went by, but some two weeks after that Lucy and I had to wait at table upstairs. Lady Fountney was having another big dinner party and Susan and Ellen, the parlourmaids, had both been taken ill in the afternoon with some sort of mystery illness.

I was terribly nervous taking up the big platters of food and even though I knew I didn't have to serve it – the footmen did that – my hands were shaking as I put down the vegetables on the sideboard. When I turned round to face the guests I was glad I wasn't holding anything – for if I had been I'd surely have dropped it – because one of the guests was David, sitting between a queenly looking woman and a man in naval uniform who were obviously his mother and father.

He saw me at the same time and his face paled to a deathly white. We stared at each other and because he was my dearest love and I understood him well I knew that he was feeling exactly the same as I was. Even though we were both half sick with love we were cursed – our paths could never meet again.

'Emily!' Lady Fountney said suddenly, making me jump. 'Bring us the mustard, please.'

I did as I was told and as I leaned forward to put the mustard on the table I felt the Honourable Mrs Becket-

Smythe, David's mother, looking at me keenly. I felt myself growing weak with terror: had she been told my name? Did she know it was me that her son loved?

'Child!' she called. 'Come here a minute!' Frightened though I was, I did as I was bid without even thinking about it. To do as others bade me was my role in life, after all.

I went to her chair in terror, waiting for her to say something about my relationship with David, but instead she put her hand up and touched the golden heart at my throat. 'Where did you get that necklet?' she asked.

The people sitting near her grew quiet, sensing a scandal. Maybe they – maybe she – thought I'd stolen it.

'It – it was my mother's,' I began falteringly. Her eyes widened but she nodded for me to go on so I stammered out the story – or as much as I knew. I told her about the shame and degradation of living in a workhouse ... and when I'd finished I realised that everyone had stopped eating and were listening to me. I hung my head in confusion; I'd surely be sacked for this.

'I will tell you why I asked,' David's mother said. 'Many years – seventeen or so years ago – I had a young cousin. She was a pretty little thing but she – she disgraced our family, ran away and was never seen again. She had a locket just like yours which had been made for her when she was born by the crown jeweller.' I stared at her incredulously, my eyes wide.

'And what – what happened to her?' I asked, my mouth dry.

'She gave birth to her child and after that wrote many times to her father to ask forgiveness. He was a hard man, though, and wouldn't have anything to do with her. Only on his deathbed did he repent, but by then it was too late – it was said that my pretty cousin had died in a workhouse. Her child – a daughter – could not be traced either, although she had been left a fortune by the grandfather she had never known.'

'Where did you get that necklet?' she asked.

She stopped speaking and looked carefully at the golden heart again. 'I would swear in court that this is the same necklet and you ...' she hesitated and the people round the table seemed to hold their breath 'you are very like my young cousin as a girl of seventeen.'

For a moment there was silence and then someone let out a cheer. 'Champagne!' a woman's voice cried. 'Champagne to celebrate the return of the long-lost grandchild!' and everyone began talking at once.

As I stood there, stunned, I was dimly aware of David getting up from his seat and coming to my side.

'Sweet Emily,' he said, taking my hand, '*now* will you marry me?'

I couldn't have spoken, my heart was too full, but for answer I flung both arms round his neck and hugged him tightly. The company of fine ladies and gentlemen cheered us and the sparkling chandeliers and glasses on the table began, through my tears, to glitter like so many stars. Yes, sometimes dreams *could* come true ...

SHADOW OF THE GUILLOTINE

June Williams

GERARD MALLET HAD FOUND it was not easy working for a man like the Marquis de Beauvoir. Vile tempered, overbearing and completely indifferent to the welfare of those who worked for him, he epitomised all that had made the common people of France come to detest the aristocrats. As for Gerard, who worked as his secretary, only one thing stopped him going on his way. He was deeply in love with the Marquis's daughter, Hortense, who Gerard thought was the most beautiful woman who had ever walked the earth.

Gerard knew that his love was a hopeless one. He was a mere clerk, whereas she was an aristocrat and the heiress to a fortune. As such, she was hopelessly out of his reach. But nevertheless, he had stayed on.

If pressed, Gerard would have admitted with some embarrassment that there was a far more important reason, other than his love for Hortense, why he stayed. After years of oppression, the citizens of Paris had risen. The prison fortress of the Bastille had been stormed and its Swiss guards massacred, and now the mobs were roaming the streets, attacking anyone who even resembled an aristocrat. In these circumstances Gerard knew it was possible that the mob might attack the home of the Marquis, which was no more than a few kilometres away from the capital. If that happened, Gerard wanted to be there to defend Hortense – even to give his life for her if necessary.

Gerard was so concerned with the state of affairs that he

decided that he must warn Hortense. He chose a morning while they were alone together going over the housekeeping books.

'You do your job well,' Hortense said, closing the book he had given her. 'Perhaps too well.' She studied him, her cornflower-blue eyes filled with concern. 'You look tired. Perhaps you should take a few days' rest and go away. I will speak to my father.'

'You would be wasting your time.' He paused. 'If anyone should go away, it is you, Mademoiselle. As you know, these are dangerous times. The mob could come here, looking for your father.' In his agitation, he had risen to his feet and was now so close to her that his senses were assailed by her heady perfume. 'I really do urge you to leave – perhaps go and stay in the countryside where it is more peaceful.'

'I have already suggested to my father that we should leave. But he is a stubborn man.' She paused to regard him contemplatively. 'I can see you are really concerned. But why should you be? Your sympathies are surely with the people.'

'Perhaps,' he admitted. 'But I do not see you as an enemy of the people.'

'Even so, I can be of little importance to you –' Hortense began.

'You are everything to me.' The words had slipped out and Gerard would have done anything to recall them. But having committed himself, he stumbled on recklessly. 'I love you, Mademoiselle. I have done so from the very beginning.' He turned away abruptly, realising the enormity of what he was saying. 'I am sorry. I should not have spoken.'

'Why do you apologise?' she said quietly. 'There is no shame in saying what is truly in one's heart.'

'But when a person of my background dares to speak in those terms to an –'

'An aristocrat? That is purely an accident of birth,' said

Hortense with a touch of impatience in her voice. 'Now please turn around, Gerard.'

Reluctantly, he obeyed her, and to his amazement he saw that her eyes were brimming with tears.

'Oh, Gerard,' she said softly. 'What a dear, kind person you are. And what courage it must have taken for you to say what you have just said. I will try and match that courage. Over the months I have watched you, and I have seen how good you are in a dozen different ways. At first, I only admired you. But gradually that respect has turned to love.' Seeing the look of utter incredulity on his face, she added, 'Yes, I love you, Gerard – far more than I thought it possible to love a man.'

'I cannot believe it,' he said hoarsely.

'Then I will make you believe it.' She moved closer to him, tilting her head back and gazing up into his eyes. 'You may kiss me, Gerard.'

At that he took her into his arms and kissed her. When he finally drew away, Gerard looked at her almost in a daze. 'Hortense,' he whispered. 'This is madness. We must never let it happen again!'

'Nonsense,' she said, with an impish gleam in her eyes. 'We shall meet every evening, when my father goes to his study.'

For the next month or so, Gerard lived in paradise. Each evening they met and then hurried into the woods that formed part of the estate. Much of the time they merely talked. Gerard told her something of his childhood, and how he had managed to obtain an education through a kindly parish priest, and Hortense spoke bitterly about her father, who, it transpired, had driven her mother into an early grave by neglect and cruelty.

'Sometimes he makes me ashamed to be a Beauvoir,' she told Gerard.

But their conversations were not always so earnest. In fact, there were times when they did not speak at all, but behaved as lovers do all over the world.

Then suddenly, Gerard's happiness was snatched away from him. He was working in the office one afternoon, when Hortense slipped into the room.

'Gerard,' she said, hesitantly, 'I am feeling a little unwell. I think therefore that it would be better if we did not meet tonight.'

Full of concern, Gerard rose from his desk and hurried over to her. 'My dearest – it is nothing serious, I hope?'

'I have a chill, that's all,' she assured him, smiling. 'But in the circumstances, I think it best I did not go out into the night air.'

'Of course.' He took her in his arms. 'I think I could bear not seeing you for just one day.'

It was then that the door opened.

Still locked in each other's arms, Hortense and Gerard looked up in petrified silence at the Marquis, who stood in the doorway, his face suffused with fury.

'You scoundrel!' His hand reached for his sword. 'That you should dare –'

Pulling the sword from its sheath, the Marquis advanced upon them, the point raised to strike. 'Stand aside, Hortense!'

'No!' Hortense cried. 'If you kill the man I love, then you must kill me, too!' As the Marquis paused, thunderstruck by her words, she added quietly, 'It is true, Father. I love him.'

Gerard moved her aside. 'Sir, I will face you with a sword, if you will give me one.'

'None of that nonsense is necessary,' Hortense said. She turned to face her father boldly. 'If you try to harm Gerard I will see to it that all Paris knows, and the reason for it, too – that you despised him as a suitor for your daughter simply because he is a commoner.'

The Marquis hesitated, and then lowered his sword. He

*Pulling the sword from its sheath, the Marquis advanced upon
them, the point raised to strike. 'Stand aside, Hortense!'*

gave Gerard a look of sheer hatred. 'I spare your life only because I have no wish for a scandal.'

Hortense gave an audible sigh of relief. Then she turned to Gerard. 'I am sorry for this.' She regarded him sadly. 'You must realise I cannot leave my father at such a time.'

'I understand,' Gerard said. He added with a trace of bitterness, 'I also realise that our love was doomed from the start.' And with that, he brushed past the Marquis and stalked out of the room.

'So you are looking for work,' Robespierre said. He flicked an invisible crumb from his satin breeches. 'Then you had better tell me something about yourself.'

Gerard told him something of his background. 'I was last in the employ of the Marquis de Beauvoir,' he finished. 'Since then I have been looking for work in Paris – without success, I fear. Then today I went into a wine establishment. The owner was kind enough to tell me that a certain Citizen Robespierre was looking for a clerk.'

'And what did he tell you about me?' Robespierre asked.

'That you were a lawyer arrived from Arras. Nothing more.'

Robespierre nodded. 'Why did you leave the service of the Marquis de Beauvoir?'

Gerard hesitated. He looked at the long, pinched face that stared at him from the other side of the desk. A cold fish, he thought. A man hardly likely to approve of his relationship with Hortense. But there was no point in withholding the truth. He told Robespierre the exact circumstances that had led to his departure. 'I fell in love with the Marquis's daughter,' he said shortly, 'and we were discovered. It was an impossible situation.'

'You are well out of it,' Robespierre said with a shrug. 'The days of the aristocrats are numbered. As for the young woman, you would be well advised to forget her.' He put his bony fingers together and looked over them at Gerard. 'I should tell you that if you have any lingering royalist sympathies, you would be of no use to me. I am a member of the Assembly, which is dedicated to their overthrow.' Gerard assured him he had none.

'Good,' Robespierre said. 'Then you may start tomorrow.' He smiled thinly as Gerard rose to go. 'The future should be interesting for both of us. For we live in dangerous times, do we not?'

Robespierre had spoken truly. A month after Gerard had joined him, the King was arrested. Gerard was appalled, and dared to say so to his employer.

'I cannot help thinking that the matter of the King could have been handled differently. Could he not have been exiled?'

'He was arrested in the interests of the public safety,' said Robespierre, 'and it is in those interests that he will no doubt be executed in due course.' He brushed the subject aside with a dismissive gesture. 'I hear, by the way, that the Marquis de Beauvoir and his daughter have fled to the country.' He gave Gerard a quizzical glance. 'I trust you are now over your infatuation for the daughter?'

'I have tried not to think about her,' Gerard said truthfully enough, though his lack of success he kept to himself. 'I have just been hoping she was in some place of safety.'

'You must be careful to keep quiet about your connection with that family,' Robespierre warned him. 'Others are not so tolerant as I am.'

That night, Gerard left the office only minutes after Robespierre. As he stepped outside, he heard a muffled cry that made him peer into the darkness, where he saw three struggling figures. He ran forward, realising as he did so that one of them was Robespierre. A raised knife, shining dully in the moonlight, was sent flying as Gerard dealt the assailant a massive blow that sent him reeling. Recovering, the man turned and fled, quickly followed by his companion. The affray had taken no more than a few seconds.

Gerard and Robespierre faced each other. 'You have saved my life,' Robespierre said. 'I do not drink myself, but allow me to buy you a glass of wine.'

'Who were they?' Gerard asked as they walked away.

'Probably assassins hired by a rival faction,' Robespierre said. 'I have many enemies.'

There were times afterwards when Gerard was to regret having saved Robespierre's life. For it was soon after that night that a dozen or so aristocrats were arrested and executed. Robespierre, now a power in the land, had signed their death warrants. More arrests were made and more aristocrats walked the steps to the guillotine, many of them again sent there by Robespierre. Appalled by the bloodshed, but powerless to do anything about it, Gerard could only hope that the tentacles of the Revolution would not reach wherever Hortense was staying.

One Sunday afternoon, Gerard visited the Marquis de Beauvoir's estate. He had gone there for no other reason than he wished to stroll once more through the woods where he had spent so many happy hours with Hortense. As he walked through them, he could almost hear her voice at his side, telling him how much she loved him, as she had so often done in those long lost happy days.

Suddenly he froze as he saw a flash of white among the trees. When it did not move, he advanced cautiously, and then stopped again, an incredulous cry of joy rising to his lips. There in front of him was Hortense, sitting in a glade. He stumbled forward, calling her name.

'Gerard!' Rising, Hortense ran into his waiting arms. 'This is wonderful . . .'

'It is more like a miracle,' he said. He held her from him. 'But what are you doing here?'

'My father was killed last month,' she told him. 'We had moved to a small village outside Nantes, but they found out who he was. They stoned him to death in the village street –' She shuddered and clung to him.

'But why did you come here?' Gerard asked. 'It is the most dangerous of places for you to be in.'

'I had nowhere else to go,' she said simply. 'When I heard my father had been killed, I fled from the village and made my way back here disguised as a serving woman.'

'Let us sit,' Gerard said. They both sat and lay back on the grass, looking at the sky above them. Then he said finally, 'When it is dark, I will take you to my lodgings. You can stay there until we have decided what is the best thing for you to do.' He kissed her gently. 'Rest now.'

Dutifully, she closed her eyes. Watching her lying there, he thought how childlike and vulnerable she looked. If only I could look after you for the rest of our lives, he thought, how happy we could be. Not for the first time he cursed the Revolution. Lulled by Hortense's presence, he too drifted into a deep sleep.

He was awakened finally by a heavy boot kicking him in the ribs. Looking up he saw two revolutionary soldiers grinning down at him. Both of them had rifles with attached bayonets. Beside him, Hortense sat watching with frightened eyes.

'Been having a little sport with an aristo, have we?' one of them said. He spat contemptuously. 'That will cost you your life, citizen.'

There were rats in Gerard's cell. Made bold with hunger, they had attacked him several times, only to be kicked squealing into a corner by his booted foot. He thought of Hortense in a similar cell, and groaned. All he could hope for now was that at least they would be condemned to the guillotine together.

Presently, a guard came to his cell. 'Citizen Robespierre wants to see you. And hurry – he is not a man who likes to be kept waiting.'

Half an hour later, Gerard was standing before Robespierre. He regarded Gerard sombrely. 'I suppose you are wondering why I wish to see you.'

'You wish to tell me my post is still open for me,' Gerard said jauntily.

'This is hardly a time for joking,' Robespierre said coldly. Rising from his chair, he began to pace the room. 'In the normal way I would let you and your aristo friend go to the guillotine without a second thought. But I am mindful of the fact that you saved my life. I therefore owe you a life.'

'Then let it be the life of Hortense de Beauvoir,' Gerard cried.

Robespierre stopped his pacing to face him. 'I will do better than that. I will repay the debt with *two* lives for the one.' The bloodless lips formed the semblance of a smile. 'What do you say to that?'

'You are being very generous,' Gerard stammered.

'I agree with you,' Robespierre said dryly. He nodded towards his desk. 'I have already signed the papers of release for you and the Beauvoir woman, who will be here shortly. Not only that, I have arranged for a guard to take you both to the coast, where you can catch the packet boat to England.'

'I can only thank you again.' Gerard was puzzled. 'But why do you do all this? Surely not just because I saved your life?'

'Not entirely,' Robespierre said. He sighed. 'Very soon, I think, my enemies will arrange for me to walk to the scaffold. When I go, I would like to think there were two people, at least, who will remember me as human, and not as an unfeeling monster. For that is how history will see me.' He put a hand on Gerard's shoulder, and then withdrew it quickly, as if ashamed of the gesture. 'No doubt I shall regret all this the moment you have gone ...'

Three days later, Gerard and Hortense were on the boat, watching the coast of France as it slowly disappeared in the early morning mists.

'I am sure we will never return,' Hortense said sadly.

'Things will not always be as they are at present in France,' Gerard said. 'It is true that you and I may never return.' He smiled fondly at Hortense as his arm tightened round her shoulders. 'But our children will ...'

NEVER ALONE AGAIN

Beverley Watts

THE SUN WAS LIKE A HUGE golden egg yolk in the sky, surrounded by soft fluffy white clouds. It looked delicious to Marjery Brown as she walked barefooted along the dirty streets of London on a roasting August afternoon in 1349. Her stomach rumbled impatiently. Two whole days had passed since she'd touched any food and her last meal, a simple supper, had been little more than a plate of thin porridge.

Marjery wiped the beads of sweat from her forehead with the back of her hand and sighed. The stench of the street in the throbbing heat was almost unbearable and she felt as if she could hardly breathe. For a moment, the simple farm girl longed for the fresh clean air of her home in the countryside, the sweet scent of hay and green, green grass. Her mind wandered back to the fields of yellow wheat and barley. She imagined the sheep out at pasture, could almost hear the bees buzzing around her head and the creak of the windmill; could almost feel the cool brown earth beneath her feet.

Suddenly a woman's shout snapped Marjery out of her daydream. From a nearby window came the warning 'Gardy-loo!' and she stepped back just in time to miss the bucketful of slops which were aimed carelessly at the stream running by the side of the road. Most of the foul mixture swirled over the cobbles, not reaching the clogged, filthy ditch she knew must be the Fleet.

The thin, bedraggled girl had been asking many strangers if they knew where she might find some work and shelter and a tinker had told her to follow the bank of the Thames till she reached the pie shop by the Fleet. They sometimes needed girls to help in the kitchen, if they were quick on their feet and strong enough to lift the heavy pans.

Just across the way, Marjery could see a thick-armed woman in a russet dress, surrounded by a small group of customers who were gathered along the wooden shop front. 'Fresh herring pies! Fresh herring pies!' she was shouting in a hoarse voice and Marjery wished that she could taste just one tiny corner of the delicious-looking flaky pastry.

Slowly, the crowd petered away and the woman stood alone, rearranging her wares. Marjery took a deep breath, tried to tidy her shabby, torn clothes and walked towards the shop front.

'Please excuse me,' she said softly to the pie lady. 'Do you have work – in the kitchen?'

Two hard grey eyes looked her up and down and a bunch of strong fingers pinched her arm. 'There's not much of you, is there?' the woman snapped. 'But we do need another hand.'

Marjery followed her down a dark passage to the large, bustling kitchen. Three young girls, no more then ten or twelve years old, were busy stacking freshly made bread, cakes and pies into an oval brick oven. Here, the heat was even more overpowering than outside and Marjery felt the blood rushing from her head.

'You know how to stack the faggots and rake the ashes, I suppose?' the large woman asked grumpily, but Marjery didn't have time to answer. She fell in a faint and lay stretched out on the black, filthy floor. When she opened her eyes again, a few minutes later, she found herself back on the street again, alone. The cold grey eyes now stared at her from a few yards away. 'Clear off!' the pie woman shouted. 'Don't want no diseases spread round here.'

Marjery had been feeling very dizzy, but she thought it was

just her hunger, and the heat. It was months since she'd got over the whooping cough that had swept through the local village. Her mother had treated her with fried mouse and Marjery had recovered almost completely. It hurt her now to think of her mother. Tears pricked Marjery's pale blue eyes as she pictured her wrinkled, weatherbeaten face at the doorway of their cottage farmhouse. Then the tearful girl pictured her father's face, too, stern and unyielding, and she clenched her fists angrily.

It wasn't that Marjery had wanted to run away and leave them, but she hadn't dared stay a day longer. Her slight figure had crept out past the barn just before dawn on the eve of her fifteenth birthday. Marjery's father hadn't understood about her not wanting to marry Joshua Jones. He was a good man, she knew, but he was three times her age at least and she did not, could not, ever love him.

There had been no arguments. When Marjery complained and refused to marry Joshua, her father simply beat her till she was covered with purple bruises all over her fragile body. The bruises had now mellowed to pale yellow rings, but Marjery could still feel the blows on her crouched frame and remember her own shrill screams which had drifted unheard, save by the owls and swooping bats, into the dark night.

Raising herself slowly to her feet, Marjery pushed a strand of hair out of her eyes and accidently brushed her neck with her hand. The undersides of her jaw felt swollen and sore, and she pressed the sites again with the tips of her fingers, wondering if perhaps she had caught bronchitis or maybe even the dreaded smallpox. As yet, her smooth skin had not been disfigured by the terrible scars.

Marjery's throat felt dusty and dry. She had seen others drinking from the river, but she could not bear to taste the sewage-tainted water. It was a muddy grey compared with the crystal brooks she was accustomed to seeing at home.

Not knowing which way to turn, Marjery wandered slowly from street to street, past row upon row of straw and stubble-covered houses, till she heard the sounds of merry music and conversation and realised that she had chanced upon a fair. Around the next corner, Marjery saw a most colourful sight. The vivid hues of the crowd's clothes mingled together to form a multi-coloured mass which moved to and fro as they jostled together.

As her legs had begun to feel wobbly again, Marjery stretched out her hand to balance herself against a post. Instead of the rough feel of splintered wood, however, she felt her own perspiring palm touch the flesh of another. Turning, she saw a young man, around sixteen years of age, smiling down at her with a kind, strong face.

With one arm looped around her waist, he gently led Marjery to the shade of a huge oak tree and seated her comfortably against its trunk. Grateful and exhausted, the ailing peasant girl leant against his broad chest and crumpled in his arms. She did not know why, but she instinctively trusted this youth. He would not shout at her or beat her body black and blue. His hands were large and solid, his nose straight and noble, his eyes a light warm brown.

'Where are you going?' he asked gently. Marjery was so weak she could hardly utter a word.

'I – I do not know,' she croaked at last, through hard, dry lips. 'I am so hungry, and my mouth is on fire.'

The boy knelt down by her side and touched her blazing cheeks with soft fingers, then felt the fever on her forehead. A deep frown etched itself along his brow. 'Please trust me,' he told her. 'My name is Luke Baker. Wait here – I am your friend.' He stood up and quickly disappeared into the fair.

Marjery feared he had left her. Sad, silent tears ran down her cheeks as she sat in the shade of the large oak. No energy at all remained in her weary bones; she could not move. There was nothing she could do but wait.

The fair grew even more crowded and Marjery had never seen such finery. There were ladies in rich scarlet dresses, gentleman in purple hose and yellow jackets. A tall and elegant woman passed by with jewelled plaits and her escort wore a surcoat of mauve and gold brocade. They were a dazzling sight. All around the town folk went about their business, trading cloth and hides or relaxing with a glass of mead or cider and a plate of sweetmeats.

A cock fight was taking place over the way and a dwarf on stilts announced that the bear baiting was about to begin. Young children played Bob Apple and Hot Cockles noisily. The light wind carried the heady smells of camphor, cloves, ginger and mace, mingled with the odour of rotting food, dropped by the revellers.

Although she tried to keep her eyes open to watch for Luke's return, her lids were far too heavy and Marjery could not help herself falling into an exhausted sleep. When she awoke it was a little cooler, the sun was setting and she could taste cold, sharp lemon barley against her lips. Luke was coaxing her to drink from a pottery jar filled to the brim with the refreshing liquid. From under his jacket, he took a piece of finely woven cloth and unwrapped some salted meat, some soft cheese and a jar of honey. He would not eat or drink himself until Marjery had taken her fill, but when she had finished and smiled at him gratefully, he'd hungrily eaten all that was left. Up above, darker clouds had gathered and raindrops, heavy and dense, were beginning to fall.

Without a word, Luke lifted Marjery in his arms and carried her to the riverside. 'I have a hiding place,' he explained. 'It's sheltered there.'

They came to a wide bridge and when he was sure that no one was watching, Luke slipped between two of the bankside supports and pushed aside a large piece of driftwood. There, in the dark rat-infested dampness, Luke had made his home. A cloak of thick velvet lay on top of his bed of rushes and he wrapped Marjery in this, laying her head on a pillow of goose down. Luke lighted a beeswax candle and the place was illuminated by its spluttering flame. There was hardly anything else in the tiny haven, except for a spoon, a knife and a metal plate.

Marjery, a little stronger for having eaten, was curious about her saviour. When she had told him briefly her story of how she had run away from her parents to escape the embraces of Joshua Jones, she asked him about his own mother and father – his real home.

'This is it,' he told her cheerfully, hiding his grief. 'My family all died when our house was burnt to the ground. It was a huge fire – six streets were eaten up – and nothing remained except a pile of ashes. I've been alone ever since.'

The two lonely young people stretched out their hands to each other and clasped them firmly. Their faces glowed with a magical feeling in the candlelight.

'I saw you outside the pie shop,' Luke admitted to Marjery. 'You looked so pretty and helpless, I fell in love with you there and then. I followed you to the fair.' She blushed.

'Do you work?' Marjery asked, wondering how Luke could have afforded his fine clothes and the expensive food they had eaten.

'No, I cannot find an employer,' he explained. 'Work is scarce and my skills are not for the land. My father was a pharmacist; he taught me all about the new spices and drugs that are coming in on ships from Venice. He had a good stock of herbs and remedies but almost all of them were destroyed in the fire.'

Luke continued in a whisper, his head hung low. 'I am ashamed,' he confessed, 'but I steal.'

Marjery looked horrified but felt sympathy in her breast.

Luke lighted a beeswax candle and the place was illuminated by its spluttering flame.

When she had left the farmyard where she had lived all her life, she did not know how she would ever survive alone. She had vaguely imagined that there would be work to find, whether it was spinning, cooking or weaving, but she had found nothing in forty-eight hours of quest.

'Aren't you afraid?' she asked, for Marjery knew that the penalty for robbers and thieves was death.

Luke nodded slowly and gently touched her cheek again. 'Yes, I am afraid,' he said, 'but I have no choice. I will find work soon and all will be well. Will you stay with me forever, pretty Marjery?'

Marjery smiled and promised that she would. Here was a boy with whom she felt she could live all her life. A tender, kind boy, who would be faithful and true as they faced life's difficulties together. A boy who loved her, as she loved him, deeply in her heart of hearts.

The two fell asleep that night, side by side in innocent slumber, holding each other for warmth in the chill of the night. No person disturbed their harmonious dreams, only the black rats rustled about in the darkness. Luke told his love to ignore them and wrapped the velvet cloak tighter around her, while he lay shivering, uncovered in the musty, dank air.

As the sun rose, Marjery was woken by the sound of Luke returning to their hideaway. He had already been up and about.

'How are you feeling?' he asked thoughtfully and Marjery propped herself up on one elbow.

'A little woozy,' she answered happily. She did not mention that she ached all over, even more so than when her father had beaten her with his belt. The damp atmosphere made her cough and her lungs felt tight and wheezy.

'It may just be a chill,' Luke told her, suspecting far worse. He knew that the plague had reached London and many thousands of people were dying from the terrible disease that had swept through Europe from China. Not wanting to frighten his sweetheart, Luke did not share his thoughts.

'Here,' he said, pouring a spoonful of thin syrup from a bottle he carried. 'Take this.' Marjery swallowed the pleasant-tasting mixture which was sweet. 'It's white horehound and honey,' Luke told her. 'Very good for coughs.' He paused for a few moments. 'Do you ache? Are you stiff and uncomfortable?'

Marjery answered with the pain in her eyes. She did not notice, but Luke's hands began to tremble. He was now almost certain that Marjery had the plague. When he rubbed her thin limbs with goosegrease and resin linament to ease the pain, he could feel the swollen glands under her armpits and below her ears, and he knew without doubt that she had the disease. It could only be a matter of hours before the end.

Knowing only that she did not wish ever to be parted from this boy who had been so loving and king, Marjery slowly began to feel more and more confused and dizzy. She became increasingly restless as her fever mounted. Faithfully Luke stayed by her side, holding her in his arms, soothing her delirium and bathing her burning forehead.

Just as the basket seller was setting up his wares for the evening fair and the minstrels and jesters began to tumble and sing to amuse the spectators, Marjery slipped into unconsciousness. A short time later she was dead. Her pale eyelids closed for the last time and Luke pressed her still-warm cheek against his own as he sobbed loudly in desolate agony at the loss of the love he had just found.

That evening, not wanting to leave Marjery to the cruel elements on the river bank, Luke lifted her now-cold frame on to his shoulder and took her to the nearest churchyard where a large grave had been dug for plague victims. So many citizens had been struck down by the killer disease that the churches had begun mass burials.

Luke did not find it easy to carry Marjery's body, even though she hardly weighed a thing. His legs were strangely unsteady; his thoughts swam around and he felt a throbbing in his belly and chest. It broke his heart to lay his love's body in the newly turned soil, but he gently lowered her into the earth and blew a kiss to wish her goodbye.

When Luke turned to leave, he found he could hardly put one foot in front of the other. His head now spun rapidly and he knew, as he had guessed from the beginning, that he had caught the killer plague, too. A deep pain wracked his whole being and every limb ached, but he smiled a fateful smile as he was filled with a strange joy.

Lying down on the flowers strewn around the grave, Luke rested his head on his arms and looked up at the moon. 'We'll never be parted, my love,' he whispered. 'Wait for me.'

The night air struck chill on his fever-wracked body and the silver orb in a gem-encrusted sky became a soft blurred light in a pin-pricked void. Then all was dark and cold ...

A QUESTION OF IDENTITY

June Williams

ANN AND SYLVIA PENNINGTON had now become such a
familiar sight to the people of Lyme Regis that no one took
much notice of them, except to bow or raise their hat as they
went by in their carriage. But for a stranger to the town, it was
a very different matter, especially for a man. Then, almost
invariably, he would start visibly and then stare after them. It
was not because they were both startlingly beautiful, which
they were, but because they were identical twins, dressed alike
down to the last detail, even to their personal jewellery.

It was a matter for wonder why neither of them had become
at least engaged. The reason was that since their father had
died, when they were seventeen, they had been forced to look
after their ailing mother. It is true that one of them could have
taken their choice from the many would-be suitors who came
calling. But this would have been unfair to the one left to look
after the mother. Although they were now twenty-two, they
bore the situation stoically enough. But lately, Sylvia had
begun to feel restless.

'Just think of it, Ann,' she said one afternoon while they
were out walking together. 'Here we are – living in the year of
1851, a time which is supposed to be a landmark in our
history. There is the Great Exhibition, which the whole world
is now flocking to see. And what will we see of it? Nothing – as
we will see nothing else of what is going on in London, while
we are forced to live in this dreary resort.'

'I think I can live without seeing London,' Ann murmured.

'Well, I can't,' Sylvia said irritably. 'My art teacher here has said that I have some talent for painting, and that I ought to go and study in London. And that's what I long to do.'

As it happened, it was only a few weeks after that conversation that the Pennington sisters' mother died. Once the funeral was over the two of them carried on much as usual. Then one afternoon, Sylvia came into the sitting room, holding an opened letter in her hand.

'I am going to live in London,' she announced. 'I'm going there to study under the painter, Armand St Dennis. You won't have heard of him, of course. But he is very famous. He is from Paris and has only recently settled in London. Anyway, I wrote to him and sent him some of my drawings. He has agreed to take me as his pupil.'

Ann put her book aside, and looked at her, stunned. 'Sylvia – why didn't you tell me what was in your mind?'

'Because I knew you would make a fuss and say I shouldn't go.'

'I say it now.' Ann looked at her sister with troubled eyes. 'A young woman with your background, living alone in London – it's unheard of.'

'Stuff and nonsense,' Sylvia said. 'Anyway, 'I'm going and that's the end of it.'

Sylvia was gone within the week. After that, over the next two months, Ann had only one letter from her, saying how well she was progressing with her painting, and what an exciting place London was to live in. Then, eventually, a second letter came. In it, Sylvia suggested that Ann should come and stay with her for a short while. Ann wrote back the next day, accepting the offer.

'Armand has taught me so much,' Sylvia said. 'And he thinks I may well be able to exhibit within the year.' She looked at her sister, her eyes sparkling. 'Isn't that wonderful!'

'It is indeed,' Ann said, smiling. From the moment she had stepped into her sister's lodgings, just off Baker Street, Sylvia had prattled on almost non stop.

'Your Monsieur St Dennis seems to have been a great help to you,' Ann said now. 'What sort of person is he, exactly?'

'He is the most wonderful person in the world,' Sylvia replied. 'He is beautiful, kind and thoughtful.' She took in a deep breath. 'And I am in love with him.'

Ann was so taken aback, she could find no words.

'He is also in love with me,' Sylvia said. 'And he has asked me to marry him!'

Ann found her voice at last. 'This is all very sudden, isn't it?'

Sylvia ignored the remark. 'There is something else. I have not told Armand that I have an identical twin sister.' She gave Ann a nervous smile. 'I know you'll think this quite ridiculous. But I thought if he met you, he would prefer you to me. You are so much more sensible and grown up than I am. So much more feminine in your manner.'

'How absurd,' Ann said. A thought came to her. 'If you were so anxious to keep me away from Armand, why did you ask me to come to London?'

'Because I was afraid you might visit London to see the Exhibition and pay me a surprise visit while Armand was here,' Sylvia said. 'Besides, I wanted to tell you *all* about him.' She added airily, 'I will bring him to Lyme Regis after the wedding.'

'That's very kind of you,' Ann said dryly.

In the days that followed, when she was not with Armand, Sylvia took Ann sightseeing. 'I will take you to the Great Exhibition,' she told Ann after they had returned from a visit to the Tower of London. 'But first I have promised to go with Armand tomorrow afternoon.'

The remark didn't register with Ann until later. Then it suddenly occurred to her that this would be a good opportunity for her to take a look at Armand. It was not just idle curiosity on her part. She was worried about Sylvia, whom she knew to be a trusting person, and therefore an easy prey for an adventurer with an eye for an attractive girl with a personal income of her own. If she went to the Exhibition heavily veiled and dressed in clothes that Sylvia had never seen before, she might be able to watch them unobserved and make her own assessment of Armand. If her impressions were favourable, it would at least make her feel a little easier in her mind.

When she arrived at the Exhibition on that fateful afternoon that was to change her whole life, she became so interested in the exhibits that she almost forgot her purpose for being there. Wandering around the magnificent edifice, made almost entirely of glass, she gazed upon the wonders which had been sent from all over the world, and understood for the first time why the Exhibition was considered to be a Trade Fair such as the world had never seen before.

Her attention was abruptly brought back to her mission when she suddenly saw them, standing arm in arm in front of the great crystal fountain that dominated the main hall. When she saw Armand's face, her heart almost stopped. Sylvia had been right. He *was* beautiful. His hair was black, his features like those of a Greek god, but without the slightest touch of the effeminacy which can sometimes be seen in their statues. Although dressed in very ordinary clothes, his bearing was so soldierly that he stood out from among the crowd. Everything about him, in fact, commanded attention.

Her heart pounded. She had always dismissed the idea of love at first sight as being an absurd one. But now she knew it was possible. For this was the very thing that was happening to her on seeing Armand.

This moment of elation, so common to people who have just fallen in love, vanished almost as quickly as it had come, when she remembered that Armand was the man her sister was planning to marry. You must put him out of your mind, she thought. When you do meet him, it will be a torture, but one you must bear. Hopefully, your meetings will be few and brief, she told herself, as she hurried for the nearest exit.

But it was not to turn out that way.

Several days later, while Sylvia was out shopping, there was a knock at the door. Ann gasped inwardly when the landlady showed Armand into the parlour. Before she could utter a word, he had brushed past her and stepped into the middle of the room, from where he gazed at her with a distraught expression on her face.

'Sylvia, I have to go to Paris at once!' he said hurriedly. 'My mother is seriously ill. Perhaps even close to death!' Ann started to speak, but he silenced her with a quick gesture.

'Don't worry. I will be back soon, I am sure, especially if it is not as serious as I think it may be.'

'Please,' Ann faltered. 'There is something I must tell you.'

'Not now —' He came forward and took her in his arms. 'I know we have so much to talk about. But it will have to wait. I must go this very minute if I am to catch the boat train.'

It was then that his lips came down on hers in a long, burning kiss that made her almost swoon. Reluctantly, it seemed he finally drew away from her.

Taking her hand, he turned it over and lightly kissed her palm. 'Goodbye, my dearest —' He kissed her once more, briefly this time, and then he was gone.

After the door had closed behind him, Ann sank weakly into the nearest chair. What am I going to tell Sylvia? she thought dazedly. Being a jealous and possessive person, she would probably think that her sister had deliberately misled Armand. Ann sighed. All she could do was to tell her the truth. Miserably, she settled down to await Sylvia's return.

He came forward and took her in his arms. It was then that his lips came down on hers in a long, burning kiss that made her almost swoon.

But Sylvia never returned.

In the early hours of the evening, a policeman arrived at the door. His expression was grave, his voice appropriately muted for the news he had to impart. In a horrified silence Ann listened to him as he told her that Sylvia had been killed in an unfortunate road accident in which she had been knocked down and run over by a hansom cab.

'She died immediately,' the policeman said in a low voice. 'So at least the poor lass suffered no pain.'

After asking her to come to the police station the next day to collect Sylvia's personal effects, the policeman departed, visibly relieved that his unpleasant task was over.

Left alone, Ann sat in the silent room, desolate with grief, the tears rolling down her cheeks. They had always been so close, the two sisters, more so than most. As twins, they had done everything together and shared everything, too – even their thoughts and feelings. Until recently they had never been apart. Now she was alone. And what of poor Armand? she thought. His heart would surely be broken.

The next week was a nightmare that Ann was to remember for the rest of her life. There was the poor, broken body of Sylvia to be identified, the funeral arrangements to be made, and finally the horror of having to watch Sylvia being lowered into her grave. With all this to contend with, she longed to see Armand again. His strength and resolution would have been a comfort at such a time, but then she reminded herself that she had no right to his support and that he still knew nothing of the tragedy.

And then a letter arrived from him addressed to her sister. Opening it, she read that his mother had made an almost miraculous recovery, and that he would be home within the next few days. It was a timely reminder that she had the unhappy task before her of informing him of Sylvia's death.

Poor Armand, she thought. If only there were some way I could help him bear the blow. But he will be so overcome with grief that he will not even think of turning to me.

As she put the letter aside, a sudden, wild thought came to her. Suppose she did not tell him of Sylvia's death? Suppose she pretended to be Sylvia? If she could take over her sister's identity successfully, she could then marry him. The idea was a shocking one. But she was doing no one any harm. Anyway, I don't care, she thought defiantly. I *know* I would make him a better wife than Sylvia could ever have been to him.

But despite all her attempts to justify to herself what she was planning to do, there were many moments when she was filled with agonizing self-doubts. And never more so than when Armand did finally arrive one afternoon, sweeping into the room with a dozen red roses in his arms.

Putting them down, he took her hands in his. 'My dearest,' he said huskily. 'I have missed you so much –'

'And I you,' she found herself murmuring. She withdrew her hands from his. 'I must put these in water.'

He watched her with a faint frown as she moved about the room. 'Is everything all right? You seem a little distant.'

'I have a slight headache, that's all.' She put the roses in a vase and began to arrange them. 'I was glad to hear your mother has recovered.'

He nodded. 'She is almost her old self again. But let us talk of you. Will you come to the studio tomorrow?'

'I think not.' If there was one final moment when she could have drawn back, it was now. There was still time for her to confess everything. She could well imagine the scene, herself stumbling through her guilty recital, while his face registered a whole series of emotions, ranging from grief over Sylvia's death to anger at her outrageous behaviour. But instead, she turned resolutely to face him to play out the scene she had rehearsed a dozen times in her mind.

'Armand – very soon I will be your wife. And that is what I want to be – a wife in every sense of the word. But I cannot be that if I continue to paint. For that reason I have decided to give it up.'

'But that's absurd,' he protested. 'To throw away your talent, just because you are to be my wife!'

'I have made up my mind,' she said firmly. 'Anyway, I no longer feel the need to paint. Possibly because I know I shall be fulfilled in other ways.'

'If that is your wish, then so be it,' he said quietly. His face relaxed into a smile. 'As it happens, I feel I would like to take a short rest from my own painting. I therefore propose to spend a little time showing you the lighter side of London.'

Armand was true to his word. They dined in some of the best restaurants, went to the ballet, marvelled at the waxworks at Madame Tussaud's establishment, and even visited that vulgar but amusing entertainment, the Music Hall. Ann enjoyed all this so much, that she almost forgot that she was living a lie – until one Sunday afternoon in the autumn when they were taking a walk through Hyde Park.

They had stopped to look at the boats on the Serpentine, when Armand said suddenly, 'I think it is about time we talked about the wedding, don't you, Sylvia?'

Ann did not answer him.

'A quiet wedding, I think,' Armand said. 'I would like –'

'Please,' Ann said hurriedly. 'Let us not talk about it now. I am a little fatigued by all the walking we have done.'

'My dear,' Armand said solicitously, 'you must rest.' He led her to a nearby bench. 'You do not look at all well.'

'I will be all right soon.' Ann stared in front of her. It's no good, she thought. I must tell him the truth. Even though it will mean that I will lose him forever.

Bracing herself, she said, 'Armand, there is something I must tell you . . .'

Sitting there, with the autumn leaves falling around them, she told him everything. Armand, she noted with some surprise, listened in silence, his face quite expressionless.

'I know it was very wrong of me,' she finished. 'But I did it only because I loved you so desperately.' She gave him a quick glance. 'All this must come as a terrible shock to you.'

'Not in the least,' he said calmly. 'I have known almost from the very beginning that you were not Sylvia.'

She gasped. 'How could you?'

'It was very simple.' He smiled. 'When Sylvia first came to me, she cut the inside of her hand with a palette knife, which left a small but deep scar. The first time I met you, I sensed there was something wrong. And then, when I looked, I saw you had no scar. So I hired a private detective, who found out for me all there was to know.' He paused and regarded her gravely. 'Perhaps I should have told you what I knew. But I was curious to see how far you would go, and to know why you were pretending to be Sylvia.'

'You know the answer to that now,' Ann said, her head bowed.

He was silent for a while. Then he said, 'Now it is my turn to make a confession. In the beginning, I think I used you to help me get over Sylvia. But in these last few weeks, I have come to love you deeply. It is a different sort of love to the one I had for Sylvia. But I am sure it is deeper, and more lasting.' He took her hand and looked earnestly into her eyes. 'I want you to be my wife, Ann.'

Ann's happiness at hearing this was almost too much for her to bear. After a long silence, while she struggled to gain her self-possession, she said weakly, 'As long as I will not just be a second best wife to you –'

'My dear,' he said gaily, 'you will be the very best wife in the world for me.' And with that, he scandalised people walking past by drawing her to him and kissing her firmly.

HIS EMERALD EYES

Beverley Watts

MEGAN TOWSER YAWNED AND stretched her arms high above her head. The cock was crowing and it was time for her to get out of bed and remake the fire downstairs. It was tempting to stay snuggled under her warm quilt, but she knew she must hurry and prepare breakfast for her father and the guests staying at the inn.

In her long cotton nightdress, Megan stumbled sleepily to the window, her breath misting in the freezing air. Thin icicles hung from the sill and it was just light enough for Megan to see that a thick white frost covered the land outside. The winter had been a hard one and blizzards had cut them off for some weeks in the cold snap just after Christmas. Now, only a few days away from the end of February 1780, Megan could still see no sign of spring.

With a nose red with the cold and a goose-pimpled skin, Megan broke the ice in her water jug to wash, cleaned her teeth with salt and dressed as warmly as she could, covering her dress with a warm woollen shawl and a coarse apron. She tiptoed downstairs and raked out the ashes of the fire till she found some still glowing, then added some more wood and blew up the flames with the bellows.

Suspended over the fireplace was a variety of pots and pans, but Megan simply slipped some small potatoes and a few field mushrooms into the outer edges of the hot ashes to bake. Then, taking a long two-pronged fork from its hook beside the brass candlesticks, she began to toast some bread.

Once the meal was prepared, Megan woke her father who lay contentedly snoring, his bald head covered by his long nightcap, and turned her mind to other chores. The guests' horses needed hay and water in the stables, so she carefully walked across to the barn, avoiding the slippery patches of icy ground.

Swinging the large barn door open wide, the innkeeper's daughter yawned once more. The sun had not yet fully risen and the sky was a deceptively warm pink. As she gathered up armfuls of hay, Megan sang to herself an old country song that she'd learned as a child. But before she could finish even the first verse, a hand was cupped violently over her mouth and she felt the sharp edge of a knife pressed against her trembling throat.

'Don't scream,' a voice ordered sharply. 'Or you're dead.'

The sight of blood on the white cuffs of her assailant made Megan believe he was not bluffing. This was no Nicker boy come to flick pennies at the windows to break them, nor even one of the brutal Scowerers who had smashed all the benches and tables in the inn a year before. They always came in groups and after sunset. Only the footpads and highwaymen scoured the land alone or in pairs – and they did not fear the daylight.

Megan felt a knee in the small of her back and was pushed forcefully face down into the hay. At first she did not dare turn around and lay on the prickly bed for what seemed like hours, but was in reality only minutes. No other instruction was issued by the intruder, so with great trepidation, Megan rolled over on her side and looked up.

The man stood limply against the barn door and was obviously badly injured. Blood oozed from a wound under his ribs, a gash on his forehead and many small abrasions on his hands. Although he was dirty and unshaven, his clothes were very fine. He wore a three-cornered hat of dark felt, square-

'Don't scream,' a voice ordered sharply. 'Or you're dead.'

buckled boots, knee breeches which fastened over his stockings, a cravat and a coat and waistcoat of excellent quality. He was not wearing a powdered wig, but his own hair was long and curled into the nape of his neck.

No longer fearing for her life, Megan's sympathies went out to the stranger. Perhaps he was no highwayman after all. She had probably startled him as much as he'd startled her, and he could simply be an injured wayfarer. His handsome face and high curved cheekbones and the lashes around his vivid green eyes were thick and dark.

'You are hurt – can I help you in some way?' Megan asked meekly. 'Have you had a fall?'

The stranger stared at Megan's innocent freckled face for a few moments and then smiled a weak but charmingly crooked smile. 'Can you tend my wounds?' he asked in a voice which was now almost gentle. 'And bring me food?'

Megan nodded and turned to pick up the two large bundles of hay she had come for. The man grabbed her wrist and held it against the point of the knife before she could leave. 'Tell no one, mind,' he hissed, and shoved her roughly on her way.

Megan really had no wish to mention her discovery to anyone else. This was her secret and hers alone. Her father had no time for her anyway. To him she was just a skivvy to wash and clean and cook at the inn. Since her mother had died, he'd spent all his time gambling over Hazard and Faro with his friends and drinking honey-bee wine or ale. The inn was on a busy narrow road on the way to Brighton where all the fashionable people went to stay, and travellers often stopped for refreshments and occasionally stayed overnight.

The ladies and gentlemen she waited on did not impress Megan. They curtseyed and bowed to each other, danced, pranced and preened, but most of them used foul language like any farmhand and spat like beggars. The women especially seemed to enjoy lashing out and slapping her at any excuse. She found their tall, white hairstyles ridiculous. Some could hardly lift their heads with the weight of miniature ships and birds woven into matted displays. It seemed like an excess of stupidity and vanity. All the pomp and display was totally unlike Megan's life of simplicity in the country. She lived a hard and honest existence, with little joy or excitement.

Megan was jealous in a way, but did not admit this even to herself. She had never been on an outing to a tea garden or to a ball. The town guests often spoke of their social lives and all the goings-on. There were weird and wonderful animals to be seen at the circuses; all kinds of glittering masked balls, hundreds of bustling coffee houses to visit. Megan had often wondered what it would be like to step on the granite cobbles of the London streets or sit in a sedan chair. Instead, here she was, day in and day out, slaving away at her father's command.

Megan walked briskly to the stables, mucked out and fed the horses, saw to the chickens and returned to the side door of the inn. Awaiting her were the dirty breakfast plates and the hundred and one chores that filled each day. To save time, Megan skimped on the polishing and cleaning and quickly scrubbed her father's shirts. As usual she poured some of the sudsy water into the weak beer that the inn sold to give it a head of froth. It made it taste rather strange but the customers were usually far too drunk to notice.

From the larder, the innkeeper's daughter stole a fresh loaf, some roast beef and a plum pudding. She took a jar of ointment and some clean linen rags to make bandages and made her way back to the barn with her heart beating hard against her ribs.

The stranger greeted her gruffly but his emerald eyes sparkled as she laid down the bounty and swung the barn door firmly shut. 'You have done well,' he told her. 'I knew you would.'

Megan felt proud of her stealth and efficiently went about the task of cleaning the wounded man's injuries. The head cut and scratches on his hands were superficial, but underneath his waistcoat, she found a deep sword wound. He could not possibly travel until it had healed.

'I suppose I had better give you some explanation,' the handsome intruder smiled. 'Have you heard of Dick Turpin? Or maybe Jerry Abershaw?' Megan gasped. Dick Turpin and Jerry Abershaw were famous highwaymen. The former had died many years before she was born, but Jerry Abershaw still terrorised coach travellers. Some people were even taking the precaution of hiring bands of armed horsemen to ride with them for protection.

'Yes, I know those names,' she replied nervously.

'Well, my name is Jake King and I too am a man of the road.' Megan shuffled a few feet away from him and could hardly believe what she was hearing.

'You have no need whatsoever to fear me,' he continued. 'I have never killed another living person or robbed anyone who did not deserve to have a portion of his riches taken from him.'

Jake smiled his crooked smile again, showing his perfect white teeth, and Megan believed every word he said. Of course, he was a good man. Those deep green eyes, looking directly into her own, they had honesty within them. She moved closer to Jake once more and he laid one of his arms across her shoulders.

'Everything I steal I give to the poor,' he explained. 'It is not right that the rich should live in their elegant houses with their walnut furniture and rich tapestries whilst so many unfortunates spend their lives in thatched hovels or even in the workhouse, drinking themselves to death on cheap gin. I've seen four-year-old children working in the fields all day and healthy young boys selling the very teeth from their mouths for money.'

Megan was enraptured by Jake's words. He spoke so fervently and with such passion that she was convinced that even if what he did was wrong, it was for a just cause. It wasn't as if he was a real criminal. This was a dream come true for her, meeting such a wonderful man – a present-day Robin Hood. And, while his impressive speech raced around Megan's head, Jake suddenly bent over and kissed her, full on the lips. A fierce kiss that seemed to make each nerve in her body tingle.

'I would like to take a wife,' he said, holding her small hand affectionately and kissing the tips of her fingers. 'It is time I settled somewhere with a loving companion. You are a lovely girl, Megan. You could make a man very happy. Have you not thought of marrying?'

Megan trembled with delight and she allowed Jake to stroke her long curly, dark hair.

'Often I have thought about a husband,' she confessed, 'but there are few young men left in these parts. Most have gone to work in the towns and those that are left are stupid or even simple. They belong in Bedlam, not behind a plough!'

Jake laughed and kissed Megan again, longer this time, pressing his curved lips upon her own soft yielding mouth.

'Can you hide me here for a while?' the highwayman asked, tracing the outline of Megan's ear with a piece of chewed straw. 'Until I regain my strength?'

Megan didn't hesitate. She recognised Jake as the 'prince' among men whom she had waited for since she was no more than a tiny girl. He was her destiny, her fate, the love of her life. 'Of course,' she agreed at once.

They talked for hours, hidden behind bales of hay. Jake told her how he had been attacked by armed horsemen and admitted that there were now more in the area, who would probably come searching for him. He asked Megan to pretend she'd seen no one, so that with any luck they would give up and move on. He had no horse; it had bolted, he explained, and he was not strong enough to ride yet anyway. When he had recovered, they would run away together to the North and Megan would never have to wait on her vicious customers again.

By the time Megan left him her head was spinning, filled with delightful rosy dreams of future happiness. They would ride through the night together, away from her brutal father and the drudgery of her life at the inn, to find freedom and fortune and a lifetime of love.

Her dreams were only a little dimmed when, later that day, she found Jake's mare, hidden behind a thicket down by the stream, waiting for her master's return. Strange that the saddlebags were still packed with jewellery and silver coins, but then, Megan thought, he wouldn't have had time to hand over his takings to the poor, not with armed men close on his heels. And the mare – he must have been a bit feverish when he'd thought the horse had run off, otherwise he would surely have remembered tethering her to a tree?

Megan forgot her misgivings soon enough in the delight of caring for him, slipping out whenever she had the chance to smuggle food or change his bandages. She gave no thought of the risk, for this was a labour of love.

Three days' later, a party of armed riders did water their horses at the inn. Megan was busy lighting the oil lamps when they arrived and they did not bother to question such a shy young girl. Her father spoke to them for some while though, and they rode off in the direction of the coast, leaving a warning for all to lock all doors and windows and to beware of any strangers.

Megan watched the horses disappear into the distance, then served her father and a gentleman guest their supper of pigeon pie with vegetables. While they ate and chatted, she picked up her embroidery and stitched the last petal of a rose, as red as the blood Jake had spilled on his pure silk and lace cuffs.

'They're looking for Jake King,' Megan heard her father say, and her ears pricked up immediately. 'I've never heard of him myself.'

'Oh, he's a bad one, that man,' the guest replied. 'He used to prowl around Epping Forest way. Must have changed his patch.' Megan remained silent but lay down her sewing.

'He held up a stage coach on Christmas Eve and killed the driver and all the passengers. They gave him all their valuables, but he wouldn't believe that they didn't have more hidden somewhere. One of the passengers lived long enough to describe what happened.'

Mr Towser spoke again. 'The search party is returning later. They're pretty certain he can't have got far away. A few days ago they almost caught him, and he was wounded in the scuffle. They said he's got a way with the women and one of his ladies is probably concealing him in her cellar. Seems he spins them a pretty story about giving his ill-gotten gains to the poor, but he's never given a penny away in his life. He's a cold-blooded, ruthless killer. Spares no one, not even small children if they cross him.'

Frozen with hurt and humiliation, Megan sat slowly rocking in her rocking chair, staring into the mocking flames of the fire which taunted her tormented soul. She did not doubt that the words she'd heard were true; they had simply confirmed her earlier suspicions. Jake had said his horse had bolted, but she'd found the mare tethered in a thicket. And the jewellery she'd found in the saddlebags – they'd never reach a poor peasant's calloused palm. She'd been a fool, an idiotic fool, to listen to his honeyed tongue. All Jake's worthy words were nonsense and she had foolishly believed them.

When the search party thundered back to the inn later that

same night, they found Megan waiting for them with a lamp. A mangy farm dog howled in the distance as she gave her brief information and the riders turned towards the barn. The sad howls of the dog continued and Megan climbed the stairs to her room where she stood at the window, watching the men take Jake away with his hands bound behind his back. She knew he would surely hang.

She could not weep for Jake, the man who had tricked her. Her mind felt numb and her eyes were dry, but her soul pined for the dark-haired highwayman of her dreams. It was to his image she clung, and to him she whispered, 'Goodbye, Jake. Goodbye.'

FOR THE LOVE OF ZEPHYR

Angus Allan

KARRAL-THE-HAG'S BONY FINGERS dug cruelly into Wilda's forearm, and there was an ugly snarl on the lined lips of the bullying crone who had brought the girl up ever since the death of her father and mother in the violent Saracen raid ten years ago.

'You are my property by right of the ancient village laws,' spat Karral. 'If I say you are to be married to Ivan, son of Mikhal, then married to him you will be!'

'But Aunt Karral! I do not *love* him! Oh, yes. I know he is handsome. He is brave, too – one of the best warriors in all the nation. But he thinks only of war, and of hatred, and the glory of his own name. He is not gentle, and kind!'

'Bah! You're nothing but a fool, girl,' snapped Karral. 'What does *love* matter? A wedding between you and Ivan would mean good for our entire family. We will share in his power and his triumphs.'

'You will share in it,' thought Wilda. 'You and your other hideous nephews and nieces.' She said aloud, 'You won't *force* me ...'

'Little you know about me, then,' cackled the hag. 'I shall bring you to your senses with spells, and potions. Helped, no doubt, by the threat of my thrashing-stick.'

Wilda hid her fear, and with Karral's evil chuckles echoing in her ears, wandered miserably through the tent-like yurts of the village to where the horses were tethered. Kingly stallions grazed contentedly in the roped-off enclosure, under the watchful eyes of Milak and his herdsmen, and the beautiful mares with their new foals roamed free on the fertile steppes. Ivan, son of Mikhal, was there, grooming the sleek black coat of his favourite mount, and now he straightened up at the girl's approach, pushing the lambswool hat back from his forehead and consciously bracing his broad shoulders, hung with the crossed belts that carried his weapons and were the badge of a cavalry leader.

'Come to pledge me your hand at last?' he said, pompously. 'About time, if I may say so.'

Wilda shook her head. 'No, Ivan, I'm sorry. Whatever the penalty, I will obey neither you nor the old woman who makes me call her my aunt.'

Ivan hurled the grooming-brush to the ground. 'Curse your impudence, girl! Don't you realise that I have only to snap my fingers to have my pick of any of the village maidens as my bride?'

'Snap them, then,' said Wilda, indifferently. 'Take Zuleika, or Sharaz. *I* shan't weep about it.'

The angry warrior changed his tune. 'Look, Wilda. I admit it. You *please* me. Your face is . . . beautiful.' He flushed. 'Your hair . . . Oh, confound it, I'm no poet! You know what I mean!'

'Sentiment certainly was never your strong point,' agreed Wilda. 'Believe me, Ivan, I admire you, like you even – but that is all. Can't you understand that I do not wish to marry you? I cannot – *will* not give you my love.'

Brusquely, Ivan turned his back on her, and the girl, sighing, walked on. If only he weren't so arrogant, so – so pleased with himself. Grudgingly, she had to admit that of all the young men in the village, he was the most attractive. But she would *not* be coerced into a marriage she did not want, for which she was not ready.

She put him from her mind, for now feelings that were

indeed akin to love suffused her being. True love, not for any of the other youths of the settlement, but for Zephyr, her pony.

He was a small enough pony. Small, light and dainty. And he was a skewbald, with a comical patch over one eye that never failed to draw mocking laughter from the horse-conscious men in the village. Their ancestral lore regarded a skewbald as bad news. An unlucky animal. Indeed, Zephyr would have been put to death at birth had it not been for Wilda's pleading. Rather untypically, the headman had given way and handed the gangling foal over to her, and now there was a bond between Wilda and Zephyr that none could ever break. Covertly, Ivan watched her as she stood stroking the pony's muzzle, feeding him with mash from the pouch at her side, whispering words of comfort and understanding in his ears. The young man ground his teeth.

'Maybe I'm better of without her as a wife,' he muttered. 'She'd give all her affection to that ridiculous-looking throwback!'

Nimbly, Wilda sprang up on to Zephyr's back, and joyously, the pony flexed his muscles and was off! The wind raced through the girl's hair as, in perfect unity with her mount, she thrilled to the gallop that took them far from the worries of the village. Suppose, she thought, that they were to keep on going. Onward, ever onward. Some far-off place where they could begin a brand new life together, over the horizon. If only that were possible!

Such were Wilda's dreams, but dreams have no place in reality, and she well knew that, beyond the confines of the village, the outside world was full of danger. To the west lay nothing but the vast expanse of forested mountains, said to be the haunt of demons. To the north, scattered outposts of her own kind – tribesmen who would take her in slavery, kill Zephyr and think nothing of it. The south? Beyond the plain, the territory of the hostile Turks, and to the east – well, that didn't bear thinking about. There, there was only the nameless terror of the slant-eyed Tartar hordes. The silent raiders whose very name drained the colour from the faces of warriors even as brave as Ivan, son of Mikhal ...

Wilda really *had* no choice. She would not marry him, and therefore the only alternative was to look forward to a life of increased misery at the hands of Karral-the-Hag.

But now, at least *now* she was free. Free as the birds she envied so much. She and Zephyr, the two of them glowing with the exhilaration of the race across the soft, springy turf.

At last, with no more than a touch of pressure from her hand on his neck, Wilda brought the pony from a gallop to a canter, from a canter to a trot. Snorting and tossing his head, he halted, and she slid from his back. He rolled his happy eye at her and fell to tugging at the clumps of grass with his strong white teeth as she spread herself beside him and lay with her hands behind her head, staring up at the clear blue sky. She thought of the nursery stories her mother had once told her; of the enchanted prince, bewitched to take the form of a horse, only to be released from the spell by the kindness of a beautiful princess. 'You *are* my prince, Zephyr,' she said aloud, and the pony whinnied softly, as if he understood ...

It was as the afternoon wore steadily on that Wilda had the first inkling of disaster. At first, she thought she was imagining it, but then she knew that the far-off sounds that came to her ears were those of battle. The distant clash of steel, the faint shouts, the cries, borne on the wind.

Gulping, she turned Zephyr's head towards home, and there, over the horizon, the heart-catching drift of black smoke rose into view!

She was not so foolish as to hurry. She knew that they had come, as had been predicted so often. The Tartars from the east. And sure enough, as she breasted the last rise, she saw her village in ruins, the yurts a mass of skeletal, smouldering poles, the horses gone, the ground strewn with still, silent bodies, pierced with Tartar arrows like the quills of a porcupine.

There was not a solitary soul left alive. Many had vanished completely – taken prisoner, Wilda presumed. She found no trace of Ivan, son of Mikhal. Karral-the-Hag lay there, cold and still – and Wilda shed a tear, even for her.

The storehouse had been looted, but the marauders had left enough for Wilda to scrape together some kind of sustenance for herself and corn for Zephyr. With a heavy heart, the girl took what she could, and turned her face towards the western mountains. Whatever the demons of the forest, they were an infinitely better choice than the savage Tartars – and wherever *they* were, crossing their path could only mean swift and painful death.

'I don't really care about myself,' Wilda whispered. 'But they shan't have you, Zephyr. That I promise!'

She was sighted before she had gone even a mile. In the fringes of scrubland that skirted the plain, four Tartars were slicing meat from a pillaged haunch of deer. Now they sprang to their feet and snatched up their captured weapons, their barbarian shouts carrying clearly to Wilda's ears as they sprang to their saddles. An outpost of the main invading force, they gave whooping chase, and Wilda crouched low over Zephyr's neck as she urged her pony to the fastest gallop he'd ever made. The whistle of an arrow above her head was followed instantly by a sharp 'ping' as another stuck a stone in front of her, sending up sparks, but the Tartars were shooting wildly, and while they were moving. There was little chance of them hitting her.

But Zephyr was tiring. Wilda could sense the effort he made to clear the fallen log spanning the track into the forest. She knew that he must rest – and soon!

Wilda crouched low over Zephyr's neck as she urged her pony to do the fastest gallop he'd ever made.

She splashed him into the torrent of a running stream to mask their tracks and, where the flow tore at the overhang of thick bushes, turned him to scramble up the steep bank. In the deep, sheltering undergrowth, she slid down and pulled Zephyr flat beside her. There was no need to hold his face steady. He seemed to know as well as she did the need for absolute silence.

Both of them heard the jabbering Tartars pick their way past above them. The enemy paused momentarily – but then, mercifully, they went on, the sounds of their horses slowly fading.

Wilda let her breath out in a long sigh. 'We'd best stay here until nightfall, Zephyr,' she whispered.

Dusk fell, and with it came all the mysterious and sinister noises of the forest. The croak and cackle of unseen birds and animals – or were they of demons . . .?

Wilda shuddered. She could only hope and pray that the gods of her people were on her side. No moon penetrated the trees above, but her night vision was good, and so was Zephyr's. Together, they cautiously picked their way along the stream, now startled by a leaping, grunting frog, now freezing as an eerie glow caught their eye, only to be revealed as some kind of phosphorescent tree fungus. Once, a crash beside them made Wilda scream – but it was just the grey, dead bough of a rotted tree, choosing that moment to fall from above. Zephyr nuzzled Wilda's shoulder, as if telling her not to be afraid. If he could have spoken, perhaps he'd have told her that the devil always makes the most of a person's fear in the grim small hours of the night.

Dawn found them deep in the forest. The stream, hardly more than a trickle among the ever-rising rocks, quenched their thirst, and both of them ate hungrily of the provisions Wilda had managed to salvage. The girl had no idea at all of the extent of the forest, nor indeed of the direction they were taking. To judge by the feeble filtering of sunlight through the top growth, they were still moving westwards, she presumed. She said aloud to Zephyr, 'We may never get out of this alive. There may not be a living soul anywhere on the route ahead.' Again, the pony nuzzled her. 'I know,' she smiled. 'While there's life, there's hope. Is that it?'

She could have sworn that Zephyr nodded his head, and despite their awful predicament, she laughed and hugged him to her. 'What a wonderful pony you are,' she said.

The terrain began to rise steeply, and considerately, Wilda walked by Zephyr's side to save his strength. From time to time, he would use his powerful forefeet to smash down tangled thickets of thorn in their way, stamping flat the cruel patches of nettle and poison-wood.

They rested when the sun was high in the sky, and now they were almost above the treeline. Wilda was aware that Zephyr's nostrils were twitching, his ears pricked, and she climbed on his back for a better view of their surroundings. 'Yes,' she said, with an anxious frown. 'You scented it, too. Woodsmoke – and see the faint blue drift of it rising not a bowshot to the right of us!'

But what did it signify? Friend? Foe? There was only one way to find out, and with Zephyr cautiously following her and instinctively placing his hoofs silently between the rocks, Wilda crept softly in the direction of the fire.

Beyond a drift of thin screw-pine and bramble they saw it. The wide clearing, the huddle of tethered horses. The roughly erected shelters of a main Tartar force!

'We'd best retrace our steps,' breathed Wilda, softly. 'There's no aid for us here!'

Her heart was hammering in her body as she watched the savage invaders at their midday meal. But then she stiffened. Over there in the shadows – beyond the horses. Men crouched miserably on their haunches, their hands linked by coils of hemp. She smothered the cry that automatically rose to her lips with a terrible effort. They were prisoners from her own village – and there among them, a rough bandage round his head, was Ivan, son of Mikhal!

Something stirred in her – a pang of pity, perhaps? Or something more? To see the once proud head bowed in despair, the strong arms shackled and helpless – and he was wounded, too ...

Wilda still wanted to retreat. Pure common sense told her that there was nothing she could do. And yet, incredibly, after all they'd been through together, Zephyr balked. He would not shift. His eyes rolled wildly, and he pushed his muzzle against her, hard.

'Come on, you silly,' she whispered urgently. 'If one of those Tartars should take it into his head to come wandering this way ...'

It was no use. Zephyr still wouldn't budge. He was as stubborn as a donkey! Wilda licked her lips. They were very, very dry. 'All right, all right. Let's think ...'

It came to her in a moment of pure inspiration. Could it have been something telepathic? Some rapport between her mind and Zephyr's? She felt for her only possible weapon – the knife she used for her food. It *might* be sharp enough.

Although she knew it was idiotic, something made her whisper her sketchy plan in Zephyr's ear. Surely it was only her fancy that he was nodding again?

Girl and pony – now Zephyr moved willingly – crept gently and silently around, keeping to cover, until they were close to the Tartar horses. One man, and only one, sat guarding them, and he heard nothing as the girl, flat to the ground, wormed her way towards the long, braided line to which the animals were secured by their halters. Heart in her mouth, she began to saw at it with her knife.

Minutes later, when the line had parted, Wilda rose swiftly

to her feet and let out a yell that would have awakened the dead. In the same instant, Zephyr shot past her, and his blaring whinny seemed to impel the plunging, startled herd to follow him! At once, the clearing was alive with the thunder of stampeding hooves, and a swirling mass of horseflesh bowled the guard flat and thundered headlong through fire and shelter, scattering the astounded Tartars this way and that!

Wilda, her knife flashing, sped for the captives, so keyed up that she was hardly aware of the shouts of recognition from the men. Ivan, especially, was staring at her as though she were a ghost!

'Wilda!' His yell was drowned in the incredible chaos as Zephyr, snapping and biting, swung the crazed herd round, back on the stunned, milling Tartars!

'Run with them! Run *with* them!' screamed Wilda. Somewhere, she recognised Zephyr's strident whinny again, and now, recovering their scattered wits, Ivan and the rest of the men were launching themselves at the flying manes of the horses that swept through them, hurling themselves up on to the backs of the herd!

Not an arrow was sent against them. With a final, exultant flourish, Zephyr threw up his heels and drove the flying debris of the Tartar campfire into the nearest shelter, while those still standing among the enemy turned all their attention to saving their weapons and their belongings.

They could not, of course, save their horses. Neither their own, nor those they had plundered.

Wilda spared the frantic barbarians one final glance, as, flushed with the hectic excitement of the rescue, she took a flying leap that landed her astride her beloved Zephyr. Triumphantly, they followed in the wake of the stampeding herd, the girl ducking to avoid the swishing branches above her head.

The flight continued headlong, through glade and clearing, across scatters of rocky scree and the splashways of mountain rivers. The echoes of the clattering hooves came back from the flanks of the rocky defile – the pass through the mountains that the horses found, by pure instinct. And then, way beyond, lay the opening above the fertile plains to the west of those supposedly demon-infested forests that had proved so harmless.

Though the pony was tired, Wilda encouraged Zephyr to overtake the rest of the galloping throng. As she came up with Ivan, son of Mikhal, she couldn't help laughing. He was not on his own proud black stallion, but on the back of a shaggy Tartar mount, scarcely more than a pony itself.

'I think it's time we called a halt, Ivan,' she said. 'We don't want to exhaust the horses.'

They were safe. Of that there could be no doubt. Safe, thanks to Wilda and Zephyr – and rich. Rich in a land where horseflesh was the main proof of wealth.

Ivan, his haughty demeanour long gone, slid to the ground. Wilda was pleased to see that, far from scorning his raffish Tartar mount, he spared the time to pat its neck and speak to it, gruffly, before he turned to her.

'Wilda,' he said at last. 'I hardly know what to say to you. I feel shamed. Oh yes, my friends and I put up a fight ...' He turned to the others, now gathering round. 'Didn't we, lads?' He shrugged. 'They were just too much for us – too many of them. And then you turn up, out of the blue! You were magnificent!'

'Zephyr was magnificent,' corrected Wilda. 'There'll be no more nonsense about a skewbald pony being bad luck!'

'There certainly won't,' agreed Ivan. 'And when we ally ourselves to whichever tribe lies ahead, to fight together against the Tartar invaders, we'll gather all the skewbalds we can find, right up there in the van of the battle!'

'But not Zephyr,' said Wilda, smiling. 'He's done his bit.'

'Not Zephyr,' agreed Ivan, with a grin. 'He's yours, and from now on his destiny – and mine – is in your hands.' He hesitated. 'It is hard for me to say this, Wilda, but I cannot ask again for your hand in marriage. I no longer feel worthy of you – you, who have the strength and courage of a man.'

Wilda, happier than she'd ever been in her life, put out her hand and gently stroked the bandaged head.

· 'Not now, perhaps,' she said softly. 'But some time – not too far off – who knows? Fate has brought us together into freedom and here, in freedom, I will choose.' She turned again to her horse, feeling the pounding of her heart, and knowing, even now, what that choice would be.

'Come, Zephyr. They are calling for us to ride in front. And then –' she looked back at Ivan, smiling, 'then we shall rest. For tomorrow a new life must begin.'

THE HAUNTED BALLROOM

June Williams

SHE HEARD THE SOUND of his horse long before she actually saw him appear, cantering down the long, winding drive on the magnificent Arab he had bought for himself on his last leave. Her heart began to beat faster as she watched him approach, the brass buttons of his naval uniform glinting like burnished gold in the afternoon sun. How handsome he looks, she thought. And to think he will soon be mine!

She continued to watch him from behind the curtains until he had dismounted and handed the reins to a waiting servant. Then she glided away and sat down. Reaching for her needlework, she bent her head over it. Much as she longed to rush into the hallway to greet him the moment he entered the house, certain conventions had to be observed – not the least of them being that one should never display one's feelings before the servants.

Presently, she heard the sound of the door being opened behind her. 'Lieutenant Farnes has arrived, Ma'am.'

Laying her work aside, she rose and turned to face the tall, fair-haired man who stood in the doorway beside the servant who had announced him. 'Robert – you're early! How nice!'

The young man bowed formally. 'Miss Cartwright –' He waited until the door had closed behind him. Then he strode forward, holding out his arms to her. 'Sophie – my darling –'

She ran to him and sank her head against his chest. 'Robert – oh, Robert! You have no idea how the days have dragged while I waited for you to come home.'

'Well, now I am here.' Releasing her, he held her at arms length, an unexpectedly serious expression on his face. 'Sophie – there is something I must tell you. My leave is only a short one. I return to the *Trident* in three days.' He grimaced. 'My Lord Nelson wishes us to try out some new manoeuvres.'

'Only three days!' She looked at him in dismay. 'Such a short time for us to be together!'

'I know.' He pulled her gently to him again. 'But in those three days we shall spend every hour we can together. Your parents permitting, of course.'

'Mama and Papa have gone to visit friends,' she told him quickly. 'My Aunt Clara has come to stay to chaperone us.' She gave him a shy smile. 'But she has already hinted she will not be *too* strict.'

'Then we shall have three days together that we will remember for the rest of our lives,' he told her.

In the eventuality, they spent those three days quietly enough. During the day, they either rode or went walking hand in hand in the nearby woods, where, as was only natural for two people in love and already engaged, they kissed a great deal. In the evening, they dined with Aunt Clara, and afterwards either played a few hands of cards or went into the music room, where Sophie accompanied Robert on the piano, while he sang in a pleasant tenor the latest popular ballards. Some might think that this was a rather tame way for two lovers to spend their time. But for Sophie and Robert, it was enough for both of them just to be in each other's company.

Although Sophie knew how short their time would be together, she was still taken unawares when she met Robert coming downstairs on the third morning, with the saddle bags slung over his shoulder. She looked at him with stricken eyes. 'It's time for you to go?'

He nodded. 'It's a long ride to my family's home. I will just have time to say goodbye to my parents before I catch the coach to Portsmouth.' He placed the saddle bags down and took her gently in his arms. 'If it is of any help, I give you my solemn promise we will marry immediately I return.'

She looked up at him, her eyes now brimming with happy tears. 'Oh, Robert. Knowing that will make the waiting a little more tolerable.'

In the long, lonely days and weeks that followed Robert's departure, Sophie tried to keep herself occupied. But living in the heart of Devon, her activities were somewhat restricted. She walked a great deal, paid a few visits, did a little needlework, and played the piano occasionally. Much of the time, though, she sat and day-dreamed of her life to be with Robert.

Nearly two months had passed, when Sophie's father, a retired sea captain, returned from a visit to London with some news for her.

'As you know, my dear, I still have a few friends at the Admiralty. So I took the liberty of calling on one of them.' He beamed at his daughter. 'They told me Robert's ship is due to dock at Portsmouth a week from today.' He stilled Sophie's cry of joy with a raised hand.

'There is something else. After I'd heard the news a thought occurred to me. You could visit our friends the Stacys, at Marsdon Hall. They have asked you often enough. As they live just outside Portsmouth, you would be there to greet Robert's ship when it came into port.'

'Oh, Papa,' Sophie breathed. 'What a marvellous idea!'

It was only afterwards that she realised that, much as she had welcomed her father's idea, her stay at Marsdon Hall was going to present her with something of a problem. The problem was Paul Stacy, the son of the house, who had repeatedly asked Sophie to marry him. She had always resisted his advances coolly, and it was partly because of him that she had been reluctant to accept earlier invitations. Although Paul was outwardly a pleasant enough man, with those dark, almost Mediterranean looks that appealed to some women, Sophie had always suspected that his outwardly engaging manner concealed a rather unpleasant person. However, the thought of seeing Robert all the sooner overcame all her scruples.

Paul was still very much on her mind when she set off in her father's coach for Portsmouth. Perhaps, she thought hopefully, he may feel differently about me now that he knows that I am going to marry Robert.

But Paul's feelings had not changed towards her, as was obvious from the moment she arrived at Marsdon Hall, to find him waiting for her on the steps of the house. He came forward, a sullen expression on his face, and opened the door of her carriage without a word.

'You do not seem to pleased to see me, Paul,' Sophie said mildly, as they walked inside the house.

'Why should I be?' he said, scowling. 'You have come here merely to meet your precious Robert. Now, if you had come to see me, that would have been a very different matter.'

If Paul's greeting had been somewhat less than gracious, the same could not be said of his parents, who were obviously delighted to see her again. After they had exchanged the usual pleasantries, Mr Stacy informed Sophie that he had arranged for a ball to be held at Marsdon Hall on the day of Robert's arrival. 'I do hope you like the idea –' he said hesitantly.

'I think it's a marvellous one!' Sophie said. 'What else can I say – except to thank you for your kindness.'

In some ways, Sophie would have liked to have been alone with Robert on their first evening together. But the idea of being in Robert's arms for most of the evening while they danced the night away was a happy enough thought to take to bed with her.

When she awoke the next morning, it was with the knowledge that in just one more day, she would be seeing her beloved Robert again. Her heart singing, she completed her toilet, dressed and then went downstairs to join the Stacys for breakfast. She was pleased to find that Paul was not there to mar her happy mood.

'He was out last night, drinking with friends,' Mr Stacy explained. 'I doubt we will see him before noon.'

Over the meal, Sophie asked Mr Stacy the question that had been uppermost in her mind from the moment she had awakened. 'What time do you think Robert's ship will arrive tomorrow?'

'It is difficult to say. Anyway, we will hear the cannon greet her when she comes in. That will give Paul ample warning that he must go down to the docks to collect Robert.'

Sophie hesitated. 'I was rather hoping to go myself ...'

'My dear Sophie,' Mr Stacy said firmly. 'It is out of the question you should go, with or without Paul. The docks are not a suitable place for a young lady of refinement to visit. To begin with, they are full of drunken sailors.'

Sophie could see that it was useless for her to argue with Mr Stacy. Perhaps it *is* better that we should meet here, she told herself without much conviction.

The following day, Sophie was up early, hoping that the sound of the cannon heralding Robert's arrival would occur some time in the morning. But it was not until very late in the afternoon, after she had spent most of the day walking around the house in a fever of impatience, that she heard the dull boom of the cannon echoing across the town.

'At last!' Sophie breathed. She hurried into the hallway, where Paul was already preparing to go out to the waiting carriage.

'I'm sorry you have to do this for me, Paul,' she said. 'But thank you, anyway.'

Paul shrugged. 'I do it because I must,' he said grudgingly.

When Paul left Sophie that afternoon, it had been his intention to carry out his task. He had no wish to incur the wrath of his father, who, he knew, was quite capable of cutting him off without a penny if he behaved like anything less than a gentleman. But certain events were to give him second thoughts on the matter.

Reaching the docks, he sought out the *Trident*, which had already berthed. Seeing a young officer coming down the gangway, he approached him. 'I wish to see Lieutenant Farnes. Would you be kind enough to tell him Paul Stacy wishes to see him?'

'He has already gone ashore,' the officer told him. 'You'll probably find him making the best of a bad situation at the Anchor.'

Paul looked at him blankly.

'Have you not heard the news? The *Trident* has only returned in order to join Nelson's battle fleet which sails on the morning tide,' the officer said. 'In view of our long absence at sea, Nelson was kind enough to grant the officers leave until dawn. Something which I propose to make the most of. Now, if you will excuse me –'

Paul was about to ask the officer if he could accompany him to the Anchor, when he paused. Suppose I do not see Robert and take him home? he thought. He will think Sophie is in Devon – far too long a journey for him to make there and back before his ship sails. The thought of Robert spending the night alone in Portsmouth, not knowing that Sophie was only a short coach drive away, gave him a great deal of pleasure. Tomorrow he will sail away, perhaps to be killed – one can only hope, he thought.

He began to walk through the gathering darkness. The scheme was not without its pitfalls. If Robert did return, some awkward questions would be asked. He dismissed the thought. With luck, the devil would look after its own. But that still left unanswered the question of what he was going to say to Sophie.

By the time he had reached Marsdon Hall, he had planned the lies he was going to tell her. Sophie met him as he came into the house, her face flushed with happiness.

'Thank goodness, you're back at last!' She looked over his shoulder to the open doorway. 'Where is Robert?'

'Still in Portsmouth, I'm afraid,' Paul said gravely.

'I – I don't understand,' Sophie stammered. A stricken look came on her face. 'He is not hurt?'

'He is well enough,' Paul said. 'I found him eventually in the company of some other officers. I told him you were here and about the ball. He said he would come later – after he had finishing drinking with his friends.' He paused. 'I'm afraid he was very drunk, Sophie.'

Sophie stood there looking at him in silence, the tears welling up in her eyes. Behind them, the orchestra in the ballroom struck up a quadrille. 'As you can hear,' she said dully. 'The ball has begun.'

'You must put a brave face on it, Sophie,' Paul said quietly. 'Come – let us go in and dance.'

The ball, which went as well as could be expected in the circumstances, ended at midnight. Sophie had gone through the motions, dancing when asked, a fixed smile on her face. To Paul, she had said little. Mr and Mrs Stacy had been very kind and were obviously concerned for her, but after the last guests had gone and the Stacys had retired to bed, Sophie went and sat alone in the deserted ballroom, hoping against hope that Robert might yet still appear. She waited until the dawn broke before she finally went to bed.

All the next morning, she waited for a contrite Robert to come calling. But, of course, he did not. It was not until the early evening that she learned that his ship had already sailed.

The bitter tears she shed were done in the privacy of her bedroom.

If all this sounds a sad business, the events that followed were the stuff of tragedy. To say that Sophie died of a broken heart might, perhaps, be fanciful. But it is true that, not long after her visit to Marsdon, she fell sick with a fever which was quickly followed by a fatal pneumonia. She put up little struggle; it seemed to her distraught parents almost as if she had lost the will to live.

As for Robert, Paul's wish that he should perish in action came uncannily true. Fortunately for his peace of mind, Robert never learned of Paul's treachery nor of its bitter consequences, for he was mortally wounded at the battle of Trafalgar and died only a few hours before his ship docked at Portsmouth. There he was buried, not many miles from Marsdon Hall.

But that is not quite the end of the story.

In the years that followed, Marsdon Hall passed through many hands, until recently, in our own time, when it became one of the stately homes of England. Among the many visitors that came to it was a young girl named Janet Clayton, who was spending part of her summer holidays with her aunt in a small cottage outside Portsmouth.

Janet's visit to Marsdon Hall came about quite by accident. She was out exploring the countryside on her moped when it began to rain, just as she was passing the gates of the Hall. Seeing a notice stating that it was open to the public, she parked the moped and hurried gratefully inside, although it was not far off closing time. There were only two or three other visitors left, and the curator gathered them together to take them round.

Janet was not particularly interested in old buildings, but as there seemed no likelihood that the rain would stop for some time, she followed the curator from room to room, listening politely, but without paying much attention to what he was saying. That was until they reached the ballroom, where, inexplicably, she began to shiver.

'It's very cold in here,' she commented.

The curator gave her a curious look. 'Perhaps that's because this room is haunted,' he said seriously.

'You have a ghost!' Janet exclaimed. 'Not a headless one, I hope.'

The curator gave her a pained smile. 'Actually, it's the ghost of a young woman.' He told them then in some detail the story of Robert and Sophie.

'Ever since her death,' he concluded, 'she has come here regularly every night, hoping that one day Robert will arrive.'

'Have you ever seen her?' Janet asked breathlessly.

'Many times,' the curator said calmly. He added, 'We would never have known the true facts but for Paul. When Sophie died, he was so overcome with remorse that he killed himself, leaving a letter which told of his part in the whole tragic business.'

Soon afterwards, the rain stopped and Janet went on her way. But she could not get out of her mind the story she had heard from the curator. She was so intrigued by it, in fact, that she went to some trouble to find out where Robert was buried. She visited the cemetery one blustery afternoon and found the grave, not without some difficulty, half covered with weeds, the name almost hidden by moss and the grime of centuries. She stood in front of it for some time.

'Poor Robert,' she said finally, in a low voice. 'If only you had been able to see her, that night of the ball.' Acting on an impulse, she suddenly knelt down and added in a whisper, 'You will find her at Marsdon Hall, where she is still waiting for you ...' Feeling a little foolish, she got up quickly and hurried away. As she left the cemetery, the wind blew gently through the trees like the sound of a human sigh.

That night, Janet slept badly. When she did go to sleep, it was only to wake again in the middle of the night. For some reason she could not explain to herself, she felt she was compelled to go that very minute back to Marsdon Hall. Rising from her bed, she began to dress.

A church clock was striking three when she arrived at the Hall. As if guided by an unseen force, she made her way over the lawns to the large window that looked into the ballroom. Staring inside, she gave an involuntary gasp. By the unearthly light of the moon that shone directly into the ballroom, she saw a woman in a high-waisted, Empire line dress in a flimsy muslin material, dancing in the arms of a handsome-looking naval officer. Strangely, Janet was not in the least frightened. And indeed, why should she be? She knew at once that it was because of her that Robert and Sophie were together again. There was no doubt in her mind now that they had summoned her to see their happy reunion.

Even as she watched, the dancing figures abruptly vanished, and Janet was left staring into an empty ballroom. She waited for a while to see if they would re-appear. When they did not, she went back to her moped. Dear Sophie, she thought, as she rode slowly away. Now at last you can rest in peace.

By the unearthly light of the moon she saw a woman in a high-waisted Empire line dress dancing in the arms of a handsome-looking naval officer.

THOU SHALT NOT LOVE!

Angus Allan

HELD BY THE SCRUFF OF HIS NECK, Richard Bezant, all fifteen years of him, hung poised for a moment in the grip of Gotobed Jenkins, the massive bailiff of Scarfallow Farm. Then, unceremoniously, he was flung headlong through the air to land asprawl in the muck of the pigsty, his lace collar besmirched, his plumed hat spinning into the swill of the trough.

'The next view of you on this land,' bellowed Jenkins, 'and I'll send ye back to your father in a dozen different parcels! Now get you gone, you Royalist whelp, and the curse of the Protector be on you and your whole rotten family!'

In tears, Sarah Martin watched from the stone porch of the big Warwickshire farmhouse as Richard picked himself up, spared the time to pluck filthy straws from his face, and gave Jenkins a deep, courtly bow. She wanted to run to his side, but her father gripped her shoulder with a hand like a steel trap, and she could feel that he was shaking with rage.

'Insolent puppy,' he spat. 'And you, girl. What d'ye mean by this secret dalliance with him, out by the old barn?'

'Father!' The girl twisted her head round. 'We've played together since we were tiny children! Whatever's happening in this poor country, Richard's still my friend! He always has been and he always *will* be!'

It was clear that Martin only restrained himself from striking his daughter with an effort. Behind him, the bloodhound cheeks of Parson Praisegod Milkwheat wobbled in disapproval, and he raised his bony hands in outrage. 'Sarah, child,' he intoned, in his syrupy, sanctimonious way. 'What possesses you to call such as Richard Bezant a friend? Know you not that he is an enemy of the state?'

Sarah, taking the risk of sending her father's fury over the edge, stamped her foot. 'Before this absurd war broke out,' she cried, 'the Martins and the Bezants were on the best of terms! How can such enmity arise in such a short space of time?'

Farmer Augustus Martin steered his daughter past the tutting minister. 'Go to your room at once! Perhaps a session with your grammars and the cane of Beldame Mutch will bring you to a more seemly frame of mind!'

'She's enamoured of that Bezant boy,' put in Milkwheat. 'I cannot conceal the fact that I found a note she had written to him. It spoke of – er – love.' The parson made a mouth as though the very word was distasteful to him.

'Is this true, Sarah?' Martin's eyes were flashing dangerously. The girl nodded, silently.

Praisegod Milkwheat turned his eyes heavenwards and shook his cropped head. 'There must be written a new commandment,' he said. 'In terms of Royalist and Parliamentarian, thou shalt not love ...'

It was, indeed, a sorry time for England. The Civil War was raging, and those who supported King Charles were bitterly at the throats of those who espoused Cromwell's cause. In many a shire, families had been divided down the middle, and brother actually fought against brother. Tearfully, Sarah Martin thought of the long, beautiful summers of what now seemed long ago, when she and Richard Bezant had roamed the woods, entranced by the rabbits and squirrels that had scurried away from them. Those glorious days when, side by side with Wat the poacher, they had been shown how to tickle and catch trout in the stream below the mill, and had learned the lore and the secrets of wild herbs and flowers. Sometimes, they had played games of Saxon and Norman with hobby-horses that Gotobed Jenkins had carved for them. Richard would have been Robin Hood, and she his Maid Marian.

But now those days were gone. Every adult – even Wat the poacher – was consumed by hatred of the other side, and in all the world, it was as though only she and Richard remained above the savage conflict that was ripping the country apart.

Sarah lay there in her bed, listening to an owl's call. She smarted, for Beldame Mutch, the governess hired by her father to give her schooling, had been free with the willow switch that she called her 'corrector'. The woman was passionately devoted to the Roundhead faction, and with her close-shorn hair, she might well have passed for Oliver Cromwell himself, warts and all.

Suddenly, there came a rattle at the mullioned panes of the bedroom window, and gathering her nightrobe about her, Sarah went over to it. The lawn outside was bathed in moonlight, and she was not in the least surprised to see her friend Richard Bezant down there, already gathering up another handful of gravel from the path.

Cautiously, she opened the latch and hissed down to him. 'Are you mad? You know what they'll do to you if they find you here!'

He grinned back, doffing his hat. 'Old Jenkins and his talk of parcels? He may be good at carving, but he's a ninny when it comes to knots! Remember how he cut his thumb on my fishing line? I've no fear of him, Sarah!'

'Well, what do you want?' she said, in anguish. She could just imagine the furore if anyone else was up late, and happened to be looking out of the house.

'I thought we might run away,' said Richard, simply. 'I have a couple of horses tethered down by the long field.'

Sarah laughed, despite herself. 'Run *away*? And where to,

pray? France? Spain? The Americas? We're not children playing games any more, Richard!'

The boy was not to be put off. 'We'll ride westwards, to Wales,' he said. 'I know from what my father says that there's a lot of folk there who don't care a jot about this war. They call it an English problem. I've actually got a relative there, and I know that he and his wife will be glad to take us in. Cavaliers and Roundheads are one and the same, to them!'

Sarah felt the blood racing in her veins. *Was* it feasible? She thought of her ties to her father. Yes, she respected him, but he had never been an affectionate man. She couldn't honestly say that she loved him. And she knew that for Richard, it was the same. Sir Humphrey Bezant was a stern, forbidding sort of individual who had always ruled his children with a rod of iron. And he was as steadfastly opposed to any relationship between Sarah and his boy as her own father. Richard had often said as much.

She came to her decision. 'Give me a quarter of an hour to dress and pack a valise,' she called. 'I'll meet you down at the long field!'

Sarah let herself out of the darkened farmhouse and ran swiftly across the grass. There he was, and they clasped hands for a moment, their eyes shining with the adventure of what they were doing. She strapped her valise behind the saddle of the big bay Richard had brought for her, and together they turned and rode for the cover of the silent woods. She noticed that he had a rapier slung at his side, and a couple of pistols in a saddle holster. Stolen, presumably, from Sir Humphrey.

'What do we say if we're stopped anywhere on the road?' asked Sarah, breaking a silence that had lasted minutes.

Richard smiled. 'Oh, I'm a clever one, I am,' he said with a wink. 'Took the time to write out a couple of passes.' He patted a pocket. 'One from General the Earl of Bowland – he's a great crony of Father's. The other from Colonel Royce, the

Cromwellian area commander. I forged their signatures jolly well, too.'

'Richard,' said Sarah with genuine admiration, 'you *are* a genius! I always said when we were playing Robin Hood that you'd have done well if you'd really lived in those days.'

Then she blushed, for he was looking at her seriously. 'When we get to Wales, and we grow up under the protection of the Prossers – that's their name – we'll get married, you and me. I mean, when we're old enough.'

Sarah nodded. There seemed no more natural thing in the world.

She said, 'Even if the war isn't over by then, and our families still hate and despise us, we'll leave the country. Go to the colonies and begin an entirely new family, of our own.'

'That's the spirit, Sarah. We won't be the only ones, I'm sure of that. Anyway, we're going to have a happier ending than the other two like us.'

'Who do you mean?' asked the girl.

'Why, Romeo and Juliet, of course,' said Richard. 'After all, the story's just about the same!'

Came dawn, and somewhere in Shropshire, they breakfasted at a wayside inn. There were soldiers there – swashbuckling men of the King, and sure enough, they quizzed the runaways. But Richard's pass from General the Earl of Bowland seemed to satisfy them. So much so that their officer, introducing himself as MacSween, actually insisted on paying for their meal.

'You be cautious,' he warned. 'Word has it' – he looked round as if anxious that the walls shouldn't overhear – 'that there's a party of Ironsides somewhere in the area, disguised as Royalist cavalry. It's said they're picked troopers under the command of Captain Silas Garran himself. Bloodybones Garran.'

'I know him by sight,' said Richard. 'Before the war he was

*There were soldiers there—swashbuckling men of the King, and
sure enough, they quizzed the runaways.*

the Lord Warden of our county. If I clap eyes on him, we'll steer clear. Thank you.'

The sun rose, brilliantly, and it was in high spirits that Sarah and her boy went on their way. Larks sang high in the clear air, and the scent of wild honeysuckle was strong in their nostrils as they trotted along the deep, shaded lanes. All at once, the war seemed far away.

Far away, that was, until they came upon the shepherd's hovel. It stood back from the road a yard or two, and though it hadn't fully burned out, someone had tried to set fire to the thatch. The door had been wrenched from its hinges, and what miserable furniture had been inside now lay broken and scattered in the ruins of the tiny vegetable garden. Sarah dismounted and ran to the shepherd, who lay groaning amidst the wreckage, near to death.

'Whatever happened?'

'Ahh, missy! They had me proper fooled! Done up like King's men, they were, so I cheered 'em on their way. Then they came back – and ... and ...'

'Bloodybones Garran,' breathed Richard.

'One of 'em dropped – this ...' The dying shepherd lifted one painful hand. 'It rolled – beneath me ...' Then he had gone, and Richard drew Sarah away.

Carefully, he unwrapped the small, oilskin-covered package he'd taken from the man's hand. It was no more than a square of parchment, covered with crabbed, minute writing.

'What is it?' said Sarah.

Richard gestured for her to be patient. 'Orders, I think,' he said. 'Secret orders that they must have learned already.' He swallowed hard, and looked up. 'It mentions my father's name. *And* yours.'

'Show me.' Sarah felt a chill run up her spine. She squinted at the tiny words, hardly legible without the aid of a glass.

Ashen-faced, she handed it back. 'So Garran's men are to

billet themselves with your family,' she whispered. 'While Garran himself makes his headquarters in my home. And what's this about treasure?'

Richard looked at the ground. 'The family jewels. The plate and so forth. Father buried it when the war began. If he's duped into thinking Garran's lot are King's men, he'll reveal it to them. Donate it to the cause. And then they'll kill him. They'll kill them all. Both my parents, all the retainers ...'

'If we ride back and give warning,' said Sarah, 'Your father can only do one thing! He'll take his men and go to Scarfellow Farm. They'll be after Garran – but they'll have to slaughter my own father, Jenkins and the others before they can take him!'

'So what do we do, Sarah?' Richard spread his hands helplessly. 'We can't warn both. Do we put it all out of our minds and pretend we aren't involved?'

'But Richard, we *are* involved! We can't live our lives pretending!' Tears of frustration had sprung to Sarah's eyes. 'We have to do *something!*'

He clasped her hand again. 'We'll ride back,' he said. 'But whatever happens – do we remain as *we* are?'

'For ever,' she said, brokenly. And then they turned their horses and were galloping eastwards, away from the rosy dream-life they had so hopefully built for themselves.

Captain Silas 'Bloodybones' Garran sat his charger at the gallows intersection of the Worcester and Evesham roads. On a sorry nag, the black-clad figure of Parson Praisegod Milkwheat faced him, an oily smirk on the hanging jowls.

'Farmer Martin is ready for me?' The Captain's voice was as harsh as his rat-trap face.

'Yes indeed,' crooned Milkwheat, unctuously. 'And the local spies have heralded your approach, never fear. As a part of Royalist cavalry, naturally,' he added. 'Your men may ride on, and soon you will be able to divest your noble self of these disgusting trappings.' The parson made fluttering, grimacing gestures at Garran's disguise.

'Quite so,' said the Captain. 'You yourself have the canal barges lined up to take away Bezant's treasure?'

'I am not one of our glorious Protector Cromwell's secret agents for nothing,' simpered Milkwheat. 'Should any accursed Royalist get free with word of your plunder, his contacts will waste their time hunting for packhorse trains, baggage wagons and the like ...'

'Excellent, Milkwheat,' smiled Garran. 'Right, lads. You know what to do. Sir Humphrey Bezant is waiting – to welcome you as heroes all!'

The party split, the main force taking the road for Bezant's manor, Garran and the parson heading directly for Scarfallow Farm. Neither group was aware that, in the heavy undergrowth of the Warwickshire border, two pairs of ears were listening.

'Now we know a little more of the plan, Sarah,' whispered Richard. 'If Milkwheat has barges ready, then they must be on the canal, maybe at Barren Valley lock.'

'What good is that to us?' Sarah was frightened, and showed it. Her friend took both her hands in his and leaned close.

'Think of this as if it were just another of the games we used to play,' he said. 'They always worked out well, didn't they?'

'But Richard. This is – different! It's *not* Robin Hood and Maid Marian any more.'

He raised his eyebrows. 'You think not? Come on – we have some hard riding to do!'

Richard's plan was simple. Uncomplicated. And the most uncomplicated plans are the ones that always succeed. He had in his possession not only his two forged passes, one

Royalist, one Parliamentarian. He also had the secret orders taken from the murdered shepherd. It was no great difficulty to go to Barren Valley lock, a region held by Cromwell's men, and pose as an officer of Roundhead cavalry, engaged on an undercover mission. There were many sons of important families, no older than he, who were on active service. Richard told the officer in charge there that the plan – he showed the order cautiously, and in private – had gone astray.

'A party will bring treasure, sure enough,' he said. 'But they'll be Royalists pretending to be our chaps disguised as Royalists. Do you get my meaning?'

'No-no,' stammered the man. 'Can you explain it again?'

Richard was patient. He hoped that Sarah, waiting for him in the woods, was not getting too agitated. 'These men,' he said, 'will load the barges. You will let them do just that. You will allow them to go off, along the canal. *My* men will be waiting at the Union Bridge to pounce and take them. Those are Colonel Royce's orders.' He brandished his forged Roundhead pass.

Now Richard went back to rejoin Sarah. Had she been successful? She had. With an arrow cut from a sapling and a crude bow from the same tree, strung with entwined fibres from her own clothes, she had fired a scribbled message through the window of the farm lodge. Into the parlour where Gotobed Jenkins would snatch and read it, and carry the astounding news to her father.

The astounding news? That Captain Silas 'Bloodybones' Garran himself was a double agent in the pay of King Charles, and not under any account to be trusted!

'The tale won't survive for long,' grinned Richard, 'but it'll carry long enough! *If* we're lucky!'

Meanwhile, in the Bezant manor, Sir Humphrey had willingly welcomed Garran's men as the Royalists they pretended to be. Until a message borne by another arrow, shot through the window of the butler's pantry, told him differently. Thus warned, he and his retainers made short work of the impostors. They thought that that was that, having been told nothing of Captain Garran. The treasure remained where it was hidden, and the captives were herded off to Royalist lines to be held as prisoners.

Garran himself, bellowing in furious captivity while Farmer Augustus Martin raved defiance at the twittering Milkwheat, thrusting the arrowed message under his nose, knew that things had gone terribly wrong. Heads would roll for this, he promised. But at the moment, his promises were as ineffectual as the battering of his fists against the cellar door . . .

And Richard and Sarah? They resumed their journey.

'So rudely interrupted,' said Richard, grinning. 'Everything is in chaos. Nobody knows what's going on, and I can just imagine those idiots down by the Barren Valley lock, waiting for the enemy disguised as friends disguised as enemy to turn up! They won't dare make any kind of move and the whole county will be in a turmoil.'

'Do you think we'll get to Wales, Richard?' said Sarah. 'Or will something else happen and force us to retrace our steps?'

'Oh – I think not. Thousand to one against,' he assured her. 'Certainly, there'll be blood spilled, on both your side and mine, before this is all over. But we've done what we can, and we'll survive.'

'He said "thou shalt not love",' said Sarah, thinking of Praisegod Milkwheat. 'What a silly little man!'

Sarah and Richard were to ride on to their happy destiny. Long after the war was over, they would be reunited with their respective families, all of them mercifully survivors. Friends, enemies, now friends again, Augustus Martin and Sir Humphrey Bezant would by that time have grandchildren to bind their friendship closer.

FOREST OF LOVE

Richard Grimsden

MALTILDA BERKELEY PEEPED around the tapestry at the end of the great hall at Dalkeith Castle and her big dark eyes shone with admiration. The enticing sunshine, streaming through tall windows of stained glass, patched the rush-strewn floor with crimson and gold and blue, colouring the surcoat and tall leather boots of Roger de Keynes, a Norman warrior to his fingertips.

Matilda sighed wistfully. If only he would look up, even give a glance in her direction.

But the thoughts of Roger de Keynes, thick-set, black-bearded, were far away from the youthful slip of a figure behind the arras.

'This is where they are most likely to be skulking!' De Keynes stabbed at the parchment map of the New Forest spread out on the long table and indicated the spot he had chosen to Sir Simon Warren, son of the lord of Dalkeith.

'This is a swamp area, filled with dense scrub and deep copses,' de Keynes went on. 'It makes an ideal hiding place. It's difficult to enter – see, this is the only path in and out, and therefore it's easy to defend.'

'We'll soon flush them out,' Sir Simon Warren growled. 'Get the men together.'

De Keynes slapped his mailed fist on the handle of the long sword at his side in a typical gesture of satisfaction that never failed to send a thrill of excitement through the admiring Matilda.

'Aye,' he said grimly. 'We'll flush them out all right.'

Matilda drew back soundlessly behind a pillar as the two men folded the parchment map and without another word strode across the hall and out through the arched doorway, passing within inches of her.

For a fleeting instant Matilda wanted to reach out and touch de Keynes' surcoat. Better judgement prevailed. That was hardly the act of a high-born lady lodged as a guest in Dalkeith Castle.

'I'm in love, I'm in love, I'm in love,' Matilda sang to herself. As soon as the two men's footsteps had disappeared down the stone-flagged corridor she skipped out into the sunlit quadrangle.

But how could she let the man she loved know that she loved him? Wasn't it absurd to feel love, yet not to be able to reveal it?

From the distance she could hear the clatter of men-at-arms and lackeys assembling before the opening drawbridge. The voice of Roger – dear, brave Roger – barked commands that echoed from stone wall to stone wall.

She knew vaguely where they were going, knew indistinctly what the knights talked about at dinner in the banqueting room. 'The local problems ... difficult peasants, led by traitors,' she had heard them say. And once she had heard them declare that the rebels must be defeated, 'for Roger de Keynes was a hard and ruthless man, and would stop at nothing to gain the victory.'

After only a month at Dalkeith Matilda knew these were troubled times.

'Remember,' her father, Sir Hugo Berkeley, had said as he'd packed her off from their Gloucestershire manor house to the New Forest castle of his great friend Lord Warren, 'remember not to meddle in matters that don't concern you. These are bad times for my Lord Warren, who must see that the King's bidding is done and all rebellion suppressed.'

Matilda, despatched to Dalkeith because the physicians declared she needed a change of air after a long bout of fever, didn't care about the King's business. Not even though the King was the mighty William the Conqueror. She cared only for the handsome, brooding Roger de Keynes, equerry to Lord Warren, from the moment she first saw him. He was so aloof, so lonely, so *enigmatic*!

And now she began to fear for him. For, she suddenly recalled, 'the King's business' was to suppress by main force the last of the pocket rebellions in the New Forest, and she had heard that these peasants were like animals, led by madmen who would kill their own mothers for a groat.

It had been going on for months, ever since the King had declared that all the villages in the New Forest must be razed and the peasants driven away from their homes so that the whole forest could be reserved for the royal hunting pleasure. This was the King's decree, and the word of William the Conqueror was law. Matilda couldn't understand why anyone should want to defy it, could even less understand why her Roger should have to risk his life to uphold it.

A wave of fear swept through her. Suppose he were struck down in the forest, murdered by a horrible, soft-footed assassin? Suppose he died, not knowing she loved him? That must not be!

Without further thought, she rushed to her chamber, threw off her fur-bordered gown, and tied on a simple jerkin and tight-fitting hose. With a short scarlet cloak thrown over her shoulders, she ran to the stables, saddled her palfrey and rode like a princess out of the castle.

She was going to find her Roger! Somehow, she must pledge to him her undying love before he fought the great battle, and leave with him a token – a lock of her hair, perhaps – as talisman to keep him from harm.

As the castle walls disappeared behind her the sun shone brilliantly on the young leaves. Matilda hummed a tune. A company of knights came riding by, their armour glinting in the bright light, and a sleek abbot on a sleeker nag murmured a smiling *pax vobiscum* as he rode past her. Soon the rutty, grass-grown track led her between trees, then deeper into the forest. Here the sun, framed above her in budding branches, wasn't so sure of itself.

The trees stretched ahead of her, endlessly. Matilda had never seen so many of them; she had no idea of the width or scale of this great royal demesne. But this was freedom undreamed of! Here she could stop to pick flowers and berries with no stern voice in her ear declaring. 'Another day, girl. Time presses.'

On an impulse she left the beaten track and, dismounting, struck off across the open heath, leading her horse. Beyond the furze and heather wild duck swished in gleaming pools framed by rushes. Here the grass grew thick and green and Matilda imagined that herdsmen had brought their pigs and sheep to pasture in such places before the King's command sent them all away.

Matilda forgot the distance, the castle, and even, for a moment, she forgot the magnificent Roger de Keynes. Intoxicated with her own freedom, she skipped over tufts of ling and sprouting bracken, singing to herself.

Then, catching the sound of a heavy crackling in a nearby thicket, she turned to look and her heart froze. For suddenly out of the thicket came an enormous boar with strong white tusks. Standing stock still, then pawing the ground ominously, the hairy beast fixed her intently with little angry eyes.

Matilda raised her hand to her mouth in stark terror, turned and, dropping the reins, fled for the nearest tree. The boar, already scenting an easy victory, grunted and charged. In a fraction of a second Matilda leapt into the safety of the branches of a spreading oak. Gasping, she hauled herself up, while the tormented animal butted furiously at the tree.

It took several minutes for Matilda to recover from her initial fright, minutes that seemed like a lifetime. As she wondered what to do next, the boar seemed to calm down. It began to roam around the foot of the tree, grunting and rooting for acorns. Once or twice it glared up at Matilda, propped uncomfortably in the branches, then went on rooting.

Half an hour went by. Matilda was glad of the shading leaves of the oak tree, for the sun was warming up, and the boar was showing no intention whatever of leaving the foot of the tree.

Another half hour ... Now she was beginning to feel the nagging pains of cramp. She thought desperately of Roger and his party of men – could he, would he come this way? Could he save her from this distress? The boar suddenly butted the foot of the tree savagely, reminding her that he wasn't going away for anything.

Slowly, painfully slowly, the sun rose to its zenith. Still the boar snorted and grunted around the foot of the tree. Matilda began to get desperate. Her horse had long since wandered off. She was far from Dalkeith Castle and wouldn't know her way back even if she could get down from the tree.

Suddenly there was a furious squealing from the boar below her. The animal had turned and was pawing the ground in preparation for a charge. Its attention was riveted on a thicket thirty yards away. All in the kaleidoscoped moment the leaves of the thicket parted and out stepped a tall, loose-limbed man with an impish grin lighting his blue eyes. Coolly, as if he were at archery practice, he raised his bow to his cheek and released an arrow. At that instant the boar crumpled untidily, shot dead between the eyes.

Matilda screamed. She wasn't sure whether it came from

Seeing the girl in the branches, he laughed. 'I seem to have killed your jailer, mistress!' he said.

surprise or relief. Startled, the tall bowman looked up apprehensively and reached for another arrow. Then, seeing the girl in the branches, he laughed out loud and strode rapidly forward.

'I seem to have killed your jailer, mistress!' he said. His voice was pleasantly soft, with a rural burr; his eyes were of the blueness of a true Saxon. He reached up to help Matilda from her precarious perch and she felt the strength of his arms as he lifted her to the ground.

'Permit me to introduce myself. Stephen of Stavringham, or, I should say, I was of Stavringham before His Majesty was pleased to eject my family from that village.'

'I'm – I'm Matilda Berkeley. From Dalkeith Castle.'

'The castle?' A cloud passed over Stephen's face. 'Naught to do with the barbarous de Keynes and his gang, I hope?'

Matilda stiffened. 'Roger de Keynes is a good friend of mine,' she said haughtily, smoothing out the creases from her dress. She was glad that Roger wasn't there to hear her say so – she remembered with a blush that he hardly knew her name. 'And you have no right to call him barbarous.'

'No right, aye, no right, mistress. I have no right to anything any more in this fair land,' said Stephen bitterly.

The notes of a hunting horn echoed across the distant heath. Matilda's heart missed a beat.

'Roger!' she breathed, ecstatically. He was coming this way – he would save her!

Stephen's mouth hardened grimly. 'De Keynes!' he muttered.

In a trice he had snatched her up and before she could draw breath to scream, he put his hand over her mouth and half carrying, half dragging her, plunged into the thicket from which he had lately emerged. Hidden in the trees was a tethered horse. Maltilda felt herself thrown across its back and almost in the same fluid movement Stephen leapt into the saddle, swung round the animal's head and then they were fleeing across the heathland.

She held on to him as if her life depended upon it – as indeed it did, for to have fallen would surely have meant a cracked skull.

They sped past a lake where herons fished in the eddies, galloped uphill into the singing woods, and over a carpet of bluebells, with sunny patches of Lent lilies lingering in the shadows. On and on they plunged into the gold and green depths of the forest. Timid deer scattered before them and once an antlered stag sprang out from behind bushes and bounded lightly down the dim aisles, all in a flick and scutter of white tails in the undergrowth.

They galloped at the speed of the wind – and then stopped as suddenly. Stephen dismounted, and pulling Matilda roughly from the steaming horse, he dragged her through the undergrowth. There before them was a tiny cottage, hidden from all the world by the thick woods surrounding it.

Stephen thundered against the door, and presently an old crone with a thick shawl masking her face came to open it.

'It is I, Griselda.' Next moment they were inside and the wooden rectangle of the door creaked shut behind them.

'Who's the girl?' the old woman demanded in a rasping voice.

'She's a friend of de Keynes,' replied Stephen. 'He's in the woods nearby, with a party of men-at-arms from Dalkeith Castle. They are looking for us, I shouldn't wonder. The rest of my men are scattered in the forest.'

'De Keynes!' Griselda, the old woman, looked hard at Matilda, then back at Stephen. 'What did you bring her here for? She'll tell de Keynes of our hiding place.'

Matilda was aware that Stephen was gazing down at her with a simple frankness she was unaccustomed to.

'I don't think you would do that, would you, mistress?' he

asked softly. 'You wouldn't betray us to Satan himself?'

Matilda coloured. 'Why do you call him such names?' she protested faintly. 'He is a good man. You have no right to bring me here like this. It's – it's kidnapping! You could hang for it!' She could hear the lack of spirit in her voice, could feel the deep blue eyes of her 'kidnapper' still fixed fully on her and stirred uncomfortably under his gaze.

The old crone spat contemptuously into the rushes on the floor and turned her back on them to attend an iron cauldron steaming over the blazing logs.

'Mistress,' said Stephen, his voice gentle now. 'Your friend de Keynes is a cruel, heartless man, who takes pleasure in the fear and terror he spreads across this shire.' All the roughness he had shown in manhandling her from the oak tree to the hidden cottage seemed to have evaporated completely. 'He has killed at least a hundred innocent men, burned the homes of a thousand English families, and turned an area that takes three days to ride across into the hunting ground for just one man, King William the Conqueror. All that death and misery, simply for one man's pleasure.'

He paused and looked sadly at Griselda, silently stirring in the iron cauldron.

'He tortured, then hanged, this poor woman's three sons. Their crime was that they refused to give up their rude little family cottage in the New Forest – refused to be turned out into the cold and rain of winter.'

Matilda shuddered involuntarily. She remembered the knights at Dalkeith Castle whispering that Roger de Keynes was a hard and ruthless man. But torture – and killing? It hardly seemed possible.

'Why should I believe what you say?' Matilda protested haughtily. She thought, I'm beginning to believe him, though. He doesn't seem the kind of man who would invent such a tale. But she had to show resolution. 'I have only your word for this,' she went on, 'and you appear to be a hunted criminal.'

For answer, the old crone whipped round from the iron cauldron and thrust her left arm under Matilda's face. For the first time Matilda saw that it was no more than a half-healed stump – the hand was completely gone. She felt her skin prickle.

Stephen said quietly, 'Roger de Keynes himself cut off her hand when she refused to reveal her fugitive sons' hiding place in the forest.'

Matilda's head sank on to her chest. She felt hot tears running down her cheeks.

'Never mind, mistress,' Stephen said gently. 'What's done is done. The King's command will be carried out, for de Keynes has the men and the power to see to that. But one day, at the right time, at the right moment, the English people will win back the New Forest, even if it takes a thousand years.'

In her confusion, she was scarcely aware that he had put his arm around her, enveloping her in his muscular strength, until his hand began to smooth her dark hair as it tumbled over his rough leather jerkin. From above the blazing logs Griselda began to fill two horn platters from the cauldron. Suddenly she paused, turning her head tensely towards the door. Her hand shook, and a ladle filled with stew split on to the fire.

Matilda looked up sharply. She sensed a sort of nervous alarm on the wrinkled face, saw the growing terror.

'De Keynes!' Griselda whispered. 'Hide! I'll draw them off! Lie quiet, for your lives' sake!'

In the sharpness of a moment she had opened the door and was gone with a speed that belied her old, bent body. Through the half-open door Matilda and Stephen could see her plunging like a young deer through a thicket. Beyond the trees was a clearing and as she reached it they heard the sound of a score of horses riding across the heathland in their direction.

Crouching on the rush-strewn floor, half covered with a rough woven blanket hastily drawn from an oak chest, Matilda and Stephen watched, like people straining to look through a keyhole, the scene in the clearing beyond the thicket. They saw the horsemen ride up to Griselda, who was bent double against a tree, and now suddenly aged again.

The men wore hunting knives at their belts, swords at their sides and bows on their backs. At once Matilda recognised their thick-set, black-bearded leader, and her heart missed a beat.

'Well, old crone!' she heard de Keynes shout. 'We're looking for outlaws and bandits who defy the King's command. Do not try to conceal your information from me, or I'll cut off your other hand! You must have seen them pass this way. Where are they now?'

Griselda raised her left stump. From their hiding place Matilda and Stephen couldn't hear her voice, could only note the intent gaze of the horseman as they peered into the distance, following the direction of the old woman's pointing stump.

'She's sending them the other way!' Stephen breathed.

Matilda felt his closeness under the rough blanket, the warmth of his breath against her cheek. She felt safe – safer than she had ever felt in her life before. She turned her head towards him and the clear blue eyes smiled back at her. Then, irresistibly, her lips moved towards his.

From the depths of the New Forest, Roger de Keynes blew a sharp note on his hunting horn, a note that sent waves of sound echoing across the heathland and into the trees.

And Matilda Berkeley never even heard it.

THE MAKING OF GENTLEMAN JACK

June Williams

THE SUN WAS NOW at its height, beating down mercilessly on the coach, making it something of a sweat box for those inside. It was perhaps not so bad for three of its occupants, for they were Australians, and therefore used to such heat. But for Constance Smythe, newly arrived from England, it was a nightmare that had started almost from the moment they had left Adelaide, to take a road that had wound on interminably between rows of dusty trees that occasionally gave way to vast stretches of dried-up land. For someone such as Constance, used to the English countryside, the depressing vistas could only come as something of a shock.

Nor had the overnight stop helped. Due to a late start, they had been forced to stay at a small township. The only hotel there had been dirty, and the landlord surly and unhelpful, apart from advising her to shake out her shoes before putting them on in the morning.

'Funnel spiders,' he had said brusquely. 'Their bite's a killer.'

It had not been the happiest of introductions to Australia, Constance decided, as she stared out of the coach window.

'Another four hours and we'll be in Bendigo.' This piece of information was offered by the leathery-faced man beside her, who had got on at the last stop, where he had introduced himself to Constance as Tim Rowley, a tin miner. He looked at her curiously. 'What takes you there, Missus?'

'I am joining my fiancé,' she told him. 'He went to Bendigo

four years ago. Now he has a sheep farm of his own. His name is Charles Hemmings.'

'Hemmings! I know the –' He checked himself and looked out of the other window. 'He's well known around Bendigo.'

The coach rattled on its way, with no one saying much, when suddenly a voice called out loudly, 'Bail up!'

The coach came to a screeching halt as the driver applied his brakes, throwing everyone from their seats. A few seconds later, a pair of pistols were poked through the window. 'Would everyone step outside, please ...'

Constance was the first to emerge, followed by Rowley, and the two other men travelling in the coach – both of them well dressed and probably business men of some sort. Outside, they were confronted by the booted figure of a tall, handsome-looking man, wearing a wide-brimmed hat and holding a pair of pistols. One of them was pointed steadily at the driver and his companion, who sat in their seats with their hands in the air. 'You two, said the raider, pointing his pistol at the two men. 'Your wallets and watches, if you would be so kind.'

His voice, Constance noted with surprise, was that of a cultured Englishman. Pocketing the wallets and watches that were given to him, he glanced at Rowley, who was beginning to undo his money belt.

'Keep it on,' he commanded, 'I'm not here to rob the likes of you.' He turned a pair of piercing black eyes on Constance. 'Nor am I here to rob a young lady.' He gave her a brief smile, before addressing the driver. 'What are you carrying in your mail bags?'

'Cash for one of the mine owners at Bendigo,' the driver said.

'Get down and put it on my horse. And don't try anything.'

He waited while the driver got down and flung a pair of saddlebags over his waiting horse. Then, sticking his pistols in his belt, he went over and mounted. With a brief wave, he was gone, disappearing almost immediately into the distance.

'That's got to be Gentleman Jack,' Rowley muttered, staring after him.

'He was certainly a very polite highwayman,' Constance said.

'We call them bushrangers over here,' Rowley said. 'That one is better than most of them, by a long chalk.' He grinned at Constance. 'He's a good-looking feller, isn't he?'

Constance said nothing but silently she agreed with Rowley. Gentleman Jack was one of the most handsome men she had ever seen. The sort of man, in fact, that in any other circumstances a woman would be proud to be seen with. She tried to brush the thought aside. But the memory of that strong, handsome face remained clearly in her mind as she went back to the coach.

They arrived at Bendigo at sunset. As soon as she stepped out of the coach, she saw Charles hurrying towards her. Briefly saying goodbye to Rowley, she ran forward to meet him.

'Constance, my dearest.' Charles embraced her briefly. 'How wonderful it is to see you again!'

'And you, Charles.' At a quick glance he seemed little changed, but she did note that his face was now more set and hard looking than it had been when she had known him in England.

Releasing her, Charles turned to shout up at the driver. 'You up there! Get this lady's luggage down – and be quick about it!'

Your manner, too, has changed, Constance thought, as she listened to him continuing to berate the driver, who was now struggling to get down one of her heavy trunks. There had been a time when he had never been less than courteous, even to his inferiors. The same could not be said of him now.

But worse, she found, was to come. Charles had brought

with him a wagon driven by a man dressed in some sort of convict garb. He was obviously ill and badly nourished. But this did not stop Charles from berating him loudly as he ineffectually tried to help the coach driver transfer her baggage from the coach to the wagon.

Seeing the shocked expression on her face, Charles shrugged it off, scowling. 'There is no other way to speak to them, Constance. These convicts are the very dregs of England, and have to be treated with firmness.'

These two incidents, small though they were, filled Constance with forebodings which, in a short time, turned out to be fully justified. Within a week of being in Charles's house, where he lived with his sister Molly, she had learned that the man she had loved no longer existed. This was not the man to whom she had become betrothed four years ago, before the death of her parents. In his place was an overbearing and self-opinionated stranger who, moreover, shamefully ill treated his convict labourers – those wretched creatures who had been shipped from England to serve their time in the colonies in the most appalling conditions.

'Have you no pity for them?' she asked Charles reproachfully one day. 'You treat them worse than it is possible to imagine.'

'They are criminals, and should be treated as such.' Charles looked at her coldly. 'And if I may say so, my dear, we will get on much better if you keep out of my affairs.'

In despair, she sought out Charles's sister, who was in the kitchen, preparing the Sunday dinner. She came straight to the point. 'Molly, what has happened to Charles? Why has he changed so much?'

Molly placed the roast in the oven before answering her. 'Power and money,' she said simply. 'It corrupts all but the strongest of men. And Charles is certainly not that.' She sighed. 'I would have written to you, warning you about

Charles and how much he has changed. But I had hoped that he would improve when you came out. I thought your influence might soften him, but I can see now that it will make no difference.'

'Then I must leave,' Constance said decisively. 'I no longer love him and I cannot marry him. I will tell him so and go back to England. I have money of my own now and enough for the fare.'

'Yes, I think that would be best,' Molly said sadly. She thought for some moments. 'Charles is going away for a few days. It would save a lot of unpleasantness if you left then. Oh, Constance –' she broke off, weeping. 'Charles is my brother, and it is my duty to stand by him. But I shall miss you sadly – if only you could have stayed a little longer. It seems so far to come to have to return so soon ...'

'I also wish –' Constance began.

Molly interrupted her. 'I have just thought of something. We have a cottage not far from here which we bought before we took over this place. It's still furnished, and has a well-stocked library. Why not stay there for a while? Charles will never know, and I could ride over and see you nearly every day. She beamed. 'What do you think?'

'I think it's a lovely idea,' Constance said.

It was a beautiful little cottage that nestled in a glade surrounded by trees in which birds constantly sang. Well supplied with provisions that Molly had brought with them, Constance was completely self-sufficient. As for company, there was Molly, who visited her whenever it was safe to do so. From her, she learned that Charles had taken the news of her departure badly, and was behaving even worse than ever towards his convicts. This disturbed her slightly, but otherwise her spirits recovered slowly, and there came a time when she was almost happy – even though there was little for her to do there, but rest, read and work on the small garden that was badly neglected.

But the even tenor of her life was suddenly shattered one afternoon, when she heard the gentle snorting of a horse. Going outside, she saw the horse standing right outside her door with the slumped figure of a rider on its back. Alarmed, she hurried forward, only to step back a pace when the rider raised his head weakly. She recognised him at once. It was Gentleman Jack!

As he tried to slide from his saddle, Constance hurried forward. 'Here, let me help you –' Supporting his weight, she took him inside and led him to a large sofa. He sank on it gratefully. It was then she noticed a patch of blood on his shoulder.

'A bullet wound. I took one chance too many.' He looked up at her and smiled wanly. 'You're the young lady on the coach! As you know who I am, you'll no doubt be going for the military.'

'I'm not going anywhere,' Constance said decisively. 'I am staying right here to look after you. After that we'll see . . .'

It took her three weeks to nurse her unexpected visitor back to health. It was an easy task to persuade the soft-hearted Molly to keep her secret when Molly came over the next day and discovered the 'guest' she was harbouring.

During that time the bushranger said very little, until early one evening when they were on the verandah, watching the sun setting behind the trees.

'I think it only fair that I should tell you something about myself,' he said suddenly. 'My real name is Michael Storm. I am the son of a judge who has sent many a poor fellow to the colonies. This did not worry me a great deal at the time. But when I came out to Australia myself, I became so appalled by the treatment meted out to the convicts that I decided I would do everything I could to help them. That is why I left my farm and became a bushranger, robbing the rich in order to pass the money on to those who had been set free without a penny in their pockets and little prospect of work. In that way, I've helped quite a number of them.' He gave her a sudden, heartwarming smile. 'You see, I'm not just another wild colonial boy, out to get rich quick.'

'I knew you were a good man at heart,' Constance said softly.

If Constance had been asked afterwards when she had fallen in love with Michael, she would have been hard put to give an answer. All she knew for certain was that at this very moment she was deeply in love with this kind, well-meaning man, who had chosen the worst of possible paths for the best of all reasons.

'All the same,' she continued in a low voice. 'You cannot go on like this. If you do, you will end up on the gallows. Your luck won't last for ever.'

He shrugged. 'If that is the way it must be . . .' He regarded her sombrely. 'You have been very kind to me. But why should you care what happens to me?'

'I care because I love you,' she said simply. She had not meant to be so bold, but sensing his inward despair, she had responded to it, causing her to say unwittingly what was in her heart. She turned away, embarrassed. 'I'm sorry. I should not have said that.'

She felt his hands on her shoulders. Slowly, he turned her around to face him. He looked confused, almost stunned. 'Constance – I have loved you, I think, from the very first moment I saw you. But I never dared hope that you could possibly love me in return.' And with that, he took her in his arms and kissed her.

Later, when they were sitting quietly together in the house, she returned to the subject of Michael's life as a bushranger. 'You must give it up as from now.' She gave him a shy smile.

'No woman would like the idea of being married to a bushranger.'

'I agree with you,' he said calmly. 'I will have to become respectable!'

'Then it is settled.' She noted with relief that he had taken the question of marriage in his stride. 'Somehow I shall have to make a new man of you, Michael Storm.'

It was at that precise moment that the door was kicked open. There stood Charles, holding a revolver pointed at Michael's chest.

'Stand up – very slowly,' he said thickly. He nodded his head in Michael's direction as they both rose. 'I suppose you know who that is, Constance. That's Gentleman Jack. I'd recognise him anywhere from that drawing I saw in a newspaper.'

'I know who he is.' Constance tried to keep her voice steady. 'How did you find out I was here?'

'One of my friends saw Molly riding this way. I guessed the rest.' Charles kept the gun levelled steadily at Michael's chest. 'What I want to know is how *he* came to be here?'

Constance told him briefly, adding, 'I'm in love with him, Charles. We are going to marry.'

'I'll kill him first!' Charles exploded.

'If you want to do that,' Michael said quietly, 'I suggest you do it outside.' His glance flickered towards his gun on the mantlepiece. 'But I wonder what will be said if you shoot an unarmed man down in cold blood?'

Charles looked at them for a moment.

'I'll make a bargain with you, Constance,' he said finally. 'If you promise to come back with me and marry me, I'll let him go. Otherwise I *will* kill him, whatever the consequences.' His lip curled in a sneer. 'A felon, shot trying to escape . . .'

Seeing the madness that lurked in Charles's eyes, Constance knew that he meant every word he had said. Michael's

There stood Charles, holding a revolver pointed at Michael's chest. 'Stand up—very slowly', he said.

life was in her hands, and there was only one thing she could do to save it.

'I'll marry you,' she said. 'You have my word on it.'

'No!' Michael cried in anguish. 'Don't do it –'

'I must,' Constance said in a low voice.

'Bring me his guns, Constance,' Charles said, with a triumphant grin. 'Then we'll go.'

There was nothing the people of Bendigo liked more than a wedding – especially if the people getting married were young, beautiful and rich. And on the surface of it, this particular wedding seemed to fill all the requirements. The only difference in this case was that the bride was desperately unhappy.

Ever since she had left the cottage with Charles, Constance's mind had been in a tumult. She had given her word that she would marry him. But as this was a vow that had been given under duress, she might have broken it without hesitation, but for one thing. She would have to leave Australia, and would therefore never see Michael again. Nor would she ever know what had eventually happened to him. So she had decided to go through with the marriage, hardly believing that it would really take place.

But now the wedding day had come. Taking the driver's hand she stepped out of the carriage, summoning a weak smile for the well-wishers gathered outside the church. Inside, Charles was waiting for her. She closed her eyes briefly. What madness had she committed, condemning herself to live with a man she hated, whose cruelty she feared?

Suddenly, there was the sound of rattling wagon wheels. Then the wagon itself appeared, its driver bent low over the reins as he forced the horse along at breakneck speed. There was a general murmur of alarm, and then everyone scattered as the wagon continued to career towards them. Everyone

245

that is, except Constance, who had recognized the driver.

'Michael!' she breathed. She had no time to say more, before he was upon her, his hand outstretched for her to take. She caught it, and was hauled into the wagon.

Michael gave her a brief grin as they drove on. 'Sorry to interrupt the wedding. But I have other plans for you.'

If anyone else, apart from Charles Hemmings, had been privy to the events that had led up to Constance's abduction, they might well have thought that this was truly a story with a romantic ending. But afterwards they would have all agreed that the abduction had turned out to be a most tragic affair.

The next morning, the people of Bendigo opened their copy of the Bendigo Clarion and read how the bushranger, Gentleman Jack, had abducted Miss Constance Smythe at the door of the church, only minutes before she was due to be married. They read, too, how a band of indignant citizens had mounted up and pursued them to the banks of a river, where the bushranger had lost control of the wagon, which had plunged into the swirling waters below. Helpless, they had watched its occupants swept away to oblivion.

'No one will regret the death of Gentleman Jack,' the writer concluded. 'But it is with great sorrow that we have to inform our readers of the loss of Miss Smythe, who, although a newcomer to our fair country, was known and greatly liked by many. The reasons for the kidnapping remain obscure.'

The people of Bendigo were shocked to read this sad story. But they lived in a country where sudden death was common, and in due course it passed from their minds, to be recalled only when they learned that Charles Hemmings and his sister were returning to England, following the sudden collapse of his fortunes.

The story of Gentleman Jack and Constance Smythe was eventually written up by a journalist who went to some lengths to find out why Constance had been kidnapped by a bushranger noted for his courtesy towards the ladies. But as he was unable to come up with the answer, the article caused little comment.

It did, however, interest a gentleman farmer and his wife, who lived far from where the event had occurred.

'It's a pity, in a way, he doesn't know the real story,' his wife commented, as she watched her husband pasting the article in a scrap book.

'Let us hope he never will,' Michael said. 'Not that he's ever likely to find out.'

Constance didn't answer him. Her mind was elsewhere, as she recalled that awful day when they had been flung into the river that had carried them for miles downstream before depositing them on a mudbank, where they had been found by a party of aborigines. The bushmen had looked after them until they had been well enough to make the long journey to the farm that Michael had owned before going into bush-ranging. Happily, from then on, everything had gone well.

Constance gazed fondly at her husband, as he browsed through the scrapbook. It was a simple life they led, but she was content. They had enough to live on, and she enjoyed working on the farm. Even more important, she had a husband she adored. No woman could ask for more.

ALL'S FAIR IN LOVE AND WAR

Richard Grimsden

WHEN MARY HEARD Dr Harry Sommerville call 'Nurse!' sharply and urgently, she knew that trouble was coming. She and Dr Somerville had been friends since they first met on the troopship from Dover to Flanders – and Harry never used that tone of voice unless he was worried. And when Harry was worried, trouble was coming.

She scrambled out of bed and into her long grey dress, and hurried down the ward corridor still pulling back her hair on to the nape of her neck. In the doctor's day-room half a dozen doctors, all in their Royal Army Medical Corps uniforms, were already congregated. A thin wisp of summer dawn light broke through the single dirty window. As Mary sat down breathlessly, Harry – or Major Harry Sommerville as he was when commanding Forward Field Hospital No.19 on the Western Front in this year of 1916 – stood up under the oil lamp that hung from the yellowing ceiling.

'In a minute you'll hear the guns,' he said. He glanced anxiously towards the window, as if its encrusted panes would reveal the visible scene. 'We've had news from GHQ in the night. There's to be a big battle in the Passchendaele area. The artillery are putting down a barrage at first light and the infantry will advance two hours later. We can expect the casualties to be coming in from then – say about eight o'clock.'

'Perhaps the advance will be successful and they'll finish up too far away from us.' The speaker was Teddy Marmond, the Forward Field Hospital's blood transfusion doctor.

Harry Sommerville looked briefly in his direction. 'You know neither side ever advances more than a hundred yards in this war, Teddy,' he said. There was still the same sharpness in his voice. 'They're putting a hundred thousand men into this attack. Every damned hospital in Flanders will be bursting at the seams before lunchtime today.'

Despite herself, Mary shuddered. She knew she had seen enough men, dead, dying, screaming, limbs torn off and heads shattered in her two years on the Western Front to be immune from all the visions of hell on earth that this Great War had provided. But she was not immune. The sights and sounds of violent death still made her want to vomit.

The panes in the single sightless window began to rattle crisply in their frames. Seconds later, a continuous deafening boom convulsed the room. The walls of the French farm that had been converted hastily into Forward Field Hospital No.19 trembled ominously, as if ready to crumble. The combined British and French artillery had begun the 'softening up' operation, which was the way the generals described their mortal rain of death on the German lines in Flanders.

Harry Sommerville's mouth tightened. 'I want everyone in working dress. The auxiliaries to get all the water stores completely filled, heating furnaces stoked up. Willie, see how many rooms can be used as operating theatres. Nurse, have the Pioneers put every available bed to use – even in the courtyard, if necessary. That's it for the moment.' They stood up, solemnly aware that the major had been raising his voice above the din of the bombardment. 'By the way, Nurse,' he said. 'See if you can organise someone to make coffee.'

He smiled across the room and as she passed him to go through the door he squeezed her hand lightly. It was only a touch but Mary felt it glow through her. He never forgets, she thought, not even at moments like this. They had been through so much carnage together now that she could scarcely remember exactly when it was that he had proposed to her and she had said yes, and then they'd agreed that marriage would have to wait until this awful war was over. Yes, it might have been a year ago. A whole year! And the end of the war was still as remote now as ever it was then.

For two years Mary Chambers had buried all her feminine instincts under the wraps of duty. At sixteen she had read in the Strand Magazine the epic tale of Miss Florence Nightingale, who, sixty years earlier, had made nursing soldiers in the Crimean War a profession of which women could be proud. Now, in this new holocaust, the Royal Army Medical Corps were accepting that women nurses could make an invaluable contribution saving lives right up to the front line.

She walked busily down the central corridor of the improvised hospital, once the cow byres of the ancient farmhouse. In these wards the farmer's cattle once spent the harsh winters. A faint light came in through the high windows at the end of each ward, enough to reveal the dozen waiting beds on each side as waves in a grey sea. There were cracks between the boards of the doors and some of the panes in the high windows were broken. But it was *her* hospital, hers and Harry's, and even Barts, back in London's Smithfield, never looked as good to Mary as did Army Forward Field Hospital No. 19.

And now all was in readiness for duty. As the roar of the artillery barrage a mile away rose to an awesome new crescendo, Mary reminded herself solemnly that all had been in readiness for several weeks for just such a day as this.

He was among the very first batch of casualties. His hair was straw blond, his eyes, constantly open, bluer than any sea. His face, in perfect repose, was of a classical young god; it betrayed nothing at all of his agony. Mary had never seen so handsome a face; rarely had she seen so ravaged a body.

He lay under a bloodstained sheet with half a dozen others, dumped by the overworked stretcher bearers on the earthen floor. A bearer, noting her absorption in the casualty, volunteered some rapid information.

''E can't talk, ma'am. State of shock, I reckon. 'E didn't 'ave a stitch on 'im when we picked 'im up – shell blew all 'is uniform off.'

The bearer gingerly pulled back the casualty's covering sheet. Blood was seeping steadily from a gaping wound in his chest. Mary felt sudden overwhelming anger. The waste! The stupidity! She stiffened, and pinned a number to the casualty's sheet.

'Number three,' the watching bearer said approvingly. 'Well, I'd better start bringing in the next ten thousand.'

Harry appeared at her side, marking off the casualties and despatching them for treatment. He came to Number Three and stood for a moment riveted by the staring blue eyes.

'Where's his I.D., Nurse?' he said.

'He hasn't anything on him, sir,' Mary breathed.

'God, he's in shock, and weak,' Harry said. 'I don't think we can save him. Take him to Teddy. He might react to a blood transfusion.'

Mary called two passing Pioneers, who lifted Number Three on to a trolley. Not so much as a flicker betrayed the casualty's torment as they lifted him none too gently. In the makeshift transfusion room Teddy Marmond set to work mechanically on the new patient.

'What's your name?' he said, as he drew blood from Number Three's arm.

The deep blue eyes smiled back at him.

'He can't speak,' Mary said, watching intently as the captain passed the blood sample on to a slide.

'Now we have a problem,' he said, as if to himself.

'Sir?'

'His blood's rhesus negative. Hardly anyone is rhesus negative. It's one of the rarest groups of all. Which is why I've only three pints of it.'

'Isn't that enough?'

'Not quite. He'll need four at least before Major Sommerville can get that shrapnel out of his chest and legs.'

'Sir, may I say something?' She heard herself speaking in a voice caught with excitement that didn't seem to be hers.

Captain Marmond was already calling the Pioneers to take away Number Three. He leaned over the casualty. 'Sorry, old chap, can't do anything for you. Try to tell the orderlies the name of your next-of-kin, will you? It helps with the paperwork.' Then, to Mary: 'What is it, Nurse?'

'Sir, I'm rhesus negative. Take my blood.'

Teddy Marmond looked at her across the casualty trolley in amazed disbelief. 'For God's sake, Nurse, don't be so damned silly.'

'Sir, you must. We have to save as many as we can. I was always told my blood group was rare and that I should give it whenever I could.' She rolled up her sleeve, as if to brook no further argument.

'Nurse!'

Suddenly exhilarated, Mary swung herself on to the couch. 'Come on,' she said. 'I want this arm working normally by the time the next batch of casualties arrive.'

As the blood dripped steadily from her arm she stared at the yellowing ceiling, visualising again the handsome, reposed face of Number Three. What was his instant fascination? Why did she immediately tremble with excitement just looking at him? Was this love – but how could one love a mute and total stranger? Dear God, she thought, if this *is* love, then free me of it as quickly as you can.

'That's it, Nurse.' Teddy Marmond unhooked the blood bottle and Mary lifted her arm cautiously. Almost before she could roll down her sleeve and straighten her dress the transfusion had begun.

Despite the stream of field casualties that kept her running all day long, Mary was still able to pay a few brief visits to the annexe, where Number Three lay under sedation. There, *her* patient slept the sleep of the heavily drugged, his blue eyes closed beneath wisps of straw hair which she carefully tidied back.

Teddy Marmond came in during one of her bedside sojourns and gave her a curious sidelong glance before examining Number Three. 'He's responding well,' he said curtly. 'Major Sommerville will operate on his lungs first thing tomorrow, but it'll be a miracle if he survives that.'

When the captain had gone Mary straightened the crumpled blanket and leaned over the sleeping patient. 'You must survive,' she whispered softly. 'You're mine now. You have my blood in you to make you live. Let your heart pump our blood! Live! Live!'

At first light the Pioneers carried Number Three on a stretcher into the makeshift operating theatre where Major Sommerville, haggard and lined from a day and a night without sleep, had operated ceaselessly on more broken bodies than he could remember.

Number Three, wide awake, grinned at the assembled medical staff, a grin that made Mary's heart leap. He fingered the numbered card on his chest.

'Dry!' he said, hoarsely.

Mary bent over him, coaxingly. 'I'm afraid we can't give you anything to drink yet,' she said. 'We have to anaesthetise you.'

Weakly the patient held up the numbered card and grinned again. 'Dry!'

'I'm sorry ...'

Mary was aware that Harry and Teddy were gazing at each other across the theatre in shocked amazement. Then Harry said between clenched teeth: 'How the hell did this happen?'

Mary looked up quizzically. 'What's the matter, sir?'

'He's a Hun, that's what's the matter. I nearly started operating on a *German!*'

'A Hun . . .?'

Teddy came forward and gripped her arm. '*Drei* is German for three,' he said gently.

A white-faced orderly said, 'He had no I.D., no clothes on him when he was brought in, sir. He must have wandered over to our side in the battle confusion.'

Another orderly said, 'He could be a spy. If he'd been wearing a British uniform, then according to the rules of war we could shoot him.'

Harry Sommerville began to peel off his blood-stained rubber gloves. 'Take him away,' he said. 'Take him down to the old pig sties to die.'

'No! No!' Mary leapt forward, clutching Major Sommerville's hand even as he peeled off a rubber glove. 'Harry, you *can't* do that! You can't leave him to die just because he's a German!' Her voice was rising hysterically. 'A life is a life.'

The line of the major's mouth showed distinct irritation. 'We have many more important lives to save, Nurse,' he said curtly. The theatre was suddenly hushed. 'Have this patient removed.'

'You brute!' Mary shouted venomously. Tears flooded her eyes. 'You're letting him die because I love him. You know I love him. It's your way of getting rid of him, so he's no longer your rival.'

Through the walls of tears she saw Harry's eyes fixed on her with strange intent, fixed in an expression of bewildered disbelief. For what seemed like the rest of the war, no one moved. Then, slowly, methodically, Harry peeled the discarded rubber gloves back over his outstretched fingers. 'Anaesthetise the patient,' he said quietly. 'And give me a scalpel.'

His calmness, his deliberateness, finally broke Mary. With a scream of torment she rushed from the theatre.

She fled for the only place of comparative refuge that she knew – to a quiet corner of the first-aid dressing compound, where there was a seat in a courtyard under the plane trees. Here, it was hard to believe this was a place of war and suffering. Hard to believe that the man she loved, loved desperately, was fighting for his life less than a stone's throw from her.

An hour later, as she sat drying her sore, reddened eyes, she felt a hand fall lightly on her shoulder. Teddy Marmond smiled down at her.

'Hello, Nurse,' he said cheerfully.

'I suppose you think I'm a stupid child,' Mary challenged him in a mixture of guilt and anger.

'Not at all.' He sat down beside her and held her arm reassuringly. 'This is a long and lousy war for all of us. Every now and then we all have to give vent to our feelings. Why should you be any different from the rest of us?'

'You're being too kind, Teddy. Nothing you say will excuse me of the crime of falling in love with a patient I don't even know. How can Major Sommerville ever forgive me for that?'

'Harry doesn't have to forgive you, Mary. He knows you're no more in love with Number Three than I am.'

'That's ridiculous. I know about my own feelings. I've never felt so close to anyone so much in my whole life. Why do you think I gave him my blood?'

Teddy laughed warmly. 'You gave him your blood because he's a human being and you've been trained to save human beings without distinguishing between them. As for love, Mary, love for you isn't love for a solitary unknown German soldier. Rather it's love for all those who suffer. Love for a man and love of duty – these are the two faces of love, and they're quite different.'

'Do you think I don't know the difference between them?'

'I think that given the sort of stress that we're all under these days, you can easily blur the distinction between them. I don't think actually that it really matters whether you understand the difference. The point is, you've saved a man's life. Number Three, or *Nummer Drei*, I should say, will have a rough time in the next three or four weeks, but he'll live.'

Mary started, and tears, this time of relief, welled into her vision. She gripped Teddy Marmond's hand.

'Oh, Teddy,' she said softly. 'Harry saved him.'

'No, Mary. *You* saved him.' He paused, deliberately. 'Your own blood and then your affection for him as a human being were the weapons you used. Perhaps the only small mistake you made was to confuse that with love in its passionate sense.'

She didn't reply at once. She was thinking of Number Three. It didn't really matter whose blood he has in him; he would live, that was all that really mattered.

'You know,' she said presently 'I think you may be right.'

'Good!' Teddy Marmond straightened himself up in a matter-of-fact manner. 'Come on, Nurse,' he said. 'It's time we got back to work.'

She didn't see Harry alone again until the next day. She had rehearsed her speech over and over again, but as soon as she saw him the words evaporated from her mind.

'I'm – I'm sorry about yesterday,' she stammered. 'I must have been completely overwrought.'

He lifted his head and gazed intently back into her eyes before taking her lovingly into his arms. 'Forget it Mary,' he whispered. 'In love and war, these things happen to all of us.'